To Be Still

The third book of the To Be Loved series

For my readers, who never stopped asking "What happens next?"
And for the man who believed I could.
We did it!

~Prologue~

When Joseph Whitby first entered into the land now presently known as Luna Pier, Michigan, in the early 1900's, standing on the sandy shores of Lake Erie at midnight, he found a lone, white wolf howling at the silvery moon. Her white silhouette in the milky moonlight was dancing on the diamond star speckled waves. Her spiritual light was shining so brightly in the distance from where he was standing in the lake woods behind her that he knew she was a heavenly creation and his curiosity towards her began to draw him closer to her.

Finding creatures like her around the world became a mission for Joseph. He longed to tame them, protect them and shield them from the unkind, ruthlessness of the humans who hunted them. Finding Luna Waya, a precious young werewolf, and a land so rich with newness and life, he knew he had found a place he and his own family could call home.

In the first six miles of pure, beautiful, untouched Michigan; on the furthest southeast beaches of Lake Erie, Joseph claimed and named his new land Luna Pier after the beauty he found there. He sought to turn his land into a thriving, busy city that would be known for the moonlit pier he built that stretched out two miles into the lake.

At the end of the main cobblestone road in the pier, lined with busy shop fronts, standing tall and sure in front of the pier, a lighthouse protects the city from the many ships that pass by headed to the mouth of the Maumee Bay in Toledo Ohio. Another lighthouse can be seen from the pier out in the midst of the lake.

Just off the pier, out on the lake; sail boats, kayaking, and fishing can be enjoyed. In the bright early mornings of the sunrise, the city comes alive on the sandy beaches, clean and fresh for all who come to walk upon them.

In his great city he has hidden many treasures, creatures, and secrets. He built his city with the riches he found wandering the world, where not only humans could feel safe in the freedom found in America, but all God's creatures.

Joseph expected greatness. He sought wisdom and knowledge. He gave freely love and protection with the powers God gave him. What he never expected, was the creation that Luna would become. His greatest work became his most reverent fear.

Be still,
and know that He is God... Psalm 46:10

~ *One* ~

Be still

June 2016

Luna Waya fell into the darkness, with absolute precision, all the way down to the rock bottom depths of the earth.

She smiled to herself as she knelt in the darkness surrounding her. Touching the cold, rocky ground below her with her bare hands, ignited a desire inside of her soul. A passion to discover and explore further into the cavern.

The empty, quietness of the cave soothed her to her core. The crisp, earthy scent of the room filled her senses with a joy unspeakable.

Luna drug her fingers in a pattern design in the rocks beneath her thinking about her past. She was tired of keeping secrets from people. Everything she did in this life was a secret. She was really tired of pretending to be someone she wasn't anymore.

The lying, the pretending, the stress of it all; she wouldn't have to do any of that here, she considered, closing her mind off to her past and letting the present seep into her existence.

Her backpack was loaded with ropes and hooks, flashlights and a helmet that would keep a human safe while caving. It was all for show, Luna told herself, in case she ran into other humans here. She was almost sure that if she were a mere human, she wouldn't need those things even then. She'd been caving and hiking so much in her life, it was just second nature to her now.

Luna had always been drawn to this cave in the mountains of Tennessee. Her family tribe had told her of the old Indian legends and how they had lived in these caves for generations. She was now a Nunnehi like they had been; a traveler through these mountains.

Stories of these caves like the one she was in now, were told in many tribes throughout the land. The Great Smoky Mountain caves were big enough to hold an entire city. Luna wanted to see and discover it for herself. She needed a place now she could make her own and call home, where no one, no humans or government, would be able to see her.

Luna shook off the dreaded feeling that came over her. There were stories the Whitby boys had told her growing up about the royal vampires that were seeking to take over the world. Stories she longed to forget now, stories that worried her.

War was coming, they had told her before she had left home. But even war couldn't stop her from finding the freedom she longed for now.

Home. Luna wanted to forget about home in the Pier. She dusted off the sandy rocks on her hands on her jean shorts. Home was in Luna Pier, Michigan, hundreds of miles from where she was now.

When she had found the entrance to cave on the outside of the mountain today, she had jumped into the darkness of the cave and fell with ease hundreds of feet below her. She didn't have to pretend to be a human anymore out here in the seclusion of the mountains like she had been for generations at home. She had no secrets here, she could be herself and that was the reason she was here.

In the silence of the cave she could hear her mother's voice calling her from when she was younger. Luna closed her eyes and listened in the silence.

"Edoa toi Waya." Her mother had called her, meaning,. 'stay still little wolf' in their native tongue. Luna longed for that freedom now. To just be still and alone.

As she stood on the rocks of the cave floor below, her cell phone started ringing and echoed throughout the cave breaking the perfect, deafening silence.

Frustrated, Luna knelt back down and dug through her pack for her phone.

Thousands of bats, flew out from hiding in every crevice of the cave, surrounding her in a screeching so loud even she had to cover her ears from the sound.

Luna didn't have time to look on her phone to see who was calling. She was blinded from everything because of the bats that were still swirling around her screaming at her. She was irate with who ever had taken her out of her own little heaven and brought her back into the reality she was trying to slip away from.

"Hello?" Luna finally announced, exasperated at whoever it was on the other end of her phone. She was ready to shake her fist at the offending bats when she remembered there was a human on the other side of her phone waiting for her to explain all the screaming happening on her end. Her tone she had used made her grimace.

She plugged one ear and said "Hello?" again trying to sound calmer as she swatted at one last lone bat who refused to leave without a fight.

"Babe. It's me. Is everything ok?"

There was only one human voice that stirred trembling emotions all throughout her body that she never could explain. He identified himself in her ear, and ripped her heart out there on the rocks she was kneeling on.

The sound of Jesse Stone's strong voice so close to her now, drew her out of her own reality as she stood up. She reached through space and time and connected their minds using her abilities. Now he was there in front of her, and she was there with him.

In one, slow, human heartbeat, Luna's entire past with Jesse played through out in her mind. She had to close her eyes just so she could see his face better in her mind.

Every gorgeous smile Jesse had ever given her. Every touch of his, every awkward hug he had given her, afraid someone would see; every damn kiss they had almost shared; memories walked around her mind like they were happening right there in front of her.

The worst memory of all, was their last moments together before she had walked away from him years ago.

Jesse questioned her again with an intensity she could hear in his frightened voice. Luna's smile widen to a degree she couldn't hide even if she needed too at the sound of his voice.

"Yes. Jesse, I am fine. I am-" Luna paused, she really hated this part. She hated lying. For a moment she tried to think of a lie and then she shrugged it off. She didn't have to lie to Jesse. It made her eyes dance the way she lit up and smiled.

Standing there, taking in her surroundings in the cave, she couldn't wait to tell him where she was. She missed this man more than she could ever admit.

She used to be Jesse's brothers wife, not anymore, she reminded herself. James still hadn't signed the papers, but that didn't mean much to Luna. She was officially not his wife. She had done the human thing and filed for divorce, she had wrote every heartbreaking reason in those papers why she didn't want to be his wife, and in Luna's book, that was the end. Whether James had accepted that or not.

Luna reached forward to Jesse in her mind like she was touching his arm, knowing wherever he was, he could feel it too. "I am hiking, in Townsend, Tennessee." Then she showed him using her powers, she opened up her mind and knew Jesse could see everything she was seeing in the cavern. The ancient rock walls, their massive depths and the way the breathtaking morning sunlight was breaking through the cave opening above her.

"And sorry-" She apologized for the offending bat who wouldn't leave her alone. "there are these stupid bats!" She almost shouted at the last lone one who kept flying back to her like a boomerang. When he bared his fangs at her, she bared hers at him and watched him fly away screeching to the rest of his friends.

She shared with Jesse through the connections of their minds her plans and that she was hundreds of feet underground looking for a waterfall that no one knew was down here, planning to turn the cave into something for herself.

Of all the humans in the world Jesse was the only one she truly cared about. The only human she could trust with her secrets. And Jesse knew all of her secrets. Except this one, she thought, biting her lip excitedly.

She missed that feeling. Being connected with Jesse. Feeling his excitement when she shared her life with him, That and she didn't have to pretend or hide from Jesse. He knew her. He knew who and what she was, she reminded herself.

Luna sighed and waited as Jesse thought about where she was. He really wouldn't be surprised by her hiking adventure and probably wouldn't even question her. But she waited, and listened with anticipation, eager to hear his voice again. Wondering why he had called her.

Luna worried briefly when Jesse took a moment with his own thoughts. She could see him sitting at his desk. He desperately needed to tell her something.

"Babe, I need to tell you something. It's Linda, your mom-"

Luna waited for him to finish saying whatever it was he started to say about her mother Linda. She even stopped and looked down at her cell phone signal to see if she had dropped his call, but she hadn't. She still had full service down here.

What made him pause, she wondered as she put her cell back up to her ear. She was ready to forget about the phone and just enter his mind fully when he continued.

"Babe, I'm so sorry-"

Again, she listened and again he stopped. But why? He sounded serious like something was wrong, but for the life of her she couldn't understand what it was.

Luna looked down at her cell signal again. She hated cell phones, they only frustrated her not being able to see and feel what the other person was trying to say.

Impatiently she sighed and waited for him to finish, as she tucked her hand in her jean short pocket. Jesse knew all he had to do was ask her to use her powers. For some reason, he wasn't though. He was trying to sort out what he obviously didn't want to say.

"Jesse baby, what's wrong?" She asked him quietly in wonder when she could tell he was still struggling for the right words.

Whenever she called him baby, he knew what she was asking for. She was asking his permission to enter his heart, to understand him better. So she pleaded with him for it in his mind.

Luna hated when humans did this, and it was very unlike Jesse, who was always so sure of everything he did to trip over something he needed to say. When she heard him sigh wearily in her ear, she knew something was dangerously wrong.

"Your mother, she was murdered this morning." He whispered softly, in his deep male bur.

Luna tried not chuckle at what Jessie had just confidently told her. She really did. She failed of course.

"Jesse come on, that's not funny." Cause it really wasn't.

Linda wasn't human, she almost told him. Luna adjust her stance and forgot about her surroundings. Her mother couldn't be murdered. He knew this, she told herself quietly.

"Babe, I'm not joking." He added, very seriously.

Suddenly, because of the confidence in his voice, the way he stated it so matter of factly, Luna knew he wasn't that facetious. Jesse would never joke about something like this.

She had to cover her own lips at his words spoken she kept hearing in her mind on repeat. Your mother was murdered this morning.

Realization hit her and made her feel like she was falling. Like blaring music was playing too loudly and she couldn't stop it.

Everything in Jesse's spoken whisper caused everything in Luna's world to spin in spirals out of control. Gravity felt heavier. A fear she had never known before, took ahold of her and wouldn't let go.

Luna bent down, grabbed her pack and then she jumped back up the narrow entrance of the cave she had just carelessly descended into and landed on her feet on top of the great mountain.

Jesse had her full, undivided attention now.

"What happened Jesse?" And in that moment, Luna felt just how far away from home she really was as she looked around the mountain side. "Tell me everything."

Jesse Stone was sitting at his desk in the Luna Pier Police Department. He had one hand in his pant pocket and the other hand he was using to squeeze his eyes shut while he shouldered the phone he was talking on.

He didn't have to picture Luna on the other end of the phone, she was there in his mind, showing herself to him. He had even felt her enter his mind and touch his arm like she had done to him in the past. Jesse could feel her tender touch like she was right here with him, creating goose flesh bumps on his arm.

He had forgotten how real it felt when she would do this.

Jesse hadn't talked to Luna in so long he had forgotten how sweet her voice sounded. Sure, they had texted, emailed, and shared moments on social media together, since she'd left. Secretly of course. But he hadn't heard her voice or felt her presence in a long time.

Luna had let him into her mind, she'd let him see where she was. Right where he knew she'd be. Out there hiking somewhere. Lost, but found. Totally blinded by the freedom she longed for.

He loved it when she did this, but he knew her world was falling apart on the other end of the phone when he told her about her mother and it was secretly killing him.

She wasn't his to console in times like this though. She had a husband, his brother James. And sometimes Jesse needed to remind himself of that. Other times he could care less. More often than not though, he hated them both for it.

Jesse eyed his brother James now, who was sitting in front of Jesse's desk, making it impossible for Jesse to let her enter his mind fully. He had to keep carrying on the conversation in front of James like they weren't using her powers.

Jesse couldn't talk to Luna the way he needed to. The way she wanted him too. He wanted to tell her he was sorry. He wanted to hold her in his arms and comfort her.

James didn't know Luna's secrets like Jesse did. James didn't know her at all, Jesse reminded himself. Not like Jesse knew her.

While he was at her mother's pet grooming shop this morning, after the fire that had taken Linda's life, after the police and fire departments had left, Jessie knew Luna needed to be contacted. But his brother, James, her husband, hadn't wanted to do it. He had asked Jesse, who was her friend, to do it.

Jesse looked at James with renewed anger. James was a coward sometimes and Jesse hated him for it.

Jesse and Luna weren't just friends. They were best friends, Jesse reminded himself with a sigh that wracked his whole body. Luna was his best friend, he told himself. Even though he knew she was so much more than that.

Jesse held the phone a little tighter now like he would if he was holding Luna. He showed her in his mind, just in case she was watching so she could see.

"It's still under investigation Babe. There are things I can't discuss-"

When Luna felt Jesse touch her through the distance, she interrupted him. "Don't play cop with me Jesse! Damn it! Tell me everything!" She pleaded with him, shaking him in his mind so he could see how important this was.

Show me Jesse. She begged him in his mind.

Luna stopped running to control him. It was there that she peeked inside his mind without him knowing. She saw his reason why he was calling her on the phone and not summoning her to his mind like they had done in the past. James was there.

Luna took a deep breath and tried to forget about that past she had with Jesse and James. She couldn't think about that right now. She needed Jesse to answer her, to tell her more.

She knew that as an officer he was bound by certain things he couldn't share, but he damn well knew if she could, she would choke the answers out of him. She may fight like a girl, but she was stronger then he was, and he knew it. She held her decorum though, James was there with Jesse, they would have to do this the human way.

She took off running again at lighting speed back to her vehicle she had left over three mountains east of where she was now, wishing she could bust out into her wolf form.

Damn all these stupid human ways, she cursed to herself, as she held the phone tight to her ear.

She needed him to say more, tell her what had happened to her mother and why. She was too far away from home now to learn the things she needed to know. She needed him to talk to her!

"I don't have all the details Babe." He started to tell her as he leaned back in the old squeaky chair at his desk, looking at the reason he couldn't speak plainly to her, hoping she could see James there in his mind in the room with him. He could hear her running now and knew just how fast she was going.

He told her what he could. "We got a call from dispatch this morning. There was a report of smoke coming out of the windows in the front of the shop.”

Jesse shook and trembled remembering the flames of the fire he had walked through in the shop searching for her mother he couldn't find in the smoke filled rooms. He could still smell the fire and smoke on him now.

"By the time we all got there, it was too late. She died in the fire, Luna."

Luna stopped dead in her tracks at this when Jesse said her name. She had to breath in and out, slowly, even though she didn't need it. It was Jesse, Jesse who had needed the air.

She was almost back to her vehicle now. But it was the way he had said her name that stopped her from moving. Jesse never called her Luna. Only Babe.

Luna looked inside his mind at the permission he had secretly given her and now she could see, feel, everything he did.

Fire. Luna could see it in her mothers shop as Jesse walked through the hot, man eating flames again remembering it for her. It was the only thing that could have killed Linda.

Truth be told, her mother wasn't what Luna was. She hadn't been reborn into a vampire like Luna. Linda's blood ran wolf in her veins though, just like Luna's. This didn't mean Linda couldn't be killed, sure it was easier to die a wolf than a vamp, but it was very hard to do.

Luna reached inside his mind as he played it all there for her. Everything he had seen, she could now see.

When Jesse had made his way out of the police station this morning as the tones dropped from central dispatch for the call at her mothers shop, he had seen flames coming out of Linda's apartment in the back beside the grooming shop. Not just the front, like dispatch had reported. The shop had been fully engulfed.

He had ran the short distance between his station and the back of Linda's shop. He was ready to kick open the back door to get in and save whoever was in the shop, had there been any clients, or workers there already, but the door had already been busted open. That alone had worried him, but he went in anyways, gun drawn.

He had searched, blindly through the white, blinding smoke and red, hot flames, but he couldn't find anyone. He had walked back out choking and gasping for breath. He never dreamed that Linda was still in there.

Linda had been discovered by the firefighters later, still in her apartment. There was nothing any of them could have done for her.

Luna covered her gasp when she saw her mother's body and fell to her knees on the grass in front of her. She closed her eyes and mind to it. She couldn't think of it anymore. She felt like she was in a state of confusion. Like she was dreaming.

Jesse had put his life in danger, risking his life for her and her mother by going into the burning shop and apartments alone. It stilled her into unimaginable silence.

Luna reached through the space between them and grabbed Jesse by his arms. "Why did you say she was murdered Jesse?" Luna questioned him in a whisper. She fell down to the earth further and had to hold it like she was Jesse with her hands to steady herself.

The shop door had been busted open when he had ran in first, Luna remembered. He had even drawn his gun as he searched.

"Who did this to my mother Jesse?" She pleaded with him for the answer hoping he knew it.

Jesse knew things. He knew things no one else knew, because of Luna. More things he had learned he needed to share with her.

His whole world had changed over the last year. The world as he knew it, was changing forever. And she had been so far away for far too long.

He looked at James before he answered her, knowing he could only share with her what James knew, and nothing more.

"There is a lot of things going on in the pier right now. I'm not sure who's doing this, Luna." Jesse sighed at that rubbing his forehead. "You should come home."

I need you to come home Babe. He told her secretly so James couldn't hear him.

Jesse knew he needed her. He had always needed her, but this was the first time it wasn't laden with desire. He needed her to find out who had done this, who was doing this. She was the only one who could. So they could stop it before it destroyed the pier.

He knew if his brother James had called her and said those words to her she would never come home. Because Jesse had said them to her, he knew she would come quickly.

But the choice was hers. Jesse knew if she decided not to, he would have to respect her decision. He waited for her answer silently. The pier and all his lonely desires hung on her next words.

Luna wiped her bloody tears away. She looked at them as they dripped down her wrist. If Jesse wasn't telling her everything right now, it was truly that bad. He wanted her to come home, but he understood if she didn't.

What had happened in the pier? What did Jesse mean when he said he didn't know who was doing this? Was there other people being murdered?

She had tried not to read the breaking news on social media lately but it was hard. The humans were broadcasting everything they learned about her kind with speculation that sickened her.

War. She could hear the Whitby's words echoing in her mind now. War, was here now.

She had been trying to run away from it all. Hide away peacefully somewhere and just be free, just for a little while. Like her people had done before her for thousands of years.

Was it really too much to ask? She had been so close to truly being free...

"Why mother? Why not me?" Luna gently wondered aloud to no one. She could painfully see her mother dying in the fire, and even though she wasn't dreaming, it almost felt like a nightmare humans talked so much about.

This couldn't be real she thought as she looked through the thick forest she was in now. The rock formations that were jutting out of the mountain, the creek that was running slow off the rocks beside her, and the way the sun broke through the trees above her. It was all the peaceful heaven she had been searching for.

Luna could hear Jesse troubled sigh. He was so connected to her that he had heard her wondering aloud. He could see the freedom she had been searching for.

She could see everything around him. She had heard his chair squeak moments ago and she knew exactly where he was, what he looked like sitting there at his desk in his uniform, distraught like her, and she knew he wanted to help her. He had risked his life for her today being the hero she hadn't known she had needed.

Jesse always wanted her. And for the first time, ever, she was going to let him have her. She needed him more.

Luna had sworn to Jesse years ago that she would never, ever come back home. Luna shook off the fear she felt about it. She shook off the pain and hatred and reasons she had left. She had to go back home.

"I am on my way Jesse. I'm coming." she said as she started to run again and then she stopped in her tracks, sliding to a halt and kicking dirt in front of her. "Jesse?"

"Yeah Babe? I'm still here." He questioned and told her softly. He knew the silence between them had been her processing everything. He had given her those moments to herself so he could be with her in some way. He could barely contain his excitement at knowing she was coming home.

"Don't tell anyone. Please? I don't want anyone to know that I am coming home."

She almost said goodbye. But Jesse had told her years ago never to say that. It was something his family did because they were firefighters. They never said goodbye, only "I'll see you soon.". It was a promise that they'd come back.

"I'll see you soon Jesse." And with that, she ended the call and ran, knowing she could trust Jesse with her secrets.

Two

Be still, leave the past in the past

Luna was coming home. They would figure this all out together.

Jesse looked at the person he knew Luna didn't want to know her secrets. He sighed wondering what lie he was going to have to tell James.

He let his phone slip free off his shoulder and caught it in his hand. He looked at the picture on his phone under his desk of the woman who had meant the world to him. The one woman in this world that was beyond his reach. Luna was his forbidden fruit.

Luna was wearing a short, white, lacy sundress in the picture on his phone. She had long, black, raven hair. She loved to braid it and to place little leather straps with feathers or charms in it. It reminded him of her heritage. Her Indian skin was soft but always ice cold. Jesse loved her skin coloring, loved the feel of her cool, super human vampire skin on his fingers. He loved to look in her golden wolf eyes.

He traced her with his fingers on his phone.

In Luna, Jessie had found hope in life that he lost in his career. He once saw the pure wonder in her eyes that life could be, that was before this land had been taken over and changed. He had seen through her what life should be, and it had given him strength to find it in his own life.

Now, Jesse wondered if that ever could be again. He had lost the faith she had given him when she had left the pier. She had taken that and so much more from him.

Luna had been leaning up against a tree in the picture against a wooded forest backdrop just south of the pier they loved to visit together. She enjoyed running ahead of Jesse and waiting for him like she was doing in the picture, just smiling, a smile Jesse was madly in love with.

James choose that moment to break Jesse from his thoughts and cough out loud to remind Jesse he was still here.

Jesse shut his phone off. It was a bad habit he had of hiding everything that had to do with Luna and him and pretend like he wasn't doing what others thought he was doing. It always made him smile though when he did it. It always turned into the right kind of wrong kind of game that he loved to play with her. To see who could do the most without being caught.

"How'd she take it?" James asked Jesse uneasy.

How'd she take it? Her mother just died you ass! Jesse almost said aloud, but kept his thoughts to himself. Jesse just stared and looked over at his brother instead.

James, who was sitting smugly in a chair in front of Jesse, started fidgeting wondering how their conversation had went.

Jesse was nothing like his twin brother James. Sometimes looking at his brother James was like looking in a mirror. The reflection was always uncomfortable to Jesse.

Jesse almost lost it and climbed over his desk to tear his brother to shreds. Instead Jesse got up.

"You're an ass James." He told his brother slamming the chair firmly behind him against the wall as he stood up.

James didn't deserve to know, Jesse thought trying not to let his anger shake him. It served James right for making Jesse call Luna.

James should have called Luna, Jesse told himself as he turned to walk out of his office. It wasn't Jesse's place. Jesse wasn't her husband. James was.

Those thoughts made Jesse want to give up on the both of them, even though his heart belonged to Luna in some sick, twist of fate. Turning his back to James, Jesse decided to walk out to his police car outside and leave James sitting there.

James and Luna had problems like every married couple. Luna's biggest problem being married to Jesse's brother was that James was the most self centered person alive. And James' problem was that Luna was now too. Neither one of them cared for the other, neither one loved the other. But somehow, what Jesse would never understand, was how they were still married to each other.

Luna should have divorced James instead of just leaving him. But she ran away instead. Leaving, Jesse to wonder if there would ever be a way for them to be together.

Earlier, the guys on the police department had said they were hungry when they had left the scene of the fire. Jesse couldn't stomach eating, but he needed the reality that waited for him at the Luna Cafe where his friends were. Now that he had notified Luna, he could go and join them.

Luna had left James years ago because of the way James was. It had nothing to do with how she felt for Jesse, he told himself as he headed down Luna Pier road to the cafe.

Or had it? It was that one thought that had plagued his mind. He had been so close to kissing her the night she had left. He couldn't help but wonder what would have happened if he had.

Would she have stayed?

Again, Jesse tried to not think about her as he looked outside of his police car as he drove through the morning in the pier. Again, he failed. Everywhere he looked he could see her there, walking around the pier. She had been there, once, everywhere he looked.

Jesse had tormented her for years after she had married James, constantly teasing her whenever they were together. Driving her crazy tempting her sexual desire for him. He knew it was there, and he knew his brother James had no idea of Luna's secret passion and desires that laid dormant in their loveless marriage.

Jesse had never touched her though. Well, touched wasn't the right word. He'd touched her so many times he almost had her crazy body memorized. But he'd never kissed her. He'd never touched her in any way that would have ruined her marriage to James.

She was still innocent of that.

The difference between Jesse and James was that Jesse loved her. James didn't.

James should have called her, not him, Jesse told himself again turning off his car, staring into the Cafe he wasn't ready to enter where his friends were waiting for him. James should have been the one telling her this private, heart wrenching news about her mother, about the pier that was being destroyed around them. But James hadn't wanted the burden of telling his wife that.

James didn't deal well with uncomfortable. He didn't deal well with women. But he knew Jesse and Luna were friends, or so he had told Jesse when he had guilted Jesse into calling Luna. Jesse hated the man all the more for it. It was just another black check mark on Jesse's already lengthy list of 'Reasons why I despise my brother James'.

Jesse got out of his vehicle and started to think of when he had started that list of check marks against his brother. It could have been when they were kids and James had always tried to put Jesse in his place like their older brothers did to them and all the things James had tattled on him for while growing up. But Jesse knew it was the summer after graduation in high school that really defined the start of his list.

Jesse and Luna had been on a 'break' that summer, or so Jesse had thought. They had gotten into a fight when Jesse discovered who Luna really was. She was afraid for him because he knew her secrets and no matter how hard Jesse tried to tell her it was fine, he was ok, she just kept pushing him away.

James had come home from visiting colleges at the end of that summer with the news that he and Luna were engaged.

That was the pivotal moment in Jesse's life that changed his and James' relationship, and everyone knew it. They may be identical brothers, but they would never be brothers again.

Jesse had tried to hate Luna for it. He really had. But he couldn't. Jesse believed in love like he believed in her. And he lived every day trying to make her love him again.

Jesse knew all Luna's secrets. He knew her. He knew her in ways no other man ever would.

He knew who she was. He knew what she was. He knew even if she wasn't, he would still love her.

Luna was funny, playful and sweet. She had a magical, giddy, comical side that Jesse adored. She never missed a beat when she joked around with him.

Jesse grinned thinking about how he missed the way she would stick her tongue out at him and cock her head sideways being goofy, or flip him off when she was cross with him.

Luna had a very compassionate heart, she was loving and tender with everyone he knew, especially his family. She worried obsessively over what everyone thought of her, wanting to be a good person and not the monster she thought she was.

Her obsession with protecting and taking care of dogs in her mothers grooming business was odd, the only odd thing he could see in her, but it was also endearing. He had just assumed it was a wolf thing. Plus, Jesse loved dogs. He loved to go in the shop and flirt with Luna and play with the dogs who were always happy to see him even when she acted like she wasn't.

Jesse chuckled at that last, even though it was odd, even though some people saw it as a fault in her, he loved it about her. She would be covered in dog hair and her own hair would be a mess from a long day of working at the shop and she still looked gorgeous to him.

One of the other things he loved about Luna, was when she would bite her lip and try not to smile at him. It never worked of course, which made her smile wider and then she would try to hide her smile with her tiny hands, and then when she couldn't, she would laugh out loud in a heavenly melody.

When she would innocently grab his face to get his attention she already had, or touch his lips to hush him distracting herself instead, or when she would touch his chest that she knew was well muscled by accident and get so turned on she would have to look away shyly. It was the only time he wished she was human so he could see her cheeks blush.

Jesse got out his car in a rush. He missed all those things about Luna. He missed her so bad he had to hold tight to the handle of the cafe door just to shake the thoughts from his mind.

As Jesse walked in the door of the Luna Cafe and saw his friends, Ken, Jerry, Josh and Tyler, he remembered one last time the look on Luna's face when she had let go of his embrace as he congratulated the both of them, James and Luna, that summer they were engaged. It was the one and only memory of her he used to think of that could make him stop thinking of her when he needed too.

She wasn't trying to hurt Jesse, it was his own fault really, for not stopping it.

What had happened between her and his brother James wasn't real though and he never understood it. It would never be what Jesse and Luna had together, and that suited him just fine.

He had been head over heels, literally tripping over himself, for Luna. Always. He hadn't even looked at another woman the way he looked at Luna.

From that summer on he just pretended to be a guy she would be ashamed of. Always telling her when he was with this girl or that. Always trying to make her jealous. Teasing her relentlessly with stories of his sex life. He loved how much it worked on her, but it sickened him sometimes how real it was.

His mother and grandmother called him a charming rake. His brothers and friends though, called him a rouge. He wasn't to be trusted with women. They all knew it was because he secretly loved Luna. Too much, they would all tell him.

Sitting next to his co-workers on the police department, trying to listen in on the conversation around the table shared with firefighters, Jesse forgot about Luna. Well, he tried his damndest too, but thoughts of her coming home excited him in ways he wasn't ready for.

He wondered, shyly for a moment, what she would now think of his new physique. He had grown out of his high school football look. He was now the size of his older Stone brothers. Asher, Jesse's older brother, was the one who had commented on it the day before telling him he even looked bigger than their older brother Curtis had been.

Curtis, Jesse had to close his eyes at the thought of his dead brother. What had been happening around the pier had happened to Curtis. Jesse knew who had killed Curtis and Linda. He could only pray now that he and Luna together could stop this before anyone else had to die.

"Her name is Emie. Joseph Whitby's sister." This from Ken who was answering Jerry's question about Asher and Emie's engagement a few nights ago at the Firemen's Banquet.

Jesse felt like his world had come to a complete stop when Ken spoke.

"Joseph Whitby's sister?" Jesse questioned Ken.

How had he missed that Emie, Asher's girlfriend now fianc , was Joseph's sister, he wondered. He had known Emie was a Whitby and that she was related to Luna's family, but now knowing she was the little sister of the man Luna had feared for years; it struck a worrisome nerve inside of him he didn't know what to do with.

The Whitby boys were vampires and so was their sister. Asher was in love with a vampire. Jesse suddenly wished he could talk to Luna again.

Ken who had been joking with Josh and Tyler about real women marrying real heroes, not cops, stopped joking at Jesse's question about Emie. He looked at Jesse confused. "You didn't know?"

Jesse was truly excited for Asher that he had met someone and was getting married. But in that moment Jesse couldn't stomach love.

Emie was Joseph Whitby's sister. How had he missed that all this time? He shook his head and sat back in his chair thinking about that. Now their families would really be intertwined. Humans and super humans.

And then there was Luna...

"No." Jesse said simply to Ken, remembering he was supposed to answer Ken's question, just as the waitress set down his favorite breakfast in front of him he hadn't ordered.

Jesse rubbed his head again. He now had developed a headache he knew would not go away easily.

Leave it to fate to throw a twist in his life. He almost cussed out loud a four letter word that Ken would have kicked him for.

Luna felt like she had just driven hundreds of miles along roadways littered with traffic through Tennessee. What should have taken her only about an hour, had taken up most of the afternoon. Accidents were everywhere.

Some cars were stopped around curves in the mountains that made it hard for her to see until she was already up on them. She had to make a path around the stopped traffic. She was glad she had a sports utility vehicle to do it all with.

Traffic on the highway though was altogether different. Once she reached I-75 just south of Knoxville traffic was at a crawl. She couldn't get any of them to get out of her way so she could drive faster.

Some people, Luna discovered, were just driving off road. So she followed them the best she could.

When she had made it as far as Knoxville, Tennessee, she gave up trying to drive any further. She had to call Joseph and ask for help.

Luna looked in her rear view mirror into the back seats of her vehicle. Everything she owned from packs to tents to her hammock was in here. She would set up camp in the trees in the mountains and just sit in silence among the forgotten forests. She hated closing the chapter of this part of her life, but she had no other choice. She would have to leave it all behind at an airport and call Joseph.

Luna hated to admit she needed his help as she dialed his number. She hated going back into her old life. Her riches untold blessed to her by the Whitby's sometimes sickened her. She knew when she needed her family more than her pride though. And right now she needed to get back to the pier.

"Jordy made arrangements for you already." Joseph told her, among other things, while she walked through the airport halls in Knoxville. She was among a hectic crowd of scatterbrained people who were too busy watching the news on the televisions to notice her talking on her cell and juggling luggage any normal woman couldn't carry alone.

Luna could hear the brotherly authority in Joseph's voice and it was a comfort she hadn't known she had missed. Joseph would know how to help her get back home to the pier.

"You could just use your powers and run back home." She heard Joseph telling her, but she'd have to leave her things behind, and she couldn't bring herself to do it. She had too many treasured things she always carried with her. Losing them, leaving them behind, she couldn't fathom it.

Joseph had not heard of Linda's death, and promised Luna by the time she got home he would have answers for her. Jordy would have a servant and a car waiting for her at the airport in Toledo.

Once she was safely on board her plane, that was due for take off any minute, Luna drowned out everyone on the plane with headphones and turned up the music on her phone. Every time Luna thought about where she was going she would cringe. She hated Luna Pier. Well, that wasn't entirely true...

She hated it there ever since the Whitby's had shown up a hundred years ago and took over their land. They made a deal with her brother Dolph of protection from the humans in the growing city Joseph was planning on making his own empire.

Sure he had made them a sanctuary on the land and protected them by building walls so they could live freely, but Joseph had turned them all into servants for his family.

Jeremy had turned her by accident into a hybrid, which none of them knew was possible. Dolph had left the land then, taking their tribe with him. Stubborn and hot headed like his fathers before him, he wouldn't be any man's servant. Luna had never heard from them again.

Luna's mother, Linda, had stayed with her. It wasn't until her mother had started a dog grooming business in Luna Pier, called Aunt Linda's Pet Grooming, that Luna's life had changed. They both needed a place of their own, a job to do that wasn't servitude to the Whitby's. They bought a building in the pier with the help of the Whitby's. They even built an apartment next to the shop.

Linda's business flourished, and at one point Linda and Luna had more business than they could handle alone. Linda had hired two young girls the same age as Luna; Talia and Miranda, who both attended Luna Pier High School.

Linda and Luna had to lie to them and convince them that Luna was homeschooled and couldn't attend regular school like them. Soon they became fast friends with Luna and wanted Luna to go to school with them.

Luna had begged Linda to allow it. To let her for once try to be normal like everyone else.

Seeing her mother in her mind, Luna let thoughts of her mother run through her heart. She had missed her mother these years they had been apart.

Luna sighed trying not to think about it, she couldn't cry on the plane. Then her plane took off the runway at speeds only she could match.

She thought of her first day at Luna Pier High School instead. Luna closed her eyes at the thoughts that entered her mind. She let the music on her phone fill her heart as her soul rejoiced at the memories she finally allowed to come back to life. It had been a long time since she had let it happen.

Luna had spent so much time running from her past. She almost chuckled at the thought that all it took was the sound of Jesse's voice to make her want to come back home.

Or was it Jesse she was running back too?

Luna had met Jesse her first day of school their senior year. Jesse had been sitting in front of her making her all kinds of nervous in their English class. He was dangerously attractive in his muscle tank top he didn't quite fit in, like his big brothers did, and gym shorts.

He had fresh tattoos on his arms he had gotten with his brothers that summer. Luna loved his tattoos. They were unique; red and blue fire surrounded in white smoke and barbed wire that cut into the stone images of crosses that identified him with the fire department his family was apart of. They weren't just ordinary tattoos like everyone else had that didn't have meaning or were all out of place. No, she whispered to herself remembering. They meant something and were perfectly designed. Etched in his skin like it was in his heart for everyone to see.

He really shouldn't have been showing them off at school. It was one of the things that set Jesse apart from other boys and his family. Jesse was untamed and he knew it. It was the curse of being the middle child, he had told her playfully once. No one ever tried to tame the middle child.

She remembered looking at his tattoos and feeling caught up in the life-like barbed wire like he was trying to trap her, the wolf she was.

He had turned around and when she looked up to face him to ask him what he wanted, their eyes met. And in that moment she knew she was his. And Jesse knew it too. She heard him say it in his mind. She felt it in his heart that had stopped when she smiled at him.

Luna had never met a human that had caused her those kind of emotions. She had never believed in love, let alone love at first sight. But there it was. All she could do was bashfully smile back at him. And Jesse always smiled back at her, knowing he was the reason for her smile.

From then on, life turned complicated. She knew Jesse's entire family from working at the shop with Linda and meeting his mother when she came in with her dog. No matter how Luna tried to keep Jesse out her life, his family just made it impossible.

Jesse had made himself a constant in her life. He knew she was different, and it bothered him not knowing why. That, and he intimidatingly wanted her. Some days Luna felt like he was hunting her the way he prowled around her for attention.

Luna's smile widen at those thoughts. She had forgotten how she used to daydream about Jesse as a wolf. Which made her sigh out loud, looking out her window into the evening night sky above the clouds. She missed Jesse in ways she couldn't describe.

Thoughts of James crossed her mind then. She had met James only once or twice in the halls at school.

James, although he was a Stone boy, wasn't as broad shouldered as the rest of them. He was tall sure, but lengthy. His choice in clothes didn't show off his natural muscled figure and his days spent without the sun showed on his skin. He didn't play sports like his brothers, he'd rather play video games and hunt in his own fantasy worlds. He wasn't good in school because he'd rather skip and be only God knew where.

James had only talked to her when it was convenient for him. Luna had never paid him much attention then.

Jesse was tall like his older brothers. He was strong like them from working out and playing sports. His golden tanned body all muscled up next to the other boys in school made all the girls' hearts melt. His messy blonde hair and casual clothes could make any girl weak in the knees.

Even though they looked alike, Luna could tell them apart easily. It was the way Jesse looked at her. The way he breathed when she was near. He couldn't hide it, the way his body reacted. It made her body react the same way.

It was the way his mind called out to her when he would lay eyes on her. The way he thought about her. She could see herself inside of him like she was looking into a mirror. No one, absolutely no one, had ever seen her so clearly, especially James.

A human tapped her on the shoulder breaking her daydreams and Luna's golden eyes came awake there on the plane. She looked to the woman who had invaded her space and dreams.

The woman looked truly frightened by the sight of Luna.

Luna almost smirked. Serves her right, Luna thought. She wasn't ready to let go of Jesse's sexy smile just yet.

Luna removed her head phones and smiled reassuringly at the woman who announced they were about to land in Toledo and Luna needed to fasten her seat belt.

Luna almost chuckled as the woman walked away. She wanted to tell the woman that she didn't need too, but she fastened her seat belt anyways.

When she landed at the airport she walked out into the throng of people. It was like it was in Knoxville. Luna shook her head at all of them and almost put her headphones back in when she noticed a gentleman standing in the crowd in a black suit wearing sunglasses, holding a white paper with an outline of a wolf drawn on it.

Luna grinned at that. Leave it to Jordy to handle her arrangements. When the gentleman stood a little taller and acknowledged Luna, he turned to motion to Luna to lead the way. He took her to her baggage and loaded everything she needed in a black SUV. He neatly guided her in the back seat where a box filled with delicious treats awaited her. She reached for the wine bottle she knew was filled with chilled, delicious blood, as the gentleman closed her door.

Luna was reaching the first mile into Luna Pier now, she looked out her window to the east and followed the six miles of Whitby land with her eyes.

Luna was home. She rolled down her window and let the midsummers night fresh air fill her. She had missed the smell of the lake wood in the pier.

Jesse and she had spent years out there in the lake woods together. She remembered the night Jesse had learned who she was. Exactly who she was, Luna thought with a silent sigh.

Luna had broken out in a run at the sound of Jesse being attacked by Collin, one of Joseph's other servants, when Jesse had stupidly and stubbornly snuck unto the Whitby's land. Collin was chasing Jesse, the intruder, off their land. Luna ran up to Jesse screaming at him not knowing he was on their land alone looking for her. She landed in his arms as he tried to protect her from the beast who was chasing him.

It was she who had to protect him though.

Luna lashed out at Collin baring her teeth as she kept Jesse behind her. Jesse wouldn't allow it. He got in between her and Collin. When he turned to look back at Luna, he saw her eyes, her golden wolf eyes no one else had ever seen, and her fangs. He knew then, what she was. It had taken him by such surprise that Collin almost had him.

Remembering that night, Luna shook her head, as they turned off the expressway into the pier. She tucked her hands under her legs and tried to relax. Jesse had to learn that night her entire life's story.

What choice had she? She had to trust him with her secrets.

Trusting Jesse wasn't easy. She worried constantly for the both of them. Collin, who had rushed home defeated and angry with Luna, had told Joseph that Luna had brought a human on their land that night and what he looked like. Joseph had been furious with her. He had wanted the human off his land that night and told her never to return with the human ever again or he would hunt him down and kill him.

She never wanted Joseph to know that it was Jesse and that she loved Jesse. She feared what he would do to Jesse if he knew. Luna decided she had to develop a secret life there in the pier. She broke up with Jesse and married Jesse's twin brother soon after, knowing she was deceiving Joseph. He would never know the difference between the two now.

She needed to be close to Jesse though. She needed to protect him from Joseph. She needed to be close to his family so she could always watch and listen and make sure he was protected.

She had made the hardest decision of her life that summer. A decision that kept her so close, but yet so far away from Jesse.

Luna looked around the pier as they drove down Luna Pier road. They pulled into the hotel in the pier next to the hospital. She made arrangements for a room there. She had no intention of anyone knowing she was here and asked the front desk lady for discretion.

There was no way she was going home to James. And she refused to go back to the Whitby's.

She walked back out to the vehicle to get her things and looked over towards the hospital. There were three vehicles parked next to each other that she knew in the hospital parking lot. Each vehicle was hard to miss, even at night. A police car that was probably Jesse's, Asher's big truck decked out with firefighter lights you couldn't miss even in the dark, and James's truck that also looked like a firefighter owned it.

She looked curiously at the three as Joseph's gentlemen shut the back hatch and left her there with her luggage. As he drove away she was staring at the vehicles across the street. Why would all three of them be there, she wondered. She scanned the parking lot again and noticed their parents truck was there too. The entire parking lot was filled with emergency responder vehicles.

That was odd. What the hell were they all doing at the hospital?

Luna took a step towards the hospital and had to stop herself. She shouldered her pack instead and loaded her luggage on a cart so the nice girl at the front desk wouldn't suspect anything. Before she walked back into the hotel she wondered what she should do. She looked back at the vehicles again.

It wasn't like she could just walk over to the hospital and ask for the Stone family. One, she wasn't supposed to be here, and two, she wasn't married to their son any more.

That thought made her angry, she thought as she marched herself into the hotel.

James was an ass. He shouldn't have made Jesse call her after all he did for her this morning. James should have called her.

If he still hadn't signed those damn divorce papers she'd given him years ago and told everyone in their family, she was going to make him sign them with his own blood in front of them all.

Once Luna was in the safety of her room she rested her back against the door before she turned on the lights. Not that she needed them on, she could see just fine in the dark.

She dropped her bags thinking of her family. There must be a reason they were all over at the hospital.

Was it possible they were just there seeing a patient? But then who? And what had happened to them?

She wondered worriedly who it might be now. Jesse had said there was a lot going on and he didn't know who was doing it.

Luna sunk down to the floor. She was torn. She wanted to see them all again, aside from her husband. Ex husband, she reminded herself.

She longed to see her family again, she thought with a defeated sigh. She missed Jesse's parents and Asher too. This last year had been hell without them, knowing they were still in morning, she knew they were going through a lot after losing Curtis last year. It had been all over their social media how much they missed Curtis.

She even missed her sisters-in-law. Izzy was the youngest and Luna's favorite. Izzy liked vampires and always wanted to talk to her about them. Luna had tried to get her to like werewolves, but Izzy liked vampires.

Luna sighed greatly then. She really had missed them all.

She needed to find out what had happened to her mother first though. She was still holding out hope that her mother was still alive. In their secret lives together they had always had to start anew every ten or twenty years with the humans. Linda might have just wanted to move on since Luna had left the pier. It was almost that time again.

Maybe Linda and Collin had run off together, Luna thought, bringing a smirk on her face. Linda adored Collin. And Collin had always been Joseph's driver. She didn't know who this new gentleman was that had picked her up tonight, but he wasn't Collin.

Reasons Luna didn't understand though flooded her mind. Why didn't her mother call her and tell Luna her plans? Why would she just disappear without telling her?

Those thoughts led Luna back to what could only be the truth. What Jesse had told her. Everything the Whitby's had tried to tell her before she had left.

Luna started playing with her long hair hanging at her sides, nervously. War was coming. War was here in the pier like it had been everywhere Luna had been.

Luna stood up. She had time to shower and clean up from her travels and make herself resemble a human again before she wandered back out into the reality of the pier. She was still covered in loose gravel from caving and had dirt smeared on her face. She needed to rinse it all away. Along with it, her freedom.

She let the warm, steamy water fall down her body as she held the wall of the shower for support. She wasn't ready to get out just yet. She needed this peaceful solitude just a moment longer.

She would start with the fire department and wait to talk to the guys when they got back, she told herself as she watched the steam rising around her. Apparently they were still awake. She would have to suck it up and face James if he came back there.

She tried not to think of the last time she had seen Jesse, but failed. Closing her eyes she looked up at the water falling out of the shower head and got lost in the trance of her mind. Jesse was close by, she could feel it now that she was back in the pier.

Luna stared at herself half dressed in the steamy mirror after her shower. She remembered the last night she saw Jesse.

He had been trying to convince her to stay as she was packing her SUV. He had slammed her hatchback shut, grabbed her arms and demanded she tell him why she was leaving.

Luna had hated him for it. She hated that he had grabbed her arms and was trying to force her to do something she didn't want to do. Only James could evoke those feelings in her.

"Tell me why, damn it? Why are you leaving?"

Luna had looked in Jesse's eyes, blood tears dripping from her eyes only he was aloud to see. She knew if she told him because she didn't love James anymore he would just tell her to love him instead and stay, but she couldn't do that to James, or their family. Loving

Jesse would have been wrong on many levels. So she told Jesse the one thing that would make him let her go.

"Because I don't love you." She had choked on her own lie, but she had said it aloud and she couldn't take it back. It had been just another lie she had to say.

Jesse had shoved his own hands in his uniform pockets and looked at her defiantly. "Prove it."

Confused, she had looked at him questioningly.

"Kiss me." He had whispered the dare at her. His lips were shaking worried she wouldn't.

They had never kissed before or shown any kind of passion in public. They had kept their secrets and told no one, not even each other.

Luna and Jesse had teased each other for years, but he had never dared touch her or do anything that could have been seen as adulterous in public before unless it was to tempt James' ire.

For one split second, one of his heart beats, she had been tempted. She almost moved her feet towards him because she wanted too. She could see herself kissing him. She had always dreamed of it, and heaven help her there he was, telling her to do it.

She almost did.

Luna pulled out her white lace sundress that was tucked deep in one of her bags she had forgotten about, pulled it over her head and let it fall down her body. She put on a garter belt to hold up her stockings and wanted to kick herself for not packing any other under garments. Not like anyone was going to see that though, she told herself, almost heartbreakingly. She slipped on her white sandals and finished styling her hair. She clipped in tiny silver butterfly clips here and there down her hair.

She ran her fingers through the length of her long raven hair. She looked in the mirror one last time before she turned and left her hotel room. She barely recognized herself anymore. This is who she used to be. Not who she had been trying to becoming. She looked so different from the ponytail she had been sporting these last few years in her hiking clothes.

She looked down at her hands. The only piece of jewelry she ever wore was a ring from her past life she barely remembered. It was stamped with the impression of a wolf, and a gold necklace Jesse had given her when they had first met. She pulled it out from between her chest and her dress. She gently rubbed her finger over the charm. It was a golden, police and fire department medallion. She smiled at it. And then, she saw there on her left hand the perfect indent of a ring she no longer wore, from the years of wearing James' wedding band.

Angrily she walked out of her hotel suit and slammed the door.

When she stepped out into the midnight in the pier, she thought about calling her driver back. She changed her mind and decided to walk to the fire department. It wasn't a long walk. She kept telling herself she was just here to find out about her mother. Then she was leaving and going back to that cave. She wasn't going to stay here. She wasn't going to worry over the people here or that the world around them was going to hell in a handbasket.

She wouldn't... she might try to take Jesse back with her, she grinned to herself in the darkness.

Luna watched as memories she had made in this place passed her by while she walked on the streets she had walked on before. The restaurant, the Luna Cafe, she had been to with everyone more times than she could count. It was a fire department hang out.

As she passed the church where she had married James she tried not to look at it, but it's presence was ever looming next to her. The gas station though, had brought back memories of all those summers her and the Stone family had filled up the boat and water crafts with gas for their adventures on the lake.

As Luna walked closer to the edge of the city, closer to the waves she could hear crashing on the Lake Erie shore line, she couldn't help remembering all those summers spent with Jesse. Luna and Jesse loved being in the water together. She had no idea why it instilled feelings in her she couldn't control. It had a lot to do with Jesse, Luna grinned thinking about it, and his dirty little mind.

Somehow, when they were alone in the water, Jesse would find ways to be closer to Luna. Closer than he should've been. Just thinking about all those years on the lake brought her body to life in a way that she had to stop walking before she tripped on the broken sidewalk.

That was odd, she thought, looking at the broken sidewalk that was in front of the church. What had happened to the sidewalk, she questioned.

Looking around she noticed there was a lot wrong with the city. Trees were missing, leaving the fields empty where they had once stood for centuries. New telephone poles and lamppost had been recently installed, but they had been left eerily unfinished.

It looked like a tornado had blown through the city and they were still rebuilding from the damage.

Luna looked across the street at the fire department. Big bold letters read 'Luna Pier Fire Department' on its front. Luna almost sighed. She was truly home now.

Luna noticed there was only one truck parked at the department. It was Jesse's. Good she thought. They could be alone. It must have been Jerry with the police car over at the hospital and not Jesse.

She walked the distance to the front red door and turned the handle and walked right into Jesse.

Jesse had been at the department for over an hour. He had been cussing up a storm, pacing, wanting to throw everything he could get his hands on.

He accidentally kicked a mop bucket up against Engine two and splashed dirty mop water all over the floor causing him to finally stop his tirade. He was about to go and get a mop out of the hose tower closet but his thoughts stopped him next to the big red front door. He had to lean back against the engine to support him.

His father, Frank Stone had died hours ago at the hospital. Jesse had lost his brother a year ago, his little sister Izzy had ran away from home not too long ago, and now his father was gone.

Jesse had tried to believe that his father would make it tonight after the heart attack. He had prayed to whoever was listening to please save his father. But even he knew his father was too far gone. Between the marina fire last year and years of smoke damage to his lungs, he had been slowly dying this last year.

Jesse remembered the night he watched Asher struggle carrying out their screaming brother Curtis whose burnt body was still on fire. He and his brothers all knew the life of a fire fighter and the dangers they faced every day, but experiencing them first hand was a kind of reality slap he could have lived his whole life without knowing.

Jesse, for the first time ever, wished he would've chosen to become a full time firefighter like his brothers instead of choosing the life of a police officer. He couldn't help but wonder if he could have done something to have helped them that night. If his brother and father would still be alive if he had.

Jesse closed his eyes at the thought it might have been him that had died a year ago instead of Curtis.

Thoughts continued to haunt his mind. Would it have been such a bad thing?

Jesse was standing at the front of Engine two in front of the bay doors. He knew the rest of his family or at least Asher was going to see his truck parked here at the department and was bound to walk in any second to try to console him. He hung his head and held onto the front of the truck gripping his hands and causing pain as the steel of the diamond plated bumper cut into his fingers.

He couldn't stand anyone else touching him. He couldn't take another hug from his mother or sisters. He couldn't stand another pat on his back from his brother Asher or James. They kept telling him it was ok to cry, but he hadn't cried over Curtis either, he wasn't about to now.

The last person he expected to see walk in through that big red door was Luna.

~ *Three* ~

Be still, look at what's right in front of you

Jesse groaned an ungentlemanly whimper at the sight of Luna in her white sun dress. He had craved her and that dress all this time she had been away. He let go of the truck he had been holding onto, astonished by the way she had hauntingly come into the fire department just when he needed her. He walked up to her and bent his knees to wrap Luna in his arms as soon as she let go of the door.

He hadn't meant to pick her up. He didn't mean to use her for a shoulder to cry on. But, the moment his tears finally let go, he couldn't stop them.

He hadn't meant a lot of things in his life, and the only thing he regretted now was her, he thought with a long drawn out sigh that shook him with the weight of his grief.

Not making Luna his the moment he met her was his worst mistake. Not stopping the wedding as he sat there drunk and watched her vow her life to James was another.

When he had seen her tonight, he couldn't help himself when he wrapped her in the comfort of his body. She was everything he needed in this moment of darkness. His own personal hell he needed to pull her into to save him.

He knew she was mourning the life of her mother, and was just as stricken with grief as he was with his father's death. He sighed into her neck and held her like his own life depended on it though.

Luna had a way of making everything in his life better when no one else could.

"I swear you're an angel sometimes Babe." Jesse choked on his every word as he nuzzled closer to her in his embrace and held her as close to him as he could fit her.

Luna noticed right away Jesse was almost twice the size he had been when she had left him. She didn't know why he was here alone or why he was holding her so tight, but she let him. She held him and did the only thing she could. She let him hold her.

It was what they did for each other; what they had always done for each other. Their bodies welcomed it, their friendship depended on it.

It wasn't like Jesse to do this though. Men didn't do this, did they, she wondered quietly. She had never witnessed anything in her life like it. She had never held anyone like she was holding him now. Like his whole world was falling to pieces and he needed her to save him.

"Jesse? Baby." She breathed, asking for his permission again into his shoulder.

Even though once before she could reach his neck on her tippy toes, now she would only be able to reach up to the bottom of his shoulder. It was very odd, she thought silently. Somehow he was big enough to crush her had she been a human.

No wonder he had bent down to pick her up.

Luna breathed him in closer wrapping her arms around him regretfully. He had grown up so much over these years without her. More than she could have ever have dreamed of. He smelled like the fire department around them she remembered, and a little differently. More- what was the word she needed. Manly? She almost chuckled to herself.

"What is it Baby?" She beckoned him again. Letting the side of her cheek nuzzle the side of his when let her down. He bent down closer to her never letting go of his embrace aground her. She almost lost it though when she felt his tear on her cheek.

Jesse never cried.

Jesse had finally let his entire body relax and breathe when she had spoken to him, called him baby like she always had in their past. He buried his nose in her hair and breathed her in heavily. He just wanted her to stay there in his arms.

Luna felt it in the way he moved, the way he breathed. He had his arms wrapped around her back so tightly and his legs were pressed into hers like a dance move. He was bending into her like he had to touch her with his whole being.

Something was very wrong. Luna could feel it inside of him. Jesse never did this.

"Jesse, tell me." She demanded of him, almost shaking him with her hands holding onto his sides. It was almost funny, she had been the one in need of saving. And yet here he was, the big oaf, with some kind of super human strength and might, needing her to save him.

The way he fell into her and was holding her, the way he was falling apart, the way he needed her, it almost made her want to destroy what ever had done this to him. He had been her hero just hours before. Now she would be his. Whatever he needed her to be.

Jesse breathed, and almost choked on his words again. He didn't know how to tell her what was happening around the world or that his father had just died. Died because of all the fires going on in the city lately that had caused enough smoke damage to kill him.

She didn't know about how Curtis had died either and he knew it was going to hurt like hell when he told her.

His father, James and Jerry; they all believed there were rouge vampires like her killing people and destroying cities all around them catching everything on fire faster than they could put it out. They were right though and because she had chosen to leave just before all this started to take place, she was safe from their rumors. Jesse sighed deeply vowing he would do everything to protect her from them.

Jesse trusted Luna like he trusted no one else, he thought as he ran one of his hands up under her hair and down her hip along her side. Knowing what she was only ripped his heart open further at times. But holding her here now, gripping her hip tighter almost like he was dancing to a slow love song with her, it restored what little faith he had lost in her.

Jesse closed his eyes shut and held her for just one more, unsteady moment, knowing as soon as the truth was out he'd have to let her go.

Luna closed her eyes and felt his moment he was stealing. She knew she'd never get this moment back if she let it slip away. So she held onto it too for him.

"It's my father, Luna." He struggled to tell her, in a silent whisper giving her permission to enter his mind. And then when he couldn't see past his father's death, he opened up his mind to her and showed her everything he couldn't say aloud.

His father had a fatal heart attack tonight. It was unexpected and sudden. Jesse had just spent hours at the hospital while the doctors tried to save his father and couldn't. He hadn't stayed long after his father had passed.

Then he remembered Curtis for Luna, dying last year in the marina fire. Jesse almost lost it again. The tremble that shook his body couldn't be helped.

He had wanted to be alone, to not think about it all, until Luna walked into the fire department, and walked willingly right back into his arms.

Now that Luna was close to Jesse, now that she could read his mind once he opened it to her, he didn't have to tell her anything else. She could read it all there in his mind. His ever present fears over the war raging around him and everything that had happened to his father and Curtis were now known to her. There were vampires, rogue vampires, hunting and murdering people. And he couldn't stop them.

In that moment it was like they had never been apart, but the knowledge of it all made Luna chillingly aware of her absence in his life. He had been afraid and needed her. He had missed her so damn much she could feel the pain of it in his soul.

Luna clung to Jesse then. "Oh Jesse. I am so, so sorry Baby."

She lifted her arms and raised them around his neck as he lifted her in his embrace. She felt his troubled heart beating up against hers and the chaos his mind was in. The state of his soul was in distress.

All she could do was hold him tighter and be everything he needed in that moment.

When he leaned in to her embrace, when he pulled her off the ground and held her impossibly closer, when she felt one last lonely tear fall from his lips unto her shoulder and fall down her arm, she placed her fingers on the back of his head and promised his soul she would never leave him again.

Jesse pulled back, setting her down he apologized. "No, I'm sorry. I know you came back home to grieve your mom-"

Luna hushed him and placed a finger on his lips. He didn't have to apologize to her. "It's ok." She whispered softly. "She probably just left to get out of the city. In a disguise, burning the shop down and all."

Luna wanted to believe it about her mother, she thought looking at his chest as she straightened his shirt. She really did. She looked up at Jesse in reassurance then. "I'm here now. We will figure this all out together, ok? I promise."

Luna got lost in his weary eyes. Jesse was tired, he was shaken to his core, he was breaking inside. He needed her.

He rested now, leaning back against the front of the engine, taking her with him between his legs while she held onto his shirt, and Luna almost started crying at the weight she felt that lifted off of him.

She wanted to take the pain of losing his father away from him but she heard the unmistakable sounds of vehicles driving up into the parking lot next to the big red door. It was Asher's truck, she recognized the sound of it. James and most likely the rest of the family were right behind him.

They both let go of each other quickly. The embrace had to end. Or at least that was how the past had always ended their embrace.

They both looked at the door and somehow their fingers found each other in one last embrace. It was a bad habit both of them had developed. To be still. Pretending they weren't touching each other, not to look at each other when anyone was around, but somehow their bodies always betrayed them.

With a heavy laden sigh at the sound of unwanted company, Jesse knew he had to hide Luna. He could tell from her reaction she didn't want anyone to know she was home.

"Here." He pushed her towards the hose closet next to Engine 2, behind her where the department hung hoses to dry after they were used in a fire.

It was the closest door he could find and the perfect spot to hide her. It was the same closet he was headed to earlier where the mops were.

He hadn't meant to go in the closet with her, but he wasn't ready to leave her side yet. In the depths of the dark closet he stood there in front of her, face to face, the sound of the big red door opening and the sound of their families voices entering the fire department next to them, right outside their door.

Jesse reached for Luna. There in the darkness he reached for her hips, grasping and feeling the lacy essence of her thin dress he loved with his fingers, pulling her slowly towards him. He breathed in her fresh scent as he towered over her as she stepped closer into him.

He closed his eyes when his nose touched her hair and tried to remember all the reasons he wasn't supposed to touch her, why he wasn't supposed to love her. His resistance wasn't that strong.

Even though every one who would be offended by those things had now come into the department just outside the closet door, close enough to hear the two of them, he bent down and enveloped her in his arms again anyways.

Luna was scared. James probably hadn't signed the papers yet. He probably hadn't even told his family she had filed for a divorce. She had tried for so many years not to let the family she cherished as her own, the Stone family, suspect or even see her love for their other son Jesse. But here they were, trapped in closet together in what could only be mistaken for a lovers embrace.

It would be a scandal the whole city would talk about. She worried she would never see any of them again. That they too, like what her brother had done to her, would want her out of their lives, and she couldn't ask that of Jesse. She couldn't let him abandon his family to run off with her. It was why she had left. She had left everyone she held dear in her life to run as far away from James as she could get. Knowing she was really running away from Jesse.

But being here in the closet with Jesse, in secret, like her entire life had always been, she longed to just hold him, to just feel him. To not let anyone from her past but him see her. Only Jesse knew who she really was. Just by the way he was holding her, trying to remember that she too was in mourning, touched her heart and broke it at the same time.

"Baby." she whispered to him softly, burying her lips in his neck trying not to kiss him there as she clung to his shirt in between them.

"What Babe?" He asked her quietly, wondering what she needed. He'd give her anything she asked.

"I just really missed you Jes-" She tried not whimper when she said it, but she did.

"Shh." He whispered softly back to her against her bare neck trying not to kiss her either. He pulled her tighter against him when he felt her shatter.

Jesse let his hand that was holding her hip pressing her neatly up against him, run softly up her side. He meant to hold her cheek and look at her and tell her he missed her too, but he heard his brother Asher outside the closet door.

"I'll grab a mop."

Jesse cussed out loud, silently. The mops were here in this closet. Asher was going to clean up the mess Jesse had made earlier. He couldn't let Asher see them so he picked up Luna wrapping her arms and legs in front him, he started up the steel ladder next to them that lead up the 50 foot tower to the top of the hoses where they were hung, and climbed as fast as his arms would allow.

Jesse breathed in heavily and clung to the ladder when he reached a quarter of the way up the tower. He stopped knowing he was out of sight over the door, resting his forehead against Luna's struggling to breathe. He didn't know how long he could stand there on the ladder holding her.

The light in the closet above them came on. They both listened and looked at each other as Asher opened the door, grabbed a mop and shut the door back. Leaving the light on in the closet.

Luna looked away from Jesse and tried not to giggle.

"Have you been working out?". She wondered aloud, looking back at him. She couldn't believe his size now that they were in better light. The way he swooped her off her feet and carried her up here. It was galant to say the least, she thought excitedly.

Jesse lifted his head to her. "A little." He told her quickly. "Firefighter, remember?" He told her secretly, raising an eyebrow to her, daring her to tease him more.

He knew any second she was going to feel his reaction to having her legs wrapped around his midsection, cradling her like he was. He tried not to look her in the eyes, knowing he couldn't look at her reaction to him, so he looked at her lips, like he had always done. Which, only made everything worse.

Luna was trying not to gulp the air around her as she felt Jesse growing harder. He was looking at her lips like he always did and she could feel everything he was feeling in that moment. She tried not to shutter, but failed.

It made him harder still.

Jesse looked down over his shoulder. "Come on Asher." He pleaded aloud to his brother even though Asher couldn't hear him.

Luna whispered in his ear softly while he was looking away from her, "How long do you honestly think you can hold me like this?"

She wondered how long it would take for him to figure out she should be the one holding him, she was stronger than he was.

He shuddered at her breath radiating off his neck and ear as it pulsated through his blood right to his-

"As long as it takes." He groaned, interrupting his own thoughts, looking right into her eyes, not willing to be affected by her even though he knew it was too late.

Asher choose that moment to walk in and place the mop and the problem bucket Jesse had kicked earlier back in the closet and shut the door.

Asher had left the lights on though. The switch was on the outside of the closet.

Jesse and Luna both held their breath and looked down at the offending mop and bucket.

Luna waited and looked at the side of Jesse's face. He was unshaven. His dark blonde hair was in desperate need of a cut. It was unlike him to be in such a state. He looked cuter like this she thought to herself wishing she could run her fingers through his hair.

Why couldn't she, she questioned herself secretly. Tonight was so different than any other night she had ever spent with him. First off being she was not a married woman any longer. Secondly, they were alone.

So finally she did what her heart longed to do, unashamed.

She ran her fingers gently through his messy hair barely touching him. She wanted to question him about his father, but Jesse turned then and looked at her.

Damn, she was beautiful, he thought to himself when his eyes finally let his mind look at her, wishing she couldn't hear his thoughts.

He groaned and had to adjust his hold on the rails of the ladder and pull them closer together as he adjusted her bottom. Her bare bottom, he noticed as his hands felt more skin than it should under her leg he was holding. He tried to squeeze his eyes shut and pretend like he wasn't hard with her so neatly pressed around his length, but he was really hard now.

Luna tried not to laugh. She had to stifle it in his shoulder and hold him against her so he could hold her better. Jesse had day dreamed of a situation like this with Luna. He had been more debonair in his daydreams, but right now he was falling to pieces.

The more he adjust her though, the more she felt it right in her over heating core.

"Baby, we have to climb down, this is silly. I think Asher is done with the mop now."

Jesse pulled back and looked at her astonished. "The lights are on. What if someone walks in?" He knew he needed to think of a better idea, but he couldn't think looking at her sheepish grin.

"Well...". Luna thought more about it. It was the best idea she could come up with. "They shouldn't be here long, right?"

They both listened as the big red door opened again followed by more voices of other firemen they both knew. They both sighed greatly. And looked back down.

They both knew that they all could be here for hours. That's how nights like this went at the fire hall. Families and friends gathered together and shared in moments. Tonight, with the loss of Frank, the chief, everyone would stay to comfort the family members as long as time allowed.

Luna eyed him worriedly sideways when he wasn't looking, Jesse should be out there with all of them.

She thought quickly about just walking out when no one was around, she could pay her respects to the family even though she knew James was here.

Luna groaned inwardly. She wasn't ready to face James yet.

"It's not like anyone else is gonna need the mop again, right?." She tried to whisper to him resting her lips on his shoulder, trying again not to kiss him there, or worse, bite him.

Jesse looked up then. "There's a landing at the top."

Luna looked up then. The motion made her neck visible to Jesse. She felt as his hardness throbbed against her and bucked uncontrollably at his new thoughts. He wanted to slowly kiss her neck.

She looked at him more directly then. It was shameful, his thoughts, she thought with a shameful smile of her own.

She had to distract him.

"It's very small-."

"There is nothing small about it, Babe!" Jesse grinned at Luna. Pulling her closer and lifting her slightly up his length to prove himself.

Luna couldn't control the reaction her body had to his movement. She had to close her eyes and bite her lip as she took in a deep breath of Jesse's essence. He was heated right to his core and it was driving her insane.

"I meant the landing." She told him in a soft moan, biting her lip harder.

She knew- well, now she knew exactly how 'big' he really was, but she never dreamed how perfectly right he was. She had only stolen glances at him before when he had worn gym shorts like he was now.

Now she was just as heated as he was at being this close together wrapped around him.

"Do you ever wear underwear?" She questioned him breathlessly, knowing the answer was no because she could always tell in the past when he wasn't. Feeling him bare under his thin material and knowing just how bare she was against him made it difficult to speak.

Jesse smiled evilly. He knew she could feel him now. "Um, I'm not the only one not wearing any tonight Babe." He told her as he ran his thumb foolishly along her garter strap, and squeezed his fingers into the bare flesh he felt on her ass cheek.

"I forgot to pack them!" She growled heavily, trying not to concentrate on his hand, or how hard he was. And, just how much she wanted this.

She tried really hard all the time not to think about how sad her marriage sex life had been with James, and how wonderfully, lovingly, different it would be with Jesse.

Jesse looked up then and broke her silence.

"If I can make it to the landing, there is an attic door we can open. The attic leads to the roof. There we can wait till everyone leaves."

He eyed her curiously then wondering what she was thinking. She wasn't paying attention to him at all. Why, he wondered quietly.

If they did that, it would mean that they would both have to let go of each other, Luna heard both their hearts and minds beckon their disappointment. Sadly, she was the only one that heard hers.

That had never bothered her before... until now. Looking at him now, she wondered why that was.

Jesse could sense it. He could feel her let out a sigh. She didn't want to let go either. But Jesse couldn't hold both their weight anymore. He had to climb, and with every step up he took, he couldn't control the feelings he felt for her.

He growled softly as he fought to climb. He could feel how her lower lips spread apart as she opened her legs wider to hold onto him tight and how neatly they fit together. He could feel her as she rested her arms on his shoulder and he could hear her moans as he bumped into her. He could feel the little movements her hips made with every step up like she was rocking back down onto him.

Jesse had to stop almost to the top and looked above them. He was a good ten steps away from the landing. He knew he could make it. He was strong enough. With one foot above the other resting there, he adjusted her again and tried not to climax at the feeling of holding her closer. Her womanhood felt so warm and inviting it made him tremble.

She was holding his head against her shoulder now, cradling him. Letting her fingers play with the edges of his hair. He was tangled up in her and it felt so damn amazing.

Luna never felt warm. She was always ice cold reminding him of who she was. But now she was just as heated as he was.

They had never been this close together. He had missed her so much he didn't want to let her go now. He hadn't even kissed her yet!

It almost wasn't fair, he told himself pressing his lips against her neck so softly he hoped she wouldn't notice.

Luna listened to his thoughts and it caused her to bite his neck. She couldn't take it anymore. She had to break his spell over them. She hadn't meant to bite so hard, but the draw of blood she tasted on her lips was sweet. She sucked it in and sealed his wound shut with her tongue. It caused a different type of hunger inside of her and a distraction for him that she hoped would do the trick for them both.

Jesse closed his eyes at the pierce of her fangs through his skin. It hurt, but it also distracted him enough to finish climbing the rest of the way. Knowing though that she had heard his thoughts and felt them too made him smirk all the way up.

"Baby." She moaned aloud softly as he climbed. She needed him to stop. She couldn't help the moan once it broke her lips. The feel of what he was doing all over again so close to her, she couldn't bare it anymore. The way he was rubbing against her, into her.

"I'm trying Babe." He laughed a little at her weakness. "I'm not stopping though." Not again, he told her honestly as he climbed faster.

When he made it to the top he tried to judge the distance to the landing next to them. He needed her to turn around and hold onto the ladder so he could scoot over to the landing and pull her over to him. But he couldn't breathe anymore from the climb. The desire to bury himself inside her was too great.

"Jesse." She said breathlessly as she reached for his face and turned it towards her. She had to concentrate so she could tell him something.

It was very hard to do between his thoughts of making love to her right here and now. He couldn't stop looking at her lips and then her breast in the moonlight shining through the top of tower.

Oh, how she wanted him to do all of those things he was thinking about right now. She was almost panting with want and desire at what his mind was imagining.

"The ladder- Jesse. It's made of steel."

Well, that explained why she hadn't tried to do this all herself, he thought awkwardly, dragging his eyes away from body and looking at her like she wanted him too. The steel against her hands would burn her.

Luna turned quickly and looked at the ladder then back at him, making him listen to her. "I can do it for a minute, but you have to hurry. Ok?"

Jesse absolutely loved it when Luna grabbed his face like this. He couldn't help but grin at her lovingly, even though his arms were burning. He placed his forehead on hers as he said "But it's gonna hurt Babe-"

Luna pushed him back to hush him. She could do this.

She touched her fingers to his lips and interrupted him. She'd done this before, touched his lips and tried to hush him when he was being silly. That was when she was sober though, when she wasn't drunk with being turned on so high.

Instead, she looked at his lips and unknowingly opened her mouth and had to lick her own lips, slowly letting her fingers fall away from his lips. It cause a tremble that went throughout her entire body. She had to suck away the venom mixed with need pooling around her tongue.

Luna wanted to kiss him... so bad she almost burst into tears.

"What?" He grinned questioning her, trying not to chuckle at her. She never did this. He had never seen her look at his lips like she was now as her fingers fell away. Was she really speechless, he wondered in amazement.

Luna looked up at his eyes then.

"Just hurry." She grinned back at him playfully, glad that he couldn't read her mind and turned in his arms with his help.

It did burn, and hurt like hell to hold unto to steel bars. But she did it. Distracting herself throughly from her thoughts of wanting and needing him.

When Jesse sat on the landing letting his legs fall off the ledge he caught her as she leapt helplessly unto him. She landed back in his lap wrapped around him again.

It was his turn now to bite her shoulder as she crawled back onto him. He was dying from the emptiness he felt as he selfishly pulled her back onto his hardness where he wanted and needed her.

Jesse grabbed her hands trying to distract himself lifting his head away from her body and her scent. He knew she could feel pain because of the steel by the way she was cradling her hands in between their bodies. He flipped her palms over slowly and kissed them each tenderly.

"Better?" He asked her lovingly, eyeing her closely in the moonlight that was coming through the vent. The light in the closet didn't reach up this far.

Luna took in a deep breath. They still hurt like hell. Jesse was the sweetest, most gentlemanly man she had ever met. He had never kissed her before. She was seriously jealous of her hands.

"No." She told him honestly, not wanting to lie, and laughed quietly with him when he did. It felt wonderful, like it always had, to be herself with Jesse. She had never had this kind of relationship with anyone, ever, especially a human.

Jesse looked to his left with his hand feeling for the attic door, then looked to his right. It wasn't on either side. Damn, he thought, resting his head against the door behind him. He was blocking the door. They were blocking the door. He wanted to kick himself for not noticing it before he got on the landing.

Luna had to stifle her laugh in his chest. She couldn't help it. Oh the irony, she thought to herself. All his hard work for nothing. She leaned forward against his chest and held his shirt in both of her hands.

Jesse laughed too. He had no choice but to put his hands back on her hips.

Luna stilled as he gripped her hips.

This was different and they both knew it. If he moved her, even an inch, it was no longer an accident or something they had to do.

Not that anything either one of them had done tonight could be consider as such, but somehow, this would be different than anything they had ever done together.

Jesse felt her still. He knew what that meant. And all of his ungentlemanly hopes melted away. It pained him to do it so he let himself think of anything else other than her.

Thinking of his father did it.

Luna listened to Jesse's heart. She tried not to let it bother her... but it did. Would she ever be able to forget that she was now allowed to touch him after so long of not being able too?

"Now what?" they both spoke to each other at the same time.

Jesse sighed and let her speak first, knowing she would have a plan. Luna always had a plan.

Luna looked down below them into the darkness, it wasn't an option.

"Oh hell no!" He echoed her thoughts even though he couldn't hear them.

Luna covered his mouth with both of her hands again shushing him for being so loud which lifted her off him a little. Which was stupid, she knew, it only made her feel giddy though because at some point she was going to have to sit back down.

She slowly did it shushing him with her hands and daring him with a look not to get hard again as she sat back down and told him "I wasn't thinking of climbing back down." She turned then and looked back at the ladder. "If I can get back on the ladder-"

It was his turn to interrupt her. She always had ideas, but they were never good ones. "Let me stand up with you. You can slide down me, bend down and go through the attic door and I'll follow you."

Luna thought about that, seeing his plan. Although it was a good one, she worried about it. "What if we fall Jesse?"

Jesse sighed then, reached up and cupped her cheek slowly with his hand, taking a deep breath as he did it looking at her, knowing he was going to grow hard again. "I fell for you along time ago Babe."

He didn't have to look down at the fifty feet to the bottom. He knew if they fell, he would die.

He knew it was her thoughts he had to put at ease though, so he told her with a grin, "I won't let you fall." His meaning was twofold. It had always been such.

Luna always felt like she was falling when he was near her. No matter how hard she tried to catch herself, she never could. She closed her eyes and bit her lips with her fang. She turned her face into Jesse's hand and cradled it with her own. She kissed the inside of his hand softly and tried not to cry.

Jesse coughed then and cleared his throat. It was time to stand. He reached under her and pulled them both up. It was time to get her out of here.

It was awkward, but they did it. Luna opened the door and crawled between his legs and had to crawl inside the attic because she couldn't stand up.

It was a tight attic; a tunnel of sorts.

She looked around as Jesse crawled in behind her. He almost had to crawl on top of her behind her to squeeze in. Luna found it amusing and had to hide her laugh as she looked for the door that led to the roof.

"You can see in here right?" He questioned her. "Because I can't see a damn thing."

Luna could see, but not the door he spoke of. "Where?" She asked as she looked around.

"I don't know. I've never been up here before. I thought it was an attic. Apparently it's a tunnel." He confessed as he held onto her, trying not to fall out back onto the landing as she maneuvered around.

This only brought him awkwardly on top of her as she spun under him and looked up.

"Ah ha! Found it." She beamed at him even though he couldn't see what she was looking at above him.

Time stopped for her when it stopped for him. He was over top of her, all around her. His hands were on either side of her. She could feel everything he was feeling in those moments there in the darkness.

Like the pounding of keys playing hard on a piano during a thunderous song, so could she feel the pounding of his heart beat for her.

Luna couldn't help herself, if she didn't ask him for what her mind, body, and soul longed for now, she didn't know if she ever could again.

She ran her hand up into his hair. Because she needed to steal his strength to do what her heart wanted.

"Ask me again Baby." She pleaded softly in a careless whisper asking for his permission. She placed her other hand on his heart and pleaded for him to remember what she was asking for. What he had asked her for once before.

She knew if she was alive her heart would be pounding like his was now, beating wildly. He wanted to kiss her. This she knew as sure as she knew the dawning of the rising sun.

Jesse closed his eyes then and swallowed hard. He held his eyes tightly together. He knew she was asking him to let her kiss him. He knew because his heart was pounding out his answer before his lips could speak of it. He knew because it was exactly what he wanted to do to her.

He could hear himself thinking 'no' also, in the back side of his brain, but his body was struggling and fighting against himself with an urgency stronger than ever before, ripping him apart.

When he opened his eyes he looked down in the darkness and he could see her there, waiting, pleading with him for what she wanted.

Jesse thought about James then. Thoughts of his brother, and every reason he had never kissed Luna before entered his mind. He had to shake his head to jar lose the trembling that quickened his heart into a frenzy he couldn't control.

He couldn't do it. He couldn't betray the man he had hated for as long as he could remember. And then, in that moment, he couldn't understand why she could.

"What are you doing?" Jesse asked in almost an unspoken whisper. Not what she was doing, but what was he doing?

Luna, stunned, breathlessly questioned him in the stillness. After all these years, after everything that had happened tonight, she couldn't understand how his conflicted conscious won out over his unstable desire.

And that's when it hit her. With a blinding flurry so sever she almost fumed with hatred, she understood. James not only hadn't signed those damn papers, he hadn't told his family about the divorce either! There was no way if Jesse knew she was divorced that he wouldn't have asked her, that he wouldn't have kissed her. She could feel it in his struggle.

"Where the hell is that damn door?" Jesse reached above him and found the latch that opened the door. He stood as he opened it and stepped up onto the roof without helping her out.

He walked to the ledge of the roof and tried to catch his breath. Tried to calm down. He still couldn't believe he hadn't kissed her. He put his hands on the ledge and waited. For what he didn't know, but his body was still struggling, conflicted with absent resolution.

Jesse turned then and looked for her, knowing she was right behind him. She was looking at him worried. Her long raven hair blowing softly in the summers night wind. She looked like his worst nightmare. She was frightened.

"What the hell are you doing?" He questioned her this time, seriously, because God help him if she asked him again he wouldn't be able to stop himself from kissing her with all abandonment of conscious thought. James be damned to his own mistakes.

Luna read his mind. To him, she was just playing, teasing him. He didn't know anything about the divorce papers. And he was so close to breaking their promises of not committing adultery, she had to tell him, stop him before he did it.

Damn James, she thought to herself. Damn him and all his stubborn ways. How could he have so selfishly not told his family. She couldn't understand how he had gotten away with it either.

Had he told everyone she was just on vacation? His family had to of known better, she wondered.

"Jesse," She was beckoning him now, raising her hands in a pleading jester for him to wait for her and listen. "I didn't just leave James and walk away all those years ago, I divorced him. It is over between us."

Over? Jesse tried to let that one word set in as he turned and placed a hand on the wall next to him. He had to let his heart rate slow down first though so he could hear himself think. He hadn't expected this answer.

Over? He understood the word better now. He was truly astonished though.

Why hadn't James told him, he wondered? What could James possibly be thinking not telling his family about the divorce?

He looked at her then for answers. "When?" He asked her in almost a plea. He had to know when as he turned back around facing her now.

Luna sighed and almost growled thinking about what Jesse thought. Why hadn't James told anyone?

She looked away then, thinking maybe James hadn't signed the papers.

Slowly, she edged closer to Jesse. "Even if he didn't sign the papers, it is still over."

She told Jesse honestly, looking directly at him as she said it. "I divorced him when I left Jesse. He's had the papers all this time. I swear it."

She needed Jesse to understand how she felt about James. She moved closer to him still. She tried to reach for him, but he stilled her with his hand.

Jesse questioned her, looking desperately at her, knowing she would know what he was asking. "Why?" It was an unfinished question he needed the answer too.

He was so close to her now and what he wanted, it almost felt too good to be true. He waited for her answer and drank in the sight of her. Like desperately wanting a drink of something you can't have. He knew if he touched her, if he let her get too close, she wouldn't get another chance to speak at all because he wouldn't be able to stop himself once he started kissing her.

Luna looked at Jesse for what felt like the first time. She touched the hand he was stopping her with and held it. He was pushing and pulling her away in ways that made her feel like she was falling. She had never needed to touch him, she had never wanted him the way she wanted him right now.

But why? And that was really what he wanted to know. He needed to know how she felt about James still, yes, but he needed to know how she felt about him, and why.

She had left Jesse, and told him she didn't love him. Only she knew the truth now. And now he needed to know it.

She had been gone for so long that the need to run to him, to envelope him inside of herself and just show him how much she truly loved him was overpowering.

She wanted it all back now. Every little piece in time she had missed. Every moment they had shared before. She wanted to do it all over again.

She wondered then, how she had ever thought being alone was what she had really wanted all this time. With Jesse, standing here in front of her, she didn't think she could ever go back to being alone again.

Luna stole one moment out of time to think. Jesse wouldn't even know it, she told herself. She needed to grasp her thoughts and hold them in front of her and just look at them for a minute. She needed to look at Jesse for just a second longer and ask herself what he was asking her.

And then she knew. It was because she loved Jesse. Yes, it had always been why. From that very first moment in time they had shared together when his eyes looked into hers and they both knew they wanted each other, to the next when his heart skipped a beat.

And then, she had to admit, as she looked into the eyes of the younger Jesse in her mind at school that day, he had stolen a piece of her heart in that moment in time when his heart stopped beating, because without her heart inside of his, her love, his never would have beat again. It was the moment when she looked at him the same way, when he realized she felt the same, that his heart started beating again through the power of her own love towards him.

And it wasn't until this moment right now, that she realized she had wasted too many moments, too much time. To many of his heart beats she could never get back. She had carelessly thrown them away.

She had never loved James! He was all kinds of wrong for her. And somehow, Jesse was all the right kind of wrongs for her.

Luna looked at Jesse, let go of the time she had been clinging too, ready to tell him everything. But Jesse's next thoughts stole her breath away.

Jesse saw a figure standing in the doorway that led into the fire department behind her. His brother Asher was standing there in the darkness. He looked back at Luna and sighed deeply, swallowing a lump of regret and wishing he hadn't broken the spell they were under together when he noticed Asher.

Jesse had seen her thinking of his question, and her hesitation to answer him was all the answer he needed. She must still be in love with James in some sort of way, he wondered silently to himself, watching Luna look over to Asher now like she always did when she was ashamed to be alone with Jesse, letting go of him said more to him than any words she could have spoken to him tonight.

Jesse tucked his hands in his pockets and leaned back against the ledge behind him, defeated, knowing she'd never answer him now. He didn't have to be a mind reader like her to understand what she was thinking. He heard it in the way she gasped at the sight of Asher.

Luna had turned at Jesse's thoughts towards Asher. She had to cover her gasp when she seen Asher for herself and read his mind. She had been so wrapped up in Jesse she missed the sound of Asher approaching.

It wasn't that Asher was there, it was his thoughts she heard. Luna's heart dropped at Asher's thoughts. He was ashamed of them. Everything Luna had worried about happening in the past, happened right before her eyes. Asher had been standing there apparently long enough to assume they were having a rendezvous on top of the fire department alone.

She was going to beat James with those papers and make him read them aloud, in front of his entire family, she told herself angrily. Especially her own words she had written about why she wanted the divorce.

She watched as Asher turned and walked away from them both back down into the fire hall.

"I'll talk to him." Jessie whispered as he came up behind her and drug his fingers slowly up her arm, then he wrapped his arms around her. He wanted to reassure her in any way he could that he would fix this.

Luna closed her eyes and leaned back into Jesse. She didn't know how much she had missed the warmth of his arms until tonight. Letting him hold her like this reminded her of how much she loved how affectionate Jesse was all the time. It felt so right.

She sighed heavily, letting the burden of Asher go. He would understand it all and more soon enough.

Luna turned in Jesse's arms. She beckoned him as she let her hands follow the tattooed path up his muscular arms to his shoulders where she intertwined her fingers behind his neck.

He looked into her golden eyes in the moonlight and knew everything was about to change. He moved a stray hair off of her forehead and knew they had a lot of other things to deal with tonight instead of this. He needed to be with his family, and she needed to be with hers. He knew he would just have to wait for the answers to his question.

"Jesse?" She questioned him after his thoughts of family, running her hands back up to his face to get his attention.

Jesse eyed her curiously when she looked intently at him.

"Where is my mother?" She asked him slowly. "I need to see her. I need to know-"

Jesse hushed her taking both her hands in his off his shoulders. He didn't want to have to show her. Ever. But he understood why she wanted him too.

"Joseph has her. He took her body from the morgue afterwards. We had to follow protocol as not to raise suspicions. He didn't want the medical examiner to autopsy her. Not with the way things are now."

When she looked away from him, clearly planning her next move, Jesse stole a glance at her. He looked in her beautiful eyes he had missed, he looked at her cheeks that he knew were ice cold and longed to warm them with his palm. Then he looked at her lips with a desire stronger now than before to kiss them softly, building with intensity like a heated flame fueled with the passion he had burning inside of him that needed release.

Anger flared and ignited in Luna as he spoke of Joseph taking her mother's body. She understood his motives. She had been too far away from home to make those decisions for her mother.

Luna looked down between them trying to think of her next move. She raised her arms and placed her hands on Jesse's chest then. She started hurting all over again thinking about her mother.

"I need to go to the Whitby's." She whispered softly.

She looked back up at him then, pleading for him to understand why she couldn't finish what they had started tonight.

"Well, Emie is here with Asher." He told her as he looked back at the doorway. "Maybe we can all go over there together tonight with them."

He almost begged her not to leave him looking back down at her. He could see her plan even though she hadn't told it to him yet. He reached for her hips and pulled her tighter up against him and emphasized what he wanted.

He couldn't let her leave alone. Not tonight. Not with the way the world was falling apart. He needed her.

Luna froze, scared. "What did you just say?"

Jesse looked at her confused.

"What do you mean Emie- Jesse?" Luna grabbed his shirt then begging him for answers. "Emillie Whitby? Why is Emie with Asher?" She exclaimed aloud looking at the door where Asher had been, then back at Jesse, begging him now to explain, gripping the front of his shirt harder.

Luna entered his mind without asking him and it was there, all of it. Emie and Asher were together.

Luna almost expired right then. What little blood she had left inside her body drained from her. She even lost her footing as her knees went weak.

"Jesse no!" She cried aloud, covering her mouth.

Jesse tried to hold her, he saw the expression on Luna's face and it worried him. He didn't understand. He looked over at the door where he just saw his brother and worried for his safety.

"I don't understand Luna. Isn't Emie just like you?" He asked her quietly, looking back down at her.

Luna shook her head no. She didn't know what to do, or say now.

"No Jesse. She is very different from me." Very different, she thought worriedly. "They are required to take certain lives, Jesse. It's why I always kept you away from them. Asher is not safe with Emie."

Luna knew she couldn't do anything to stop Emie here, she thought as she pulled away from Jesse to collect her thoughts. Well, she could, but the wrath of Emie's brothers would destroy her first. She couldn't fight them all. She had to go to Joseph and plead for her family. Plead for their lives.

She worried though as she looked back over at Jesse. What she had always worried about was Jesse. She worried now she had made the wrong decision as she held onto him with one hand. She gripped his arms tight then. She should have run away with Jesse a long time ago.

Luna looked back at the door to the fire hall like Jesse was doing, then she looked up at him. "I need to go see Joseph. Can you take care of Asher?"

Jesse looked at Luna worried. He hated her leaving, but he had learned along time ago that he couldn't follow her into her world alone. He didn't know how to deal with Asher, but he would do everything to protect him.

Luna thought about that too. He needed to be with his family right now, he couldn't go with her. She hated leaving him also. Their thoughts almost unnerved her. The idea of running from here with Jesse was more tempting now.

She knew she needed to deal with Joseph alone first. She needed answers.

"Just stay safe Babe, please."

"I'll see you soon." Luna promised him. She reached up on her tippy toes and placed a kiss on his cheek, then turned to leap over the edge of the fire department. If she didn't walk away from him now she wouldn't be able too. She had to hurry.

One second Luna was there, kissing his cheek so softly, wrapped safely in his arms, reassuring him everything was going to be ok with her sweet smile, and the next, his hands that where holding her hips were empty and she was gone.

Jesse tucked his hands in his pocket and looked at the fire hall doorway. He sighed and headed for the door.

~ *Four* ~

Be still, and listen

Asher was pacing inside of his office. Jesse could see him from out in the meeting room where he was with a group of his family. Jesse watched as Asher stopped, put his hands on his hips and hung his head.

Clearly Asher was thinking, Jesse told himself.

When Asher looked up and out into the meeting room, he locked eyes with Jesse.

Jesse excused himself from his present company and headed towards Asher knowing it was him Asher had been thinking about.

The slamming of Asher's door behind him sent chills down Jesse's spin. He couldn't remember the last time he had been scolded by his brother. Jesse stood his ground though and tucked his hands in his short pockets and waited for Asher to speak first as he rounded his desk and faced Jesse.

"What the hell are you doing?"

Jesse tried not to chuckle as he looked away from Asher, but failed. He had just said those same words to Luna.

"You son of a-"

Jesse held up his hand and pointed his finger at Asher, interrupting Asher with a very serious look. "Don't finish that sentence, Asher.

"First, because you know damn well mom is not a bitch. And secondly, because I'm not doing what you think I am."

Asher kept his voice down but he made his question crystal clear to Jesse. "So you're not having an affair with our brothers wife on top of the roof of the fire department?"

Jesse looked at Asher then and smiled. Luna wasn't James's wife anymore. His heart almost danced around at the thought. "No, Asher, I'm not having an affair with her."

"What the hell were the two of you doing then?" Asher raised his hands at him exasperated

How long had Asher been up there, Jesse wondered. "They are divorced Asher. Luna served him with divorce papers she had filed before she left him all those years ago. James knew everything was over and had been for a long time, but he ignored her pleas to work on things. I remember her trying Asher. I remember her setting up appointments for them to get counseling, she tried to make things right with them, but James wasn't listening. She left, divorced him and he never told any of us this."

Asher listened. He almost started pacing again. He shook his head when he looked away from Jesse taking it all in. "Why didn't he tell us this?"

Jesse widen his eyes at Asher and shrugged his shoulders. He could never explain James habits. He didn't care too.

Asher stuffed his hands in his pockets then. "So you just decided to move on in and-"

"No. Asher. Wait. You walked up on the end of the conversation. She is here because Linda died this morning."

Asher looked at Jesse again like he was furious for not being informed of this also.

Jesse put his hand up then and explained. "I called her first after it happened so I could get her home to be with her family. Then I went to breakfast to discuss things with Jerry."

Jesse thought more about how his day had played out. He tried to remember why he hadn't called Asher. He thought out loud as he spoke to him. "You know how the chain of command runs during an investigation Asher. I couldn't just call you and tell you everything. It wasn't my place."

Asher knew this, he thought defeatedly. Just because Jesse was his brother didn't mean Jesse could tell him everything about work. Sometimes Jesse was a cop, and other times he was a firefighter. Today he had been a cop.

"Plus... " Jesse hung his head then and sat in the chair in front of Asher's desk. He hung his head and rested his elbows on his knees and folded his hands together. "That's when I got the call from mom about dad."

Asher sighed heavily then. He had been up north with Emie when all this happened. He hated that he had left his family the way he had. Especially with the way things were happening now. He had just wanted a moment alone with Emie away from her family.

He walked behind his desk and all but threw himself in his chair. When he started taking things out of his pockets; his keys that were too big to sit with, his phone and radio off his hip so he could sit down and relax, Jesse spoke up again.

"How's mom doing?"

"She's holding up. Stronger than most of us." Asher knew she wasn't. Knew she needed to go home and be in peace so she could grieve.

As for his father's death, Asher couldn't feel bad about it. The only thing bothering him now was what his father had told him on his deathbed. Which reminded him of Emie. Which reminded him of Luna.

Those thoughts only made Asher wonder if Jesse knew their secrets. And if so, how long had he known.

Asher looked up at Jesse and smirked. Jesse had neatly changed the subject on him. "Let's go back to your indiscretions."

Jesse looked at him more seriously this time. He refused to be corrected like a child. "I want to be with her Asher. Your gonna have to get used to it. I love her. I've always loved her."

"I know." Asher grinned at Jesse not looking at him. He took of his ball cap he had on backwards and placed his hands on top of his head and leaned back in his chair trying to relax. His shoulder was killing him from the eight hour drive back home. Sitting like this took the strain off it.

"How?" Jesse asked him surprised.

Asher adjusted back in his new chair that Emie had bought him that was still too small for his body. He eyed Jesse and cocked a wide smile at his brother.

"How many times have I had to tell you to stop looking at your brothers wife the way you do? You stop breathing Jesse when you're around her. If anyone mentions her name, your face heats up and turns three shades of red like you're guilty of just thinking about her."

Asher leaned forward then, letting go of his head and placed his arms on the desk in front of him. "When you talk to her Jesse, you act like no one else is around. You're so careless about your feelings towards her. You always have been."

Jesse didn't know whether or not that was a scolding, but he liked it. He did everything Asher had just said right then in front of him. He had stopped breathing listening to Asher, his face was heated and he could just see himself in Asher's eyes all turned on and red. And even now he could care less if anyone could hear their conversation or not.

"I'm not dad Jesse and you're not a child who I can tell what to do anymore. You're a grown ass man in love with the wrong woman. I can't stop you, but I can tell you that you better be less careless when it comes to her. I could tell from the way she reacted up there that even though things with her and James are over, she still loves and respects this family, and I'll be damned before I let you ruin that for her."

Asher put his head down thinking about his sister in-law. She had been apart of his family for a long time now.

"Luna is an amazing lady Jesse. James never treated her like one. She deserves your discretion right now to keep your feelings under control until she has time to fix what James is trying to undo. If he hasn't told anyone this it's because he is being stubborn and prideful.

"You need to let her tell everyone what has happened. Mom and the girls and all our friends. They need time to process this before they witness what I walked into on the roof. Then they will be able to accept the two of you coming together."

Jesse sat back at that. He was not a patient person by any means. He hated waiting. He had been waiting for her forever it felt like already. Now she was so close to being his and he couldn't have her. It was frustrating to say the least.

There was a faint knock at the door, followed by the door opening. James walked in. He looked at both brothers urgently and said "You both need to come out here right now. I need to show you something. There's something you need to hear."

When he closed the door and walked away, Jesse looked at Asher worriedly. "Did you tell him already?" Jesse questioned him jokingly.

"No." Asher told him seriously shaking his head looking just as confused as Jesse was.

They both stood and walked out into the meeting room.

Jesse was leaning up against the door frame of the radio room. Everyone he loved was standing in the crowded radio room or around him listening to the county dispatch. Something similar to this event had happened a few weeks ago during a tornado storm. But nothing could compare to what they were listening to now.

Monroe County was under attack. Police, fire and emergency personnel were being dispatched from every corner in response to the storm that was now raging around them. What had happened in most major cities around the world today while they had been living, was happening now to them closer to home.

Emie and Asher, his mother Cyndi, James, Jesse's other sisters and their husbands, Jesse's grandparents, Ken and Miranda, a young couple on the department Derrick and Amanda. Jerry, Josh and Tyler his co-police officers on the department, and everyone who had come to the fire hall on this night to support the Stone family for the loss of their Chief, Frank Stone were all gathered like a flock, huddled, quietly listening to the radio.

They all knew what they were listening to and didn't know what to do about it.

One radio dispatch had everyone in the office looking at Jerry and Jesse concerned for the safety of Grimm, a paramedic they all knew, who was talking now on the radio. He was talking to Helana, the dispatcher, describing not only what he saw going on in the street in front of him, but also what others had been trying to say and couldn't.

"There's a body laying in the street." Everyone could hear the urgency in Grimm's voice as he ran up to the body.

"I'm examining him. I can't stop his neck from bleeding from the wound! It looks like he's been bitten by something. He's bleeding out."

One minute he was talking quietly over the radio, trying to save the life of the man on the ground and the next you could hear him running. His keys shaking and the sound of a shotgun being loaded as he continued talking wildly. "He was dead! He had no pulse! He was lifeless, Helana."

"You have to get out of there Grimm!" Helana begged him over the radio.

The next sound on the radio made everyone in the room jump, scared to death of the frightening sound. It was the shot gun going off.

Everyone in the room could picture the young paramedic who had been running for his life, fall silent, like he was whispering very softly, like he was afraid for his life when he spoke next.

"When he opened his eyes, they were bright red. They were no longer human eyes. He started chasing me, screaming at me to help him. Then he started to growl as he caught up to me.

"It was like something out of a damned horror movie!"

Everyone in the room heard the helplessness in Grimm's voices.

The next transmission from the medic was almost like he was scared to death, while he was running. Again. "I had no choice Helana. I shot him in the head."

And with his last transmission, everything just stopped. For the first time since the emergency dispatch system had begun, it had never just stopped.

Asher and Jerry both tried to adjust the channels and frequency, but it wasn't until Jesse had tried to call central dispatch on the phone that they all realized the truth.

And then the power went out at the station and everyone felt the eerie feeling all the firefighters felt.

When Jesse flipped the switch to turn on the generators in the other room, Ken and Miranda broke the silence everyone surrounding them was enchanted by. Both of their girls were at home alone waiting for them to return home.

"Kenny! The girls-." Miranda pleaded with Ken begging him to go get them.

Ken, Asher and Jerry left in a hurry without thinking to go and bring the girls to the department.

Jesse informed everyone else they too should do the same for their families while he locked down the fire hall. He watched as James sat in the radio room, distraught about something.

Jesse consoled his mother and sisters. He talked with other friends who had come in and informed them they could stay with his family here if they wished. There were plenty of cots to go around.

Keeping everyone together just seemed like a good idea tonight. It was what they did during situations like this. What his father had taught them to do. The fire hall was home when home isn't safe anymore.

When Asher walked back in with Ken's girls, he looked up towards the roof stairway and headed for it. Jesse knew Asher's favorite place to sit and smoke and think was on top of the fire hall on the roof. Probably where he had been going when he had walked in on Luna and him, Jesse thought to himself.

Jesse watched as Emie followed Asher up the stairs. He remembered what Luna had said about Emie being a death angel. Jesse was curious now, so he followed the two of them up the stairs.

Jesse wasn't surprised when he looked out the doorway and saw them in a tight embrace. Every couple he knew were embracing right now. He thought about leaving them alone, and felt bad for being up here.

What he hadn't expected was for Emie to look at Asher and nod her head at Asher like Luna had done to him in the past. It was an acknowledgment of understanding and Asher hadn't spoken a word to her.

Jesse knew that meant that Emie could also read minds like Luna. She was answering an unspoken question of Asher's. Jesse shook his head worriedly for his brother not knowing how to protect him. He leaned against the door frame and crossed his arms trying to listen in on them and watch over his big brother.

Jesse watched as a man jumped on the ledge of the roof next to them. His first instinct was to reach for his gun, but he realized too late he didn't have his uniform on.

Emie turned towards Jesse then. She bared her fangs at Jesse in a low growl. She hadn't meant too, but if Jesse would've had a gun, he would have shot her brother Jeremy.

Jeremy stepped off the ledge and grinned at Jesse. He cooed at his little sister reassuringly. "Nah. He's not that fast. Yet." Jeremy stated simply with a wink towards Jesse.

"Come a little closer kid. You and I need to have a talk." This time Jeremy eyed him in all seriousness as he stood in front of his little sister protecting her. It worried Asher, but Jeremy stayed him. He needed to make a few things very clear to Jesse.

Jesse looked to Asher for help understanding what he was supposed to do as he walked forward, compelled to obey Jeremy. Asher looked at him irritatingly like he was upset with Jesse again which confused Jesse further.

"Jesse, this is Jeremy Whitby. Emie's brother." This, Asher told his brother thankful he hadn't shot Jeremy.

Jesse gulped at the air around him as he got closer to Jeremy. He could hear Luna's voice inside his head. Death angels. He looked at

Emie's big brother and had never felt so threatened by a man in all his life.

Jeremy Whitby was tall. Taller than Emie, as tall as Asher was. Most men were not like Jesse and his brothers. Being of such a height made life awkward for Jesse sometimes. Meeting someone of like height, in such a threatening manner, made Jesse feel smaller all the same.

Jeremy carried himself in a manner Jesse envied. Jeremy was strong, and sure of himself. He looked human in his jeans and tight black t-shirt, but looks could be deceiving, Jesse reminded himself.

He saw an exchange between brother and sister. Emie looked irritated at Jeremy and Jeremy was menacing, big brother smiles for his sister. Jesse wasn't sure what was about to happen, but he was sure of one thing. Luna would save him. It was the only thing he was sure of anymore.

He wouldn't have guessed it when he woke up this morning that he'd be standing on top of the fire hall with not only one, but two vampires like Luna. But here he was.

Suddenly he craved a smoke break with Asher.

"First things first. Since my sister won't state the obvious-".

Emie nudged Jeremy hard enough that it should have sent him over the edge if he were a human. "Stop being a cad Jeremy. He already knows what we are."

Jesse was completely and utterly bemused. He had almost shot this guy and now he wanted an introduction?

Jeremy cocked a grin at Jesse's thoughts in the moon light flashing his best vampiric smile. He looked pointedly at Jesse in answer to his unguarded thoughts. "Oh, little brother, I want so much more from you." He told him with a wicked wink.

This time Emie did knock him over the edge. What almost sent Jesse into shock was when her brother reappeared like he was floating.

He had wings! Angel wings. And he was floating back to the edge of the ledge laughing at Emie. For an unguarded moment, Jesse could see Jeremy and Emie's angelic wings, and then they disappeared like he had just imagined it.

"Honestly, Jeremy! Can't you be serious for once in your life?" Emie looked at Jesse apologetically. Then at Asher.

Asher was covering up a smirk he knew was going to get him knocked off the edge for too and told Emie honestly "Oh come on, it was a little funny. Jeremy knows better then to play with his food."

Emie flicked Asher on his ball cap sending it off the ledge for his jest about her brother.

"Oh!" Jeremy bellowed in laughter at Asher's playful banter. "See Emie! That is why I haven't killed your boyfriend yet." This

Jeremy said proudly, sitting on the ledge, with a huge grin his face while he looked at Asher with pride.

"Will someone please tell me what the hell is going on?" Jesse finally said to all of them, tired of all this.

Jeremy finally addressed Jesse cordially, coughing in his hand like a human would do. "Jesse, my name is Jeremy Whitby. As you already know, I am Emie's brother, and, I am a death angel like Luna told you."

This stunned and confused Jesse further. "How did you know-"

Jeremy raised up his finger and pointed at his wings behind him to interrupt Jesse. "Angel, remember?"

When Jesse acknowledged that, Jeremy continued. "But, we are not a danger to your family. Asher is... the chosen one, if you will." This Jeremy said looking over at Asher, then he looked back at Jesse, jumping off the ledge in front of him he took up a relaxed stance leaning back against the ledge. "He is important to our family.

"As his family," Jeremy said, addressing Jesse's worries. "that makes every one of you; your family and your friends, all very important to us. We will protect you, care for you as our own. You have nothing to fear."

Jesse took a deep breath then. He could feel himself relaxing now that he knew that.

"As for Luna, that's why I'm here."

Jesse looked at Jeremy then very seriously. He was worried something was wrong and waited for Jeremy to explain.

Jeremy looked at Asher, then back at Jesse. His little brother was as sharp minded as Asher was. Nice. Jeremy told himself. He liked Jesse already.

"She is with Joseph now, learning the same thing I am telling you. When the time is right tonight, I will take you to her. But, for now-"

Just as Jeremy was about to reach out and take Jesse's hand, Emie stopped him. She touched Jeremy's hand with hers and steadily said to him "No.".

Jeremy looked at his sister then who had quietly stopped him from showing Jesse everything with the help of Joseph. The past, the present, and his future.

Jeremy sighed at his sister. "Ok." He knew she knew what she was doing, and the decision was hers to make.

He looked at Jesse then. "But, one day...". This he winked at Jesse who he couldn't wait to share things with. Jesse had a sense of humor that matched his. It was hindered now by all that was going on in his life. "you'll understand this. One day you'll thank me for all this."

Jeremy turned and looked at Asher then. "Sure you're not ready yet?"

Asher crossed his arms knowing what Jeremy was asking of him. And as ready as he would ever be, he knew right now wasn't the time. He had a family he needed to help, and he needed Jesse to help him with them all. Neither of them could do that as vampires.

"We're sure." he spoke for the both of them.

~The Whitby Mansion~

Luna started walking down Lakewood drive towards the Whitby home. She could have ran, she could have flew, she even could have just disappeared to the human eye and ended up at the mansion on Joseph's front steps.

She chose to walk instead.

Luna wanted to take in every essence of her home. The pier. She walked by the houses of people she knew. She walked by the homes of many pets she knew. Pets she had spent so many years taking care of.

It was almost like she had never left. She couldn't shake the feeling that she had though. She had been gone a long time.

Luna shook her head in remembrance as she kept walking towards her destination down Lakewood Avenue. She needed to focus on where she was going.

Walking past the house of Miranda and Ken brought back the memories of her past, which only led to thoughts of Jesse again. Ken and Miranda had been the best of friends to Jesse and his family. They even accepted her as one of the family.

She wondered quietly to herself as she walked away from their home, if they had known who she really was, would they have accepted her still? Would they accept her when they found out?

Luna sighed in the summer evening air around her as she picked up her pace. She missed so many humans from her past life. She longed to be done with this nonsense of the Whitby's against the Stones so she could return to what little bit of a life she had left now.

Jesse's face was there in her mind again. She couldn't un-love Jesse. No matter how hard she tried. Loving Jesse was as easy as breathing.

When she was standing before the gates of the Whitby land, she wasn't surprised when the gates opened on their own. Joseph must have been waiting for her.

Luna stood on the bridge that lead into the Whitby land, just staring into the darkness past the gates, watching as the lake woods swayed in the breeze. She needed to see Joseph and have words with him, but there was no one else on the face of this earth she feared more than Joseph Whitby.

Joseph could be domineering and gentle, he was also a force not to be messed with. With just his gaze he could bring the strongest of men to their knees.

With every storm comes thunder and lightning, and Joseph Whitby was like a hurricane when he was angry. Eventually, you knew he was going to run out of wind and rain that he blinded you with, but waiting for it was like waiting for the eye of the hurricane. You knew the calm would only be for a time. And when you ran out of time, he would sweep over you again with a fierce, surge that was more then before, that would make you fall flat on your face and beg for it to be over.

Tonight, Luna planned on being just as fierce.

Ignorance was her friend for right now, but when she found out the truth, she was going to rain down a pain on the Whitby's that would be heard throughout all the earth. Her wrath could only be kindled if the flames of their deception didn't consume her with vengeance.

She couldn't understand why the Whitby's had chosen Asher. Asher was like a big brother to her. Why was Emie with him? What did she want from him? Luna couldn't let Emie take his life.

Frank and Cyndi had always been a parental figure to her in the short time she had known them. Their daughters were like sisters to her. Their entire family was like family to her. She couldn't let the Whitby's destroy them.

Had they been the ones who took Frank's life? She wondered suddenly worried.

When thoughts of Jesse entered her mind, Luna tried not to let her fears of the Whitby's control her. She didn't know how to protect the ones she loved, but she wasn't about to run like hell again away from them. No, this time she would stay and fight for them. Fight until her powers made sure that they would be safe again.

She walked into the Whitby land with a determination to know why Joseph and Jordy hadn't told her all of this before it had happened. Then she wanted answers for the Stone family.

She swore Joseph kept all things secret only to benefit his family. Well, she'd had enough of that for one lifetime. Joseph owed her in ways she was going to make him repay.

Luna walked through the woods and deeper into their lands. She took her sandals off when she stepped on the sandy beach close to the mansion. She could smell the lake wood in the wind swirling around her. The softness of the warm summer breeze on her skin warmed her through. The mix of lakewood, sand and fresh lake grass filled her nostrils, enchanting her.

Luna wanted to shift and run as a wolf. She wanted to be free, just for a moment.

Luna looked out on the calm moonlit, diamond sparkling lake and sighed. Looking out over the breathtaking lake on nights like this was like a vision of heaven.

She had missed this place she spent a lifetime calling home. She remembered the ease of the days spent in peaceful solitude, not fearing the humans or the government of this land. She had been free... It had only lasted for a short time though. This place belonged to the Whitby's now.

She stopped and looked out on the shores of the lake, out into the deep of the night. It felt like a lifetime ago that she had been truly free.

If Joseph had only accepted her and her family. If he had only set aside his need to build his empire and family so high above her own, they might all have lived together as one.

The Stone family had accepted her like that. They had welcomed her into their family when she had married James. Even though her marriage had fallen apart, Luna had never stopped loving them.

Luna kept walking towards the mansion and when it came into view, Luna stood in the wake of it's enormity. She knew Joseph was waiting for her within. She even knew where he awaited her presence. In his den. With his new creations; Lelu, Lycan and Thorp, who were named after famed werewolves of old, would be there to protect him from Luna.

She almost laughed as she walked up the stone steps that led to the back doors of their home. He was going to need more than wolves to protect himself from her tonight.

Joseph could feel the moment Luna had entered his land. He could feel her raging storm brewing with every step closer she took to his home.

It was killing him that she was taking her sweet ol time.

Asher's father, Frank Stone, had revealed enough tonight of what he had learned about the Whitby's to his sons before he had died that they could destroy everything Joseph held dear in life.

Everything Joseph was trying to protect.

Asher hated Joseph now. With all due reason he didn't understand why Joseph had done the things he had done so many years ago.

Joseph wanted to strangle the life out of Frank while he had been dying tonight. He had even thought of turning Frank into a vampire just to teach the old man a lesson and making sure he lived a life of torment instead.

Frank had thought the Whitby's were evil monsters. He had no clue who Joseph and his siblings were. The man had never taken the time to get to know any of them.

Joseph had let the man die in misery though. God could deal with Frank now. And Joseph didn't care anymore what happened to the man. Frank wouldn't be saved by God when he got to heaven, his blasphemy towards God was too great to save him, and Joseph was pretty sure hell didn't want Frank either.

Joseph had his head bowed in his hands on his desk. He was still trying to figure out where he had went wrong in life with the Stone family.

When Joseph heard Luna's soft footsteps on the marble floor just outside his doors, he looked up and was reminded of the young girl she was when he had found her and her family here. Linda and Luna shared a family heritage that went back in time further than his. The history of her family had been unknown to even the scholars of this land. A time before nations had even been formed, before the wars of this land had been waged over.

Luna still looked every bit as youthful as Emie, but her true age, her astounding wisdom, exceeded even the likes of his own. Where he longed for prosperity and wealth for his family, she longed for peace and freedom that belittled his best intentions.

When the double doors of his den opened on one side, the storm she had been waging in the form of one so soft and gentle, seemed harmless in her wake.

The look in her red, golden eyes said she was here for suffering and torment though.

Joseph had feared the wrath of his little sister Emie before the way he feared Luna now. He knew now why the house had been so silent. Everyone had abandon him knowing Luna was coming. His siblings were even silent in his mind now.

Lelu and her brothers, Joseph's pets, now paced behind his desk in search of a safe place to hide behind their master.

Joseph looked at them shaking his head. "Pups." He jested to them, wishing he too could crawl under his desk.

Joseph acknowledged Luna with a nod of his head towards her in greeting. "And what do I-".

Joseph coughed, literally choked on his words. He wasn't pretending. He truly was without voice now. Staring at the woman who had done it to him, Joseph knew she was more powerful than even Jordy had visioned.

Luna stared intently at Joseph as he spoke, using her powers to rob him of the speech he was going to use on her, with just her gaze. He knew damn well why she was here. There was not going to be any pleasure had from this visit.

"Tell me why, Joseph?" Words Jesse had spoken to her earlier, fell from her lips like they had his. She needed to know all the reasons why he had hid this future from her, or he would be damned with all the excuses.

Joseph cleared his throat again listening to her thoughts. "We didn't know Linda was next, Luna. Or the pier."

"What do you mean next?" She bellowed at him. The door behind her she slammed fully as she walked further into the room without touching it, letting him hear and know that he was officially trapped by her. "What's going on? What secrets are you and your brothers hiding?"

With her last statement she almost pleaded with him for the truth. If she was ever going to know what happened to her mother, she needed to know this first.

Joseph looked away from her down at his desk, trying not to show his fear to her. "While you were busy running away with your tail-"

Oh! He didn't! Luna thought, loud enough to stop his words and make him look at her.

"Don't be condescending with me Joseph!" She told him pointing her finger at him making her point crystal clear, stopping him before he said something that would irate her further. "I wasn't running away from my responsibilities! I was running away from you! And you damn well knew it!"

James hated her because of what his father, Frank, had told him about Luna and the Whitby's. If it hadn't been for Joseph and all his meddling with the Stones, she could have had a future with James.

James had been deceiving her from the very beginning. And it wasn't until she had caught James cheating on her that she had discovered the truth. James knew what she was. And it had been all Joseph's fault.

"You know why I left! I sent you a copy of those damn papers!

"I wasn't blessed with the gift of knowing the future like your brothers. I had no idea this was going to happen to my mother." She leaned more menacingly towards him. "But your brothers did!".

Luna had him there.

He hated that Jeremy had given her so many gifts, but he was almost grateful she hadn't been given the ability of visions. He still hated what Jeremy had done to her. Jeremy had only wanted a taste of her, but he'd turned her in his curiosity.

Joseph did know why she left. The why's still bothered him though. He stood then, placing his hands daringly on his desk and let her feel his power over her. He needed to make something very clear to her.

"First: we didn't know exactly what was going to happen. You can't fault us for that. Secondly: you could have told me you loved Asher's brother Jesse instead of lying to us all about James!"

Luna looked up to the man who stood over her from behind his desk, dead in his eyes. Venom was dripping from her fangs at the sound of Joseph's voice speaking of the ones she was fighting for. She had to reign in her monsters to keep from killing him.

She placed both her hands on the desk in front of him determined now. "You could have told me the plans you had for their family when I married James."

Damn, Joseph thought, watching her fight back. She had him there again.

Joseph stuffed his hands in his pockets, not willing to back down to her. "Would it have changed your mind?"

Luna thought about that. She knew he knew the answers. She hated that Joseph had found her one weakness so quickly, but she could see Jesse in his mind, and she could only fear for him now.

Joseph smiled then, pointing his finger at her for emphasis. "And that is why we didn't tell you. It wouldn't have mattered. It wouldn't have changed a damn thing. You do what you want to do, no matter what I say Luna. You always have. And I've never stood in your way."

Luna stood to her full height then and watched as Joseph looked at her in his mind. She could see all her worries in her that he saw. She could see Jesse there in his mind. He knew her secrets now.

She had deceived him in the worst way possible.

Joseph, knowing he had her right where he wanted her, watched as she thought about it. He leaned in as he spoke again. "Do tell; why in the hell did you marry one when you loved the other?"

Luna couldn't help it when he pressed her for the truth. Her thoughts betrayed her. She had lied to Joseph about her feelings for Jesse because she would have killed him if he ever tried to hurt Jesse.

Luna had sworn never to tell the humans about them. Jesse knew things she was afraid for Joseph to find out about. If Jesse had ever revealed the truth about them, she couldn't fathom the consequences. And Joseph would have to protect his family. He would have fought back.

Joseph knew this already. She would have killed him. But not before he had killed Jesse.

He placed his hands back on the desk in front of her. He told her his secret he had been hiding from her. "I already knew this Luna. Way before he entered on our land that night. I swallowed my pride along time ago and let you have your way."

Joseph laughed then trying to lighten the mood. "The man lives Luna."

Joseph placed his spread hand on the desk for emphasis and said more quietly this time shaking his head at her. "And I need you to understand this."

He looked at her sideways, trying to get her attention. "We won't stand in your way if you want to be with Jesse. Not because I don't want to die, but because I want you to be happy."

He stood back up then and sighed. He let her see it inside of him. He had been disappointed in her for trying to deceive him, yes. And he understood why she had done it. Now, he just wanted a truce.

Luna could see it in him, there was something else lingering inside of him he was hiding. She tried to remember that night. Tried to remember the fight she had with Joseph. He could have killed Jesse that night. But he hadn't. Why?

Luna looked directly into his soul. What plans did he have for Jesse?

Joseph hated that Luna had his abilities to see inside of him. She could push past all his powers and take what she wanted. He had to give it to her.

"You'll have to forgive me, but my loyalty lies with my sister all this time and her future."

Joseph watched as Luna thought about that. She regretted it all now knowing what she knew about Asher and Emie. They were truly happy together, and Asher deserved to be happy.

Luna couldn't help her feelings for Asher's family or his brother. Joseph gave her the bone she was hunting for and hoped it would be enough to state her.

"We have promised Emie protection for his family and his friends now. She loves Asher like you love Jesse. And because of her, we will keep that promise." He tried to tell her this so he could ease her fears for them.

Luna worried for Jesse's family still and she knew Joseph could feel it. "His family is good and kind Joseph." Luna looked at him pleadingly for their lives.

She still didn't trust him.

Joseph kept his thoughts to himself this time. He wasn't sure how much to reveal to Luna just yet. Frank Stone was someone Joseph had wanted to see taken more than once.

Looking at her, the Luna he truly knew, the young woman who was standing before him now, all rage and thunder, as powerful as she was, he knew she was vulnerable now.

Her family had abandon her years ago, like Emie's father and mother had done to her. Luna needed Jesse's family. She loved them like her own.

"Some of them are, yes." And with that he let her figure out which ones he was speaking of. He made sure she seen James in his mind also and pushed it further into her so she could feel what he wanted to do to James.

Joseph walked around from behind his desk while he told her what she had come here to find out. She wanted to know who killed Linda. Joseph had learned the news today from Jordy. As he showed Luna in her mind, he walked over to his side table and started to pour them both a glass of chilled blood from the wine bottles Emie had brought to him tonight.

He set Luna's glass in front of her and watched as she stared at it afraid.

"The royals are taking over the United States now, like they have been trying to do for generations. That's what's been going on around the world while you were out waltzing around in love with the wrong man." He waited for her to condemn him for his jest while he sipped from his glass before he finished.

The royals invoked fear in all of them. He watched her drink heavily from her glass, worried and finally sat down in the chair in front of his desk. He refilled her glass and sat back down to sip on his.

Good, he thought watching her. She understood the enormity of it all now.

"The royals, the ones your family had been running from are now here in this land. They've destroyed all the other nations slowly, stole from them, and brought with them what they need to make this land theirs."

Luna knew the legends of her family's past. They had lived south of this land, on islands far away from here and had overseen the royals in the west take over nations one by one. They had defeated them once, but had lost so much of their own homeland in the process, cursed to never have it back.

When they found this land, they were seen as savages. The governments in the west overtook them easily with the help of the royals until the tribes had nothing left but to surrender. The loss her family had bore from the war had taken generations to recover from. They had become stronger. Some had moved further north to the outermost reaches of Canada where the humans could not live. Some had stayed here in this land as they crossed through, only to lose it to the Americans.

Her family's numbers had multiplied, but the Royals had done so too. The evilness and destruction of the royals had always been what her family had feared the most. What many like her family had hid from all these years. More so from the curse they laid upon her family.

When she had been turned into a vampire, a new creation in her family's eyes, they had disowned her, afraid she had become like the royals. Everyone except for her mother, Linda. Their family had left the Whitby's land, turning their backs on Luna and Linda.

"You have been searching for the places where you knew many of your tribes family had hid once, in solace of the new people here. The royals have been in control of the governments here all along with the Americans. They have been building this land on the backs of the Americans, leading them, directing them, in the paths they wanted them to go in, so when the time was right, they could destroy them. Bring them down to their knees and take from them all they hoped and dreamed to accomplish.

"Taking over the world Luna. That is their end game. Those caves you were seeking out, have already been taken by them. It's a wonder you weren't captured while you were there."

Luna grasped the soundness of his words.

It all made sense now. The news, everything on the internet; it had been the royals all along.

"They are stalking us now, here in Luna Pier. Hunting us. Using us. Setting us up so the humans will destroy us. Or so we will all destroy each other before they do." Joseph sighed downing what was left of his drink. "They are coming. To destroy us all."

Luna almost wept at the truth. It was true then. Joseph had showed it to her. Her mother was really gone. "So the Royals murdered my mother?"

Joseph sighed again at this. He didn't know the answer to that question yet. Why they wanted Linda, a werewolf, was beyond him. Unless they just wanted her out of the way.

He had wondered the same thing about Curtis when he had died. They had never found the rouge teenagers that had started the Marina fire.

"I don't know, yet, Luna. You have my word; the moment I find out, you will be the first to know."

She looked at Joseph for help now edging forward in her seat closer to him. She was truly scared now. "What do I do now Joseph?"

Joseph looked at her and for the first time tonight he relaxed. She was truly alone in this world now. She needed him.

He needed her more.

"I have a-"

"Wait!" She interrupted him, changing her mind. Joseph always had a plan. She had learned that well from him. "I have to know first," Because she really had to know. It was why she had come back home. Before she could go on with life, she had to lay her mother to rest.

"Where is my mother's body Joseph?" She pleaded softly to him.

Joseph sighed deeply then. He turned in his chair and patted the head of Lelu who had nudged his thigh. Her white fur was standing up now. She could feel her masters fear.

Without looking at Luna, he shivered at the vision of what she was going to do to him, "I had to bury her. She is in the cemetery."

Luna's eyes turned white when she processed his words. The blood that was in her body evaporated in the heat that filled her with anger. All she could see was hot burning flames around her.

Her people didn't go back in the ground like the humans did. It was blasphemous. He knew this!

Joseph knew the moment her eyes turned white she had used up all her blood. He also knew she wanted blood in her anger and all she could see now was his. He started praying harder then he ever had, that Luna couldn't... he closed his eyes then knowing she could and hoped she wouldn't kill him. All he could do now was bow his head and submit to her.

Jesse slammed his locker door shut. He was upstairs in the bedrooms of the fire department and was growing tired of waiting for Jeremy to help him find Luna. He had changed into his uniform he kept here at the station and secured his guns tightly at his sides so he could head downstairs and help Jeremy with his plan.

Jeremy explained to Asher and Jesse that under the entire bay where the fire trucks were, was a pit large enough to hide everyone and store things they would need to pass the time until his family could get everyone safely to the Whitby land. Tonight and the next, they would be safe underground where no evil could find them.

Jesse had helped Emie and Jeremy clear the room in the east bay of the department so they could open the pits under the fire trucks where they could hide everyone from the rogues tonight that were waiting right outside.

Once Jeremy and Emie busied themselves in the bay, Jesse snuck out the back doors. He knew they knew where he was going, and he knew they would stop him if he was in danger.

When they didn't, Jesse kept going.

When Jesse got in his truck and shut the door he looked out the door window. A vampire was standing there looking in his window.

"Shit!" Jesse cussed aloud, reaching for his guns at his side.

Jordy entered Jesse's mind through his door. The dizzy feeling over took Jesse and he had to stop to listen to what Jordy wanted. He stuffed his hands in his pockets outside the door so he looked more relaxed than menacing for Jesse.

Jesse, I helped you once before when you were young. I sent Luna to you before Collin could kill you.

Listen to me now and do as I say.

Jesse closed his eyes at Jordy's words with his hand still on his gun belt. Images of the night he had foolishly wandered onto the Whitby land looking for Luna played out for him in his mind like he was watching a tv screen. Jesse knew Jordy was telling the truth, no one else knew of that night, so Jesse listened to him and relaxed looking back at him through the door window letting go of his gun.

These Whitby boys were sure a sight, Jesse thought to himself. Jordy stood as tall and proud as Jeremy did looking like the mirror image of his twin brother. But the uncanny look of the super humans they were showed in their unblemished features.

The difference between them was as clear as day to Jesse. Jeremy had that look that defined him as one of the guys. Easy going and relaxed. A little cocky and playful.

Jordy though, Jesse thought to himself, looked serious. Someone you didn't mess with.

Jordy groaned inside himself at Jesse's thoughts. He didn't have time for this.

Do not go to our land tonight looking for Luna. Luna left and is now at the cemetery. Joseph had Linda buried there earlier today.

And Jesse,

Jesse had turned to start his truck in a hurry to get to the cemetery where Luna was, but he paused at that last with his hand on his key in the ignition.

You have to tell Luna you love her.

"She knows this already Jordy." Jesse said out loud looking back out the window. But Jordy wasn't there any more.

The silence was almost deafening.

He didn't know what Jordy meant, but he knew once he found Luna tonight he was going to do exactly what Jordy had said.

Luna was his whole world, and if she needed to know he loved her, out loud, then so be it.

He wasn't ever going to let Luna leave him again, he told himself as he put his truck in gear and drove away from the back of the fire hall. If telling her he loved her meant she would stay, he would do it on bended knees and plead with her.

He would do anything to keep her safe.

This Jesse felt so deeply inside of his soul he knew he had to do it. He couldn't live without her anymore.

Jesse shifted gears looking out his windows into the darkness of Luna Pier without the street lights on, an eerie feeling that life would never be as it was again crept inside of his soul and the only thing that could save him from it was Luna.

He couldn't drive fast enough to get to her.

Jesse had no idea how he was supposed to do this as he reached the cemetery tearing through the grass taking a shortcut. Loving Luna was easy, but tonight he didn't know why loving the vampire she was felt like unknown territory. Sometimes he forgot she was a vampire. She looked and smelled so much like the human he envisioned her to be. And the wolf he dreamt of in his dreams.

Pulling in front of the cemetery he noticed the gates had been busted open, then he saw Luna in her white wolf form in his head lights, digging up a grave. It almost made Jesse rethink what he was doing here.

Luna was huge, he remembered as he looked at her. She was shaking her fur out in anger as she dug through the ground. Scattering earth and dirt all around behind her.

It wasn't until she stopped and looked at him in his truck through his head lights that he realized he had missed her. Then he watched as she went back to digging.

For a split moment he couldn't figure out why she was digging up her mother's grave. Then he remembered the stories she had told him when they were younger. Because they were travelers in this land, they were not to buried on this land. They were to be carried back home to their land and laid to rest there.

Jesse sighed out loud at her, frustrated. She was being stubborn and she knew it, he told himself as he got out of his truck and walked forward to where she was. That's why she was angry with Joseph. That's why she had to know where her mother's body was. She couldn't leave well enough alone.

There was no way she could take her mother back home now. And she knew it.

He locked his truck as he walked away from it, with the way the world was now, he didn't want any surprises when he got back into it.

By the time he made it to where Luna was, she had already made it down the six feet where Joseph had buried her mother. Jessie peeked over the edge into the grave and watched just as Luna looked up at the moon.

A soft howl broke her lips as she closed her eyes. He too looked up and when the skies released the rain Luna beckoned from them, he knew she was grieving deeply.

When it rained like this, without warning, he knew it was Luna's sadness. She had the power over the earth to make it so because of who she was born to be. When it thundered with no lightning, like it was now, he knew she was angry because of the vampire she was. He never wanted to know what else she was capable of. This was enough.

He bent down and leaned on his knees so he could watch her better in the rain inside the grave.

Luna was sitting on top of the casket she had uncovered. Joseph had at least given her a proper burial. It wasn't steel, but it wasn't wood either. She jumped on it a few times with her front paws, trying to see if she could at least make a dent.

"Babe, let me help."

Luna looked up to where Jesse was then. She snarled at him, the human he was. He couldn't help it.

"Don't snarl at me!" He shouted at her stubbornly through the rain, wiping it from his eyes so he could see her. "Damn it! Come up here and get me." She needed his hands, not her paws to do this last part.

He had his guns now. He knew he could use them if he had to open the locks.

He took off his coat when she made the decision, just in case she decided to change back so he could cover her nakedness.

Luna jumped the six feet up to where he was. She huffed and snorted at him through the rain, shaking it off her fur.

She watched him as he worried standing in her presence, only for a second though, and then he relaxed. He had only seen her like this once before, in her wolf form.

Luna cocked her head sideways at him studying him. She was afraid he would be afraid of her, and was surprised when he wasn't. Sometimes his bravery with her was impressive. He was captivated by her.

She nuzzled into his chest not meaning to make him lose his footing, loving the way he chuckled and ran his hand through the fur on her neck.

Jesse took a moment to run both of his hands through her wet fur around her neck. He let his fingers find the source of warmth there under her fur from the rain. Her white fur was soft, like powder between his fingers. His eyes couldn't believe what he was doing. He playfully looked at her in the moonlight when she looked at him. Even like this, he was still madly in love with her.

Luna couldn't believe what he was doing either. Some times Jesse could be so adorable and sweet it would take her by surprise.

In her wolf form she stood face to face with him. He ran his fingers through her white fur up to her ears when she placed her forehead on his chest. He swore he heard her sigh as she took in a deep breath of the night around them, her breath for the first time he could see as it rose in the night around them.

When she finally changed, he had to look up away from her body and hand her his coat. His body had reacted to the sight of her naked belly and long bare legs through the opening of his coat. Her toes were buried in the grass under her.

Luna knew she didn't have time for this. She wanted it yes, but she didn't have time for it. Any second they could be found out here alone and Jesse was in danger.

Joseph had told her earlier that it might not be Linda in the casket he had buried, and that was the only thing that had saved his life tonight. She needed to know now for sure that the body in the casket was not her mothers.

"I don't need your help Jesse. I can do this myself." She told him pulling his coat around her, putting her arms in his sleeves she jumped barefoot back down in the grave.

Luna looked at the casket and waited before she dug into the metal. She sent up a silent prayer hoping her mother wasn't inside.

Luna busted her fist through the metal. She didn't need to see the body that laid within to know it wasn't her mother. Even though the smell of burnt flesh sickened her, she knew it was not the scent of her mother.

She sat down on the casket taken back again at the reality of all this. She closed her eyes looking up heavenward, letting the rain fall on her face and wondered what on earth she was supposed to do next.

Babe?

She opened her eyes and looked for Jesse at his silent call to her watching as the rain fell between them. She stood up and jumped back up to the ground and lowered her head trying not to let Jesse see her weeping, but she failed. She almost fell to her knees with the weight of her anguish.

The answered questions plagued her now. Luna had no idea where her mother was. Had she been kidnapped? By the royals? Had she ran for her life and set up a stage for her escape?

Luna let the pain wracking through her take over. She put her face in her hands and just cried. She had no idea where to even start looking for her mother.

Jesse stood in front of her, not sure of how he could be of help. He could barely even see her in the rain now. He raised his arms up towards her. He wanted nothing more than to take her in his arms and hold her.

Luna? He beckoned to her softly, his soul to hers.

Luna heard his thoughts. She had to get used to this feeling that she could now accept from Jesse the love he had longed to give her.

She almost laughed out loud in joy but she couldn't stop the choking sobs.

Walking towards him she let him hold her, and in return she held unto his strength and let it seep into her. His warmth she could feel between them and her body reacted to it as she wrapped her arms around his waist.

Jesse rocked her in his embrace again like they were dancing. It was what he always did when he held Luna. It was how he distracted himself from wanting her. How he made her feel better thinking about a song for her to dance to with him.

Luna had thought she could do this alone, but she couldn't. He was the only one who could help her right now. He was the only one she had left.

Jesse held her, knowing she heard his thoughts. He hoped she could feel how much he loved her as he held her close to his heart. Luna hated the cold, but she loved his warmth. It was all he could give her now in her moments of grief, like she had done for him.

Luna felt like she had nails in her heart. Her soul hurt. The world around her was losing the battle between good and evil. She didn't know what she was supposed to do.

She felt so alone now in this crumbling world. She needed her mother. Luna needed to find her. She didn't know where to start though.

She hoped, she prayed, that God would just give her this moment in time to hold on to the only thing that was keeping her from dissipating into nothing. Jesse's love meant more to her than anything else in this world and was the only thing keeping her grounded.

Luna wrapped her arms around his waist tighter and tried not to crush him.

Jesse buried his head in her hair on her shoulders. All he wanted to do was touch her now. The angel she was. He held her head in one of his hands and wrapped his arm around her back pulling her into his warmth. He could feel her cold bare skin against his body where his coat on her was open. He knew how she loved the feel of his warmth and he gave it to her freely.

Right as he was about to speak, to tell her how much he loved her, how he understood her loss and he would be here for her, she spoke before him.

"It's not her."

Luna breathed in his scent quietly. The smell of his warmth, the beat of his blood rushing through his heart, was warming her through. She waited as Jesse processed her words. She had missed him so much she never wanted to let him go.

Jesse closed his eyes tight. He had been ready to pick her up if she fell from her wounds of losing Linda. He was elated for her knowing it wasn't her mother.

He moved her hair away from her neck and rubbed his face against her skin there. When she moved her shoulder so he could do it, it made him grin.

Knowing it wasn't Linda laying in the grave made him realize they needed to go. He didn't know how vulnerable she was out here, but he was very vulnerable at the moment.

Luna looked up at Jesse and pulled away from him. "You shouldn't be here." She told him as she wiped away her tears. "I have to go away again. I have to find her Jesse."

Jesse looked down at her stunned. Disbelief formed in his own eyes when she looked up at him. His mouth started to slowly open, truly stunned into silence at her words. His mouth started to water as he stood there looking at her.

She hadn't said "we", she had said "I". It said everything she couldn't tell him.

She was going to leave him again. She couldn't take him where she was going and she damn well knew it.

Luna bit her lip to stop it from quivering with her fang. She had never meant to hurt him so. She reached for his shirt as he started to back away, she needed to make him understand she had to find her mother.

Jesse let go of her. He took a step back and turned almost slipping in the mud down into the grave. When she reached to steady him, he shook off her hold and walked away for a minute.

"Baby-"

Jesse turned and stopped her from lying to him. He knew what she was going to say.

"Don't!" He hollered at her facing her, the rain was drenching him now. Lighting cracked at the thunder in his voice and surprisingly he didn't jump at the start he felt.

It tore her empty heart open to hear him shout at her. It wasn't like Jesse. James, yes, but not Jesse.

Jesse pointed his finger at her. "No!" He hadn't meant to shout at her, again, but he felt defeated where he stood.

Luna looked at him angered then by his words. She refused to let him do what only his brother could do to her. But then she felt his heart break and she almost died inside.

Jesse whispered to her, in almost a plea, because his heart wrenching inside his chest robbed his voice of speech. "Don't go, Luna." Jesse lingered on each word, on her name he never spoke, he even shoved his hands in the pockets of his uniform as his tears mixed with the rain on his face dripping off him.

Jordy's last words to him struck a chord in his heart. He looked at her this time, not seeing the woman he had desired all this time, but his best friend.

He couldn't lose her again. It was too much. He couldn't take it anymore.

There was unknown dangers out there now that scared the hell out of him. The thought of her leaving, again, the thought that he could lose her this time was too much to bare.

He had no idea how to protect her, but he would die trying.

"Damn it, Babe!" he begged her with one hand looking in her eyes, lifting it up not sure why he had, pausing, not knowing how to say what he felt. "Make me like you so I can go with you!" He didn't know where that thought came from, but there it was.

He looked her right in her eyes, standing his ground and pleaded more with her. "But God, damn it all! Babe, don't go! Don't leave me again." And he meant it when he used God's name. He needed God now. He needed God to stop her from leaving him again.

Jesse stood taller then and walked right up to her. He grabbed her face like she had always done to him, and let the words he had kept trapped in his heart all these years finally go. Slowly he let the words fall from his lips, begging her with them to hear him.

"I love you Luna."

He moved an inch back away from her almost falling to his knees in a plea letting go of her. "I love you so much I-"

Jesse looked through the blinding rain at her. She was standing there wrapped in his police coat in the drenching rain, her long black hair soaked through. He didn't know what he was trying to say. He just wanted to keep repeating it to her over and over again until she finally understood it.

"I've tried not to-." He started to say, but it shook him.

Jesse looked up at the sky above them. He couldn't say the words "not to love you". They didn't exist for him.

He looked at her then, surrendering to it all. "It's fucked up, I know!" He laughed as he thought about it. It was true. Especially here, now, after everything they had been through.

Every damn time he tried not to love her, it only made him love her more.

"I've loved you for so long, Babe."

He stepped closer to her and begged her again with his hands cupping her face. He had to make her understand. "I love you, Luna. Please, don't go." He begged, sobbing like a child.

Luna had been stunned into silence by his every word. She had expected a scolding, or a set down when he had hollered at her like James would have and said something that would have broke her heart coming from Jesse. She hadn't expected Jesse to be pleading with her to stay instead, telling her he loved her the way he was.

He had never said it to her before.

Oh, how she loved him. It made her soul ache.

She pushed forward into his hands on her face and didn't stop till she kissed him. His permission be damned.

Jesse was taken by surprise. He had expected her fingers on his lips shushing him like she always did, not her lips kissing him when she came at him.

Jesse held her face as she kissed him, letting her kiss him so tenderly. He pulled her closer into him, held her hips and then he picked her up into his arms. It brought him to his knees, their weight in the rain, but he crushed her into his body wrapping her legs around him and he helplessly kissed her back. Devouring her mouth with his.

She had finally kissed him. After all these years she had finally done what he had asked, what he had wanted. She was loving him back. She was proving it to him. She was agreeing to love him.

Luna took from his lips everything she had ever wanted from him. She felt inside of him, felt his emotions and desire stirring. Her own reaction from the sweet metallic taste of his lips, the sweet essence of Jesse filled her whole being.

Jesse held her head with one hand and pulled on her lips, her kiss into his. Not in all his feverish dreams of her he had in the past could they compare to what he was feeling right now.

He snuck his hands inside his coat and cupped her bare hips pulling her closer to his hardness. When her lips parted at his touch he deepened his kiss, he took her hands and placed them around his neck and fell to the ground with her wrapping her around his body, pushing himself into her so she could feel him, right where she was supposed to be.

"Jesse." She moaned aloud trying to break his kiss. She needed him to listen to her still, but he was kissing her neck now, begging her to shut up in his mind as he kissed her lower under his coat. Luna could only grin and try not to laugh at his thoughts as he turned her on higher there on the muddy grass.

She almost screamed out his name again as he pushed further into her. He was cupping his hand under her now, pulling her bare bottom up, pushing her closer to him still. She could feel his desire now between her bare legs like before.

All she could do was claw at his head and back for more as he kissed her so thoroughly again.

Jesse had never imagined this in all his years of wanting Luna. He'd imagined every possible scenario with her, but never in the rain on the muddy ground above what should have been her mother's grave. He could barely even think of it all now. He was so lost in this moment.

All he could do was feel. Feel her under him, wrapped around him, all up into him. Her ecstasy was flaming all over him now. Driving him mad with need.

He kissed her fully, like he had always dreamed of doing. He couldn't stop himself.

"Please, stop." She had to stop him. She placed her hands on his face and touched their foreheads together stopping him. They needed to leave this place. She needed him to listen, she needed to protect him from the dangers around them. And she couldn't do that drunk on his kiss.

Jesse looked down at her. "Only if you swear to me Luna. I'm not letting you-"

Luna shushed his words with her lips. Her heart couldn't bare him begging her anymore. She had to smile at his eagerness though. She had no idea how she was going to get away from him ever again, but she had to get him somewhere so he would listen to her instead of kissing her. Or so she could figure out what in the hell she was going to do next.

The sound of a man clearing his throat took Luna off guard. She would have leaped and changed into a wolf, if Jesse hadn't been on top of her. Instead she bared her fangs and looked up into the face of a vampire standing over her.

~ *Five* ~

Be still, let go and fall

"Well, well. What do we have here?" Jeremy grinned down at the two lovers.

When Jesse got back up on his knees he hung his head in surrender, Luna listened into his mind and discovered that Jesse and Jeremy had already made acquaintances earlier in the evening.

Good, she thought as she stood up and rounded on Jeremy, making sure Jesse's coat didn't come open in the process. She wouldn't have to make introductions before she killed Jeremy and buried him in the grave she had just opened.

Jeremy and her had unfinished business. He was the one who had turned her into this freakish monster who couldn't control her anger or her hunger, just like the monsters who were out here killing the ones she loved.

Luna would have her revenge, now.

Jeremy rose his hands up in surrender towards her before she could do exactly that. "You need me, Luna."

Jesse didn't like the way Jeremy said it flirtatiously to her in his good ol boy accent. He made sure he announced it clearly in his head so Jeremy would hear it. Sure enough, Jeremy looked at him and winked before he finished his conversation with Luna.

Luna stood to her full height and walked menacingly towards Jeremy showing off her powers with thunder from above her, making sure Jeremy knew just how powerful she was now since the last time they had seen each other. She smiled evilly to herself when Jeremy started backing up. She even pushed up the coat sleeves for effect.

"Luna! Listen damn it!" Jeremy pleaded with her, almost tripping as he stumbled backwards in haste.

Luna chuckled out loud when he tripped backwards over a head stone and landed on his back side.

Jeremy let himself fall. He even surrendered and laid down on his back letting out a sigh. He deserved that.

He'd never met a vampire who could scare the hell out of him like that, except his sister Emie. He'd only met Luna once in his life, she had only been a sweet little werewolf then and that was when he had turned her into a vampire. Now that he could see her in all her glory and power, he knew not to mess with or touch her.

This was all just pay back now for what he had done to her. He could almost hear his sister and brothers laughing at the images they were seeing now.

Jeremy looked at Luna then and asked permission to stand up.

Luna crossed her arms together, looked at him and wondered if the punishment of showing off her powers was enough for her. Jeremy was surly humiliated now. No one had ever made him feel like that before, she thought greedily to herself.

Luna reached her hand out towards him and offered to assist him. When he put his hand in hers Luna bent towards him and looked deeply into souls eyes. "Don't ever cross me Jeremy Whitby." She sent a jolt of power through him that caused a chilling tremble all throughout his body. She sent fear raging through him so he'd never forget what it felt like to touch her.

Jeremy took her hand and as she spoke he realized she had the same powers as Joseph. She could hurt vampires and push her will, without even using her wolf abilities to tear him to shreds piece by piece. He'd have to obey her.

He kept his smile to himself as he stood up. It would be fun toying with her though, he thought sheepishly.

Jesse stood and walked over towards the two, he wondered if they had even realized how far away from him they had walked. They were half way across the cemetery now.

As Jesse walked, he looked at the head stone Jeremy had tripped over. It wasn't just anyone's grave they were standing over. It belong to a friend of his.

Talia Kruse's name on the head stone made his heart hurt as the memories of her played out in his head. Talia had worked for Linda and Luna growing up.

She had been a dear friend to him. He smiled thinking how Talia had tried her best to get Luna to like Jesse all those years ago at the shop.

Jesse noticed when Luna looked in the direction he was looking. He watched as she sighed at the memory of Talia also.

His cousin Darryl had come home last summer to attend Curtis' funeral. Darryl and Talia had been school sweethearts growing up. Jesse remembered the pain he had seen in Darryl's eyes while he had been home over the loss of Talia he still felt after all these years. It felt like a lifetime ago that she had died in the crash right before graduation.

Jesse looked at Luna and they shared a moment together. If he ever lost Luna like that...

Jeremy asked Luna who the grave belonged too in her mind. He could tell it was someone important to them.

Luna explained it the best she could in his mind as she turned to tell him who Talia was.

Jeremy nodded his head towards her in silent acknowledgement.

Luna reached for Jesse's hand and took it softly in hers, while she asked Jeremy aloud what he was doing here. "What do you want Jeremy?"

Jesse looked down at Luna who was looking at him and holding his hand in the rain. The rain had slowed somewhat, telling him that Luna's sadness had subsided a little. He was grateful for it and kissed the top of her head pulling her into an awkward hug.

"I know where Linda is." Jeremy announced proudly.

Luna and Jesse both looked at Jeremy.

Jeremy tried not to smile when he knew he had their full attention. "Well, Jordy knows. She's in Tennessee."

Luna opened her eyes wide at Jeremy, angry with him. "What the hell is wrong with you two? This isn't a game Jeremy. Why didn't you tell me this when I was there?" She rounded on him fully and stared him down, bringing him down to his knees.

Lighting struck right beside him, blinding Jeremy with its bright light. Thunder roared around her words.

Jeremy begged forgiveness in front of her powers. "Please, let me explain." He raised his hand to her to stop her power. It felt like the thunder was in his head vibrating through his soul.

Jesse smirked at Jeremy and was impressed with Luna. He'd felt something similar to that with Luna at times. She must have never pressed as hard with him in the past.

He watched as she placed her hand behind her and tilted her finger back and forth at Jesse. She was signaling to him hush secretly.

Looking over at Jeremy, Jesse wanted to laugh at him for messing with her. He should have known better. Jesse thought it served him right for all Jeremy had done to him earlier.

"Tell me where she is Jeremy! Now!"

The rain, the wind, everything stopped. The silence of the night surrounded them all.

Jeremy looked up at Luna. Jesse wasn't the only one impressed. He wanted to inquire more about her powers and whether or not she had stopped the storm, or if it had stopped because of her, but he also knew now wasn't the time.

"First, I need to take you to the shop. And for heaven's sake, please stop." He begged her. But the pain raged further inside of him when she noticed that he tried to push his will on her and mistakenly tried to make her do his own will.

Luna pushed her will further, she dug inside his mind for his secrets he was hiding. It was the only power he had against her. As frustrating as it was, she stopped and let him have it. She'd get the answers she needed one way or another.

"Promise you'll tell me everything if I take you there?" She questioned him, pushing her power once more into his soul holding him captive and making him look at her until he promised.

"You have my most solemn vow." Jeremy vowed to her softly needing to breathe for the first time in a hundred years.

Luna watched as Jeremy bent his head low in a bow of reverence when she released him. She let him go and turned back to Jesse while she let Jeremy get up on his own.

"Would you be so kind as to offer us a ride?" She asked, grinning selfishly at Jesse.

When Jeremy was about to question her why, she hushed him with her finger pointed at him. She smiled, still looking at Jesse when he complied.

Jesse looked at her and grinned. He stuffed his hands in his pockets and cocked his head at her. "I'm dying to know why though?" Because honestly the two of them could be there faster if they just ran there. Riding with him in his truck would be torture for them.

Luna grinned back him. She loved he was enjoying this just as much as she was. She hadn't been able to use her powers like this in forever. She looked fiercely at Jeremy warning him to behave then she looked back at Jesse lovingly.

"Because I promised you I wouldn't leave you and I can't leave you alone out here. It's not safe. So you get to come with us." She grinned more proudly at him this time.

Jesse turned sideways and looked to her as he held out his hand for her to lead the way to his truck. "Lead the way Babe."

~Aunt Linda's Pet Shop~

Luna was standing in the dark, badly burnt bathroom of the grooming shop, putting on a pair of scrubs the girls had kept in a locker to wear when they were grooming. She had lost her favorite dress somewhere on the Whitby land when she had broken out in a werewolf, running into the woods.

She braced her back against the wall after she had changed and tried to cool down before she returned to the guys who were walking around the shop that had been destroyed by the fire.

She wanted to destroy Jeremy, but she needed him apparently. She couldn't believe the two Whitby boys knew where her mother was, had known all along, and had kept it from her.

Curious now to know the truth, she walked out towards the guys, she found Jesse shining his flash light looking at the disarray around them. She handed him his coat and walked over to Jeremy who was standing where a wall used to be that divided the shop from Linda's apartment.

Jeremy was still contemplating Luna's powers. He knew that as a werewolf she had powers over the earth, but he hadn't known the extent of her powers as a vampire yet. He looked at her questioningly as she walked up to him.

Now isn't the place for this conversation in front of Jesse. She told his mind. Jesse doesn't need to know that you are responsible for me being a vampire.

Jeremy noted her thoughts but he couldn't leave it alone. "I remember the night it happened Luna." Jeremy said aloud defying her plea, looking into the apartments away from her.

It had been so long ago in their past it almost seemed like it had never happened. He had not spoken to or seen Luna since. He had been banned from her presence by Joseph.

Defying her now probably wasn't a good idea, but he had to know something.

Jesse looked at them, curious what they were talking about. He knew it was something important just by looking at them both.

Luna looked at Jeremy then, making him look at her so he could feel her anger towards him.

Jeremy almost smiled at the look on her face. She could scare anyone with that look.

"I didn't know what I was doing, Luna. I had been so consumed with my new life and this hunger for blood. I had desired just a taste of you. The wolf you are."

Jesse reluctantly listened, but he didn't want to know this.

Luna looked at Jesse. She apologized to him, then she looked back at Jeremy. "You're being a cad Jeremy." She growled at him when she walked up to glare at him, tucking her hair behind her. She desperately needed a ponytail.

"You need to know that I know that I was wrong. I know this now. I need your forgiveness for this, Luna."

Luna hung her head at this revelation. She felt like she was dancing with the devil, but she knew he was just being playful. Looking back at him she extended her hand and waved it at him wanting to be done with all this. "Is this really what you require before you tell me the truth?"

"Yes." He stated simply, looking at the beautiful, playful creature in front of him. If his heart wasn't already taken, he would seriously give it to this woman.

"I can't help you until I know this Luna." Jeremy told her honestly.

"Technically, this is all Joseph's fault." This he stated proudly trying not to think about her, looking away from her. "He never warned us about you when we moved in. It was Joseph who finished the job before I could kill you, making sure you lived.

"He had plans for you. None of us knew the creation you would become when it happened."

Jesse wanted to be angry. He turned around away from them and put his hands on top of his head trying to concentrate on his breathing. He wanted to hate Jeremy for toying with her like this. But he didn't know the man. All he knew was at some point Luna had been Jeremy's victim, and it did things to him he couldn't control.

Jeremy reminded Jesse what he had shared with him earlier. One day you will thank me for all this.

Luna sighed at both of their thoughts. "Fine. You have it. Now tell me where she is?"

Jeremy smiled widely at her. He had worried for years about the matter.

"She was taken here, in the back of the shop." Jeremy nodded to the room next to them. "She was in the laundry room doing laundry when they busted the door down."

"Why didn't you warn her?" Luna almost yelled.

Jeremy calmed down then. It was time to be serious now. He let her see how their powers worked. "We can't see everything Luna. Only the things we look for." He showed her in her mind, how Jordy hadn't seen that they would take Linda here until after it had happened. "We don't just know the future, we have to look for it.

"For months, he's been trying to wrap his mind around some of his visions. Like nightmares, he tries to sort them out as he searches for things. A lot of which he has tried to share with Emie and Joseph, but he can't get them to listen to him.

"While you were looking for those caves, we didn't know when it would happen. We've been leaving a curiosity in you to search out those caves for years because we knew they would be hiding them there. We were hoping you would discover them before it happened."

Jeremy sighed inwardly. Apparently it had already happened, he thought to himself looking around at the damage caused by the fire.

"Hiding who there?" She questioned Jeremy quietly. Who else besides her mother had been taken.

Jeremy let Luna see the three women in Jordy's visions. The one woman he hadn't known who she was, until tonight, just that she was an angel. Now that he knew who she was from the cemetery, Talia, he let Luna see who the woman was. Then he showed her about Emie. It had been the secret they all were hiding from Asher, waiting for it to happen, hoping that Luna could help them save her also.

Luna couldn't believe it. She seriously was stunned into disbelief at it all. Her mother, Talia, Emie would all be taken, and there was nothing any of them could do about it.

"Luna?"

Jesse took Luna by surprise then, he said her name asking for permission, breaking the unwanted spell Jeremy had over her showing her the visions they had been having.

Jeremy looked at Jesse, confused at how he knew they were speaking amongst themselves, but continued talking to Luna out loud this time. "Joseph told you about the vampire royals. We haven't discovered where the kings are hiding, but some are there in those mountains. Hiding under radar from the humans. I believe they have trapped some vampires there holding them prisoner. Ones they are trying to use and steal power from so they can create others. They've been kidnapping humans also, using them to do testing.

"They are harvesting humans there Luna. Making blood. They run test on them, make new creations on the ones who have powers, and the ones that don't they hang them up and let blood drain out of them, slowly, keeping them alive."

Jeremy watched as Jesse held his breath and looked away disgusted.

"It's all apart of the plans to take over the world. This is how they are going to do it. They're not just killing humans, they are holding them prisoners. It's a fate worse than death."

Luna closed her eyes at the images Jeremy was showing her. There were worse things going on he wouldn't speak aloud of in respect of Jesse.

Jesse couldn't believe what Jeremy had just said. He looked at Luna then for answers.

Luna looked at Jesse. She hung her head and looked around where she was standing. Tears started to form in her eyes and dripped down her cheeks. This was bigger than her. She couldn't fight against this.

She took a deep breath and tried not to tremble. "What am I supposed to do Jeremy?"

Jeremy was honored by her words. They meant she was trusting him, even if it was just a little bit.

"I brought you here so you could feel the reality of it all. Linda was kidnapped here by them. Just like millions of people have been. They set fires like this to cover the evidence from the unsuspecting humans. Creating a fear in them.

"I will take you as close as I can get you to her. I'm hoping between the two of us, we can rescue her and find the information we will need to free everyone else."

Jesse thought about that. He looked at Luna and asked, "What about turning me-". He stopped talking when she interrupted him looking at him. She had pushed a weight on him he couldn't describe. Now he could see the blood tears falling on her face. She was sad again.

Luna let the rain fall again from the clouds, hoping it would wash the blood off her cheeks. She lifted her face up towards the rain coming down through the burnt out hole in the roof above them. "There's not enough time Jesse."

Jeremy agreed aloud. "There's not Jesse. It could take years to get you prepared for what you would be facing."

Jesse walked away from them angry. He couldn't handle this.

Luna looked at Jeremy demandingly. "Tell me everything you know, Jeremy, now."

Jeremy walked forward then and placed his hand in Luna's. It was just easier this way. He showed her everything he knew.

When he was finished, Luna spoke slowly to him in a hushed whisper. "You're going to stay here. You're going to protect him. And if you fail, I will destroy you."

Jeremy knew she was telling him the absolute truth of a decision she had already made. This was what she was going to do to forgive him. He nodded his understanding to her, but shared with her the future she would have if she went alone.

If they take me, I can get closer to them. It shook Luna to think of it, but it was the only plan she could come up with.

Before he took his leave from them, he shared the future of the night with her. No one would find them here tonight, he told her with a wink towards her, just in case they wanted to be alone.

Luna watched him as he disappeared, confused by his last vision, but she walked over to where Jesse was leaning against a blackened door frame where there was no longer a door. She leaned back against the other side of the door frame facing him, resting her arms behind her.

Jesse turned and faced her. He crossed over to her slowly and put his hands above her. He placed his lips on her forehead softly and kissed her, dreading the feelings welling up inside of his heart. They hurt.

"Have mercy on me Babe." He whispered, begging her as she wrapped her arms around him. "Don't go Luna." He whispered to her, letting his arms fall around her.

Luna closed her eyes. She could feel his warmth. It was radiating off him like steam in the rain. She could smell not only the essence of the burnt building around them, but the scent of Jesse. He smelled of cologne mixed with earth from the rain.

Luna ran her hands up his body. "Jesse? If you were me, and it was your mother, what would you do?"

Jesse closed his eyes and put his hands on her hips pulling her towards him. He kissed the top of her head as she wrapped her arms around his neck. He knew he would do the same thing. Even as a human, if one his family were missing, he would move heaven and hell just to find them.

"Promise me Luna. Swear it to me that you'll be ok?"

Luna squeezed her eyes tightly shut. She knew it was a lie. She hated lying to Jesse. More tears formed in her eyes and fell steadily down her cheeks. "I swear it Jesse. I'll be fine."

Luna tried not to let the images Jeremy had showed her fill her with fear. Of what the royals would do to her if they caught her.

When Jesse started to shiver, not because he was cold, but because he was scared, she looked up at him. She knew what he needed. Knew tonight, she was going to give him everything he had ever wanted from her.

She surrendered to him.

Luna reached up on her toes and kissed his lips softly.

Jesse cupped her face when she kissed him. He pulled her hard into his kiss and didn't stop until he was heated through.

Luna let her feelings for him overpower her. She let them flow inside of him so he could feel it too.

Jesse pushed her back against the frame of the door and lifted her arms around his neck. He was about to pick her up and wrap her around him, never breaking his kiss, when his radio went off at his side.

Jesse felt the vibration of his radio along with the transmission of his Chief, Jerry.

"Jesse! Where the hell are you?"

Jesse almost jumped out of his skin at the way Jerry had broken the serene silence between them. He felt like stomping his booted feet, cussing up a storm and throwing his radio. Instead he pulled Luna in harder and kissed her like he hadn't heard anything at all.

When Jerry beckoned again over the radio, Luna made him stop.

"Jesse." She scolded him breathlessly.

Even though now he was kissing her neck, she tried again. "Jesse, please." She begged, not wanting to push him away because he was kissing her ear and it felt so heavenly.

Again, Jerry bellowed over Jesse's radio. "Jesse! Answer me, Jesse! What's your location?"

Jesse growled out loud but he stood up straight and made a face snarling at her that mimicked her look at him earlier, while he reluctantly answered Jerry on the radio.

"What's wrong Jerry?"

"Where are you?" Jerry demanded.

Jesse paused and looked at his radio and wondered what he was supposed to tell Jerry. He looked at Luna for help.

Luna shrugged her shoulders at him and whispered to him "You should be there Jesse." She lowered her head then and placed her hands on his chest. The truth that was there with both of them sadden her. "You shouldn't be here with me."

Jesse drew his brows together in a determined look. "No." He stated simply to her. Then he radioed Jerry back.

"I'm just grabbing a few things. I'll be back soon." He grinned when he finished as he grabbed the only thing he wanted.

"Jesse get your ass back here right now! That's an order! It's not safe out there alone."

Jesse looked at his radio and wanted to throw it.

Luna whispered to his mind and showed him that his family was right there with Jerry and they needed to hear his reassurance that he was ok.

"Who's side are you on?" He asked her looking at her seriously and gave her his best crooked smile winking at her teasingly.

Luna smiled and hushed him with her fingertips on his gorgeous evil smile and joking comment. He always knew how to steal her heart with his sweet endearments, even though they were totally out of place and half backwards in all seriousness.

She ran her thumbs across his lips caught up in the moment, lost with him in front of her and couldn't help looking at his lips, that had so roughly kissed her just moments ago, that now were dripping with desire watching her look at him like she was. She was drawn to them like a moth to a flame now. She brushed her thumbs across them again thinking of how she had always wanted to do that, but never could.

Their lips slowly came back together again in the stillness until Jerry interrupted them again.

"Jesse!" Jerry persisted over the radio.

Jesse broke the kiss and pulled Luna closer to him and kissed the top of her forehead, praying God would give him the strength not to deck Jerry the next time Jesse sees him.

He was finally alone with Luna. He could finally kiss her, make love to her, do whatever the hell he wanted to do with her, but Jerry wouldn't shut up!

Luna covered her silent giggle in his neck at his thoughts.

"I just need five more minutes, damn it!" Jesse hollered back over the radio, more to himself than for Jerry.

Jesse groaned aloud then, worrying about offending his Chief and remembering belatedly, thanks to Luna that his family was listening to him. He looked at Luna and apologized, begging her to wait.

"Jerry, listen, I know it's not safe out here, but if you keep hollering over the radio and announcing that I'm alone, incapable of protecting myself to whoever else is out here with me, you're going to get me killed. Please just shut up. I'll be back soon."

Luna was truly impressed and showed him that with an impressive look on her face. He had come up with the perfect response without having to lie or tell the truth about where he was. She wished she could learn how to be so suave like he was sometimes.

After Jerry responded with an "Ok." to Jesse, he unhooked his radio from his belt and let it fall to the ground. He was determined now to kiss Luna the way he wanted too. He took off his gun belt in front of her, let it too fall to the ground.

Luna wanted to stop him. He was unbuttoning his shirt now and ripping off his bullet proof vest. She could see it in his eyes as she tried, by saying his name and putting her hands on him, but when he reached forward and kissed her lips shushing her, she couldn't stop him.

Jesse showed her in her mind that Jeremy had shared the nights future with him. She could spare him the five minutes he was asking for. They were safe here.

The way he was kissing her, the way his mouth was making love to hers, Luna wanted so much more tonight than she could have of him.

"Jesse-"

Jesse broke the kiss and closed his eyes when she spoke. "Luna. Shut up."

He waited, then he opened his eyes again. Her smile was the most beautiful thing he had ever seen. Her fang was seductively biting her lower lip.

He grinned back at her letting his finger graze the tip of her fang. "Five more minutes Babe. That's all I'm asking for."

When she smirked at him unbelieving his comment, he started kissing her again until she started moaning. He dug his fingers into her bottom and pulled her up closer to him, pressing up into her with his hips. He wanted to make her want him like he had always wanted to do. He wanted her to know what he wanted.

When she broke his kisses, and moaned his name aloud at the feel of him pressed up into her, she begged him for more when he started kissing her neck.

"Four more." He ordered breathlessly.

When she leaned back he let her go and made his way into her shirt with his hands and searched for his prize like he was unwrapping a gift he wanted more than anything. He found her breasts bare and raised them to his mouth sucking on each nipple hard, sucking on them like he was drinking from them, reveling in the way she loved it.

Luna rested her head up against the door frame Jesse was pushing her against. She looked up into the sky through the burnt out roof and let the cool mist of the rain cool her cheeks as Jesse left her nipples cold and damp to the night air around them.

"Three more." She stated to him simply.

Jesse was determined now to make her forget about time and place. He kept kissing her lower, down her abdomen, as he got down on bended knees there in the middle of the burnt out shop, in the cool misty rain, til she finally relented. He didn't stop kissing her till he ran his hands down her hips and thighs dragging her scrub pants sensually down her legs, and spread them apart opening her to him.

Jesse looked up seductively and hungrily into her eyes then. He willed her to remember what he had told her years ago he wanted to do to her.

Luna looked breathlessly at Jesse. She was in awe of the way Jesse was making love to her. In one night Jesse had managed to love her more tenderly than anyone had ever done to her before.

Jesse had told her in the past how he loved to make love to a woman with his mouth. She'd never experienced it before and he had known it. He had teased her so many times the way he had described it to her, that Luna had desired it. She honestly couldn't believe what was about to happen to her.

She knew she shouldn't let him. He needed to be safely hiding away with his family from the storm that was coming. But she couldn't deny either of them this stolen moment.

Jesse looked at the woman who was spread open for him, like a feast ready to be devoured. He had no idea if his five minutes were up or not, and he could care less at this point. He was in his own peace of heaven with Luna. He was going to take his sweet ol time with her.

Luna tried not to make a sound at the touch of his lips on her lower lips. She had to bite her lips every time she moaned at the touch of his tongue on her. Tears filled her eyes at the pleasure of it all. Every time she almost climaxed, he would pause, and then slowly start all over again licking and sucking every inch of her womanhood.

The very last second before her body lost control Jesse stopped.

With rugged breathing she opened her eyes and looked at him pleading for more.

"I know, Babe." Jesse told her as he stood trying to unbuckle his pants. He was gonna make love to her right here even if it killed him.

Jesse's radio went off again on the ground next to them. This time it was Asher. Jesse hung his head knowing his five minutes were officially up. He reached for the door frame above her and almost crushed it with his bare hands trying to regain his composure.

Luna reached for Jesse's face as he bent over her struggling to breathe. She could hear inside of his heart how he had longed for this day. He longed still for this moment they were stealing together to never end.

"Jesse!" Asher bellowed again, louder than anyone ever had over the radio.

Jesse looked at Luna, really looked at her. He thought for a split second about ignoring Asher, then read the look on Luna's face as she adjusted her scrub pants and interrupted her thoughts before she voiced them. "I know, I know. I shouldn't be here."

Jesse sighed inwardly and picked up his radio. "What Asher?"

"I need you here." Asher demanded.

"I'm fine Asher."

"Moms not." Asher stated simply.

Jesse sighed at that. He let go of Luna, put his hands on his hips and looked up into the rain that was now drenching him. Luna was trying not to cry, but the rain couldn't contain her sadness.

He knew he needed to go back. Their mother had just lost her husband, she was probably worried to death about her son right now.

He looked to Luna. He needed her to go back with him.

"I'm on my way." He told Asher, holding Luna's gaze with his.

Thunder rolled quietly above them.

Luna watched Jesse. She whispered to his heart what she couldn't say aloud. Because he was only a human, he couldn't follow her tonight. And because she was a vampire, she couldn't follow him tonight.

Their worlds were that far apart.

She couldn't be alone, trapped, with all those beating hearts. She needed to feed tonight.

Jesse read the look on her face and heard her whispered thoughts. She couldn't go with him. She'd spent her life in the human world, but she'd never been trapped with them like she would be down at the fire hall tonight. He sighed greatly again. He hated this part. He hated saying goodbye to her again.

His heart literally sunk in his his chest causing a heavy weighted pain.

Luna made the rain stop. She looked at his bare chest through his open uniform shirt and walked the distance from where she was to where Jesse was standing alone. She ran her fingers up his chest. She felt his fears and chased them away.

When she looked up at him, she wrapped her arms around his neck and looked up into his sweet eyes tenderly.

"Jesse, this morning I was standing alone in a cave. Believing I was searching for a life that was destined to be. I've been alone for a long time out there."

Luna looked at where his heart was and placed her hand there. "I don't want to be alone without you anymore Jesse. Let me go, let me find my mother, and I swear it to you, I'll come back to you."

Jesse loved what she said to him. He placed his palm on her face sweetly and looked at her with renewed relief in what had happened between them tonight. Just a few hours ago he had been alone at the fire department wishing he had her back in his life. And now here she was. Just as in love as he was.

"Promise me you'll try to stay alive?" He begged her moving her hair off her face that had fallen forward.

Luna couldn't lie to him again. She told him the one thing she knew that would quiet his worried heart. "I love you Jesse Stone."

"Prove it." He grinned, daring her.

Luna reached up on her tippy toes and placed a kiss on Jesse's lips. She let the heat build inside of him with her kiss. Took his lips inside of hers and kissed him, holding onto him for dear life.

~ Six ~

Be still and walk by faith

Asher was sitting at his desk thinking. Trying to decide what to do with a department full of people who were about to descend into dirty, greasy truck bay pits. People who were his friends and family. People who depended on him to protect them. People he would die for.

The burden was great. The weight was so heavy.

Asher felt the sweet hands of the woman he loved wrapping around his shoulders. He closed his eyes and took a deep breath at the feel of her loving essence.

"Don't fear my love." Emie tenderly placed a kiss on his neck and spoke again, filling Asher with hope and taking the weight of his burdens from him. "Have faith. You can do this superman."

He could feel Emie's love as she grinned into his neck. Her jest was sweet and comforting, but his fear was overpowering him.

"What if I fail Emie?" Asher asked her, exhausted.

Emie didn't even hesitate in answering him. She whispered behind him, hoping he would understand this and carry it with him forever. "Don't fear failure, Asher. Fear not doing anything at all."

He was a firefighter. He knew this.

Asher squeezed his eyes tightly shut at Emie's words. He couldn't un-hear her words even if he tried. She was right. Absolutely right.

He vowed to the heavens she spoke of, to never let her go. To never-

Just as Asher was vowing his life to loving Emie, about to show her just how much he would always love her, his brother James walked in his office.

James cleared his throat at his intrusion, apologizing to Asher. He couldn't help but notice the way Emie was whispering in Asher's ear when he had opened the door. He could just imagine the evil she was stirring in his brothers head.

She was going to be the first to go, James told himself quietly.

Emie patted Asher's shoulders. "I promised Katie that I would read her a story before she has to go down in the pits to help her relax. I'll leave you two alone."

Emie tried not to look at James. She could tell he was staring at her and thinking things he shouldn't be. He hated her, just like Frank had.

She nodded curtly to him when he waited for her to leave Asher's office.

Asher stood as Emie walked around behind him trying to leave. He reached for her fingers and pulled her back into him. He placed a kiss on her forehead and whispered to her he loved her.

I know Asher. Emie whispered to his mind as she looked up to his sweet face. She winked at him, letting him know she knew everything about him.

"I love you more Asher." She whispered out loud. Loud enough so James could hear her. She wanted him to know she loved his brother. She even pushed her will upon him so he could feel it.

Asher was tempted to swat her behind as she walked away for being so cute. She always won the at the game they played, seeing who could tell each other that they loved the other more. He didn't deserve her love.

He caught the look on his brothers face and changed his mind.

"What's wrong James?" Asher watched as the door closed behind Emie and watched as James wrung his hands and sat at the desk, looking so much like his twin that had sat just like that hours earlier, it creeped Asher out.

James didn't know much to tell Asher. Or even what to tell him. "It's Jesse."

"What about Jesse?" Asher sat down harder then he wanted to at James words.

"When we were getting everyone ready to go down into the bays, Jesse left. Jerry has been calling to him on the radio, but he keeps avoiding him. Moms worried about him."

Asher closed his eyes and rubbed his hair out of his face pulling it up behind his head as he sat back in his chair with his hands on top of his head. There were a lot of things he and James needed to talk about tonight. This wasn't one of them.

Asher leaned forward and grabbed his radio off the desk and called to Jesse. When he responded and Jesse said he would be right back, Asher felt better knowing he was safe.

He knew where Jesse was. He was with Luna. And Asher couldn't fault him for that. But he made sure Jesse knew what he was doing to their mother. She didn't need to be worried about her family tonight. She had enough to deal with.

"James, you and I need to talk."

James rubbed his hands together between his legs. "About what dad tried to tell you tonight?"

Surprised, Asher asked, "You heard what dad and I were talking about before he died?"

"Yes." James acknowledged somberly.

Asher sighed at that. Frank had told Asher about what happened to him years ago when he first encountered Joseph Whitby. About who and what they were. James shouldn't have been listening to that.

"What did you hear?"

"Dad told you the same story he's been telling me for years."

Asher was shocked to learn this. He sat forward in his chair, resting his arms on his desk and looked at James to continue.

"When I was in high school, when Jesse met Luna, dad didn't want them together. I learned why one night when Jesse disappeared and dad came to me. He told me that the Whitby's were vampires. Like the ones we are hiding from now."

James knew from the look on Asher's face that Asher knew this already. He wasn't sure how to take that. So he continued.

"He told me Luna was one of them."

Asher gulped for air. He almost choked on it. He had to cover his mouth with his hand and look at James over his hand.

"That summer, when Jesse and Luna broke up, dad wanted me to start talking to Luna. He wanted me to find out all I could about them. He told me if I held my thoughts from her, she wouldn't be able to read my mind. He explained everything to me about them Asher. All that he had learned. And he was right. She is a vampire.

"So are the Whitby's, Asher." James stopped talking. He could tell by the look on Asher's face that he knew this already too. James was afraid of Asher now. What if he was planning to become one of them? What if this was all was some sort of trap?

But James had to try. Asher was his brother. He had to try to convince him.

Asher could hear Emie in his mind. He stayed her, and begged her not to come back in. He would deal with James.

Asher wanted to flat out deny it in front of his brother. But he knew he couldn't. James knew to much. He had to learn more of what James knew. If he was planning anything.

"Go on."

James cleared his throat and continued. "The more time I spent with Luna that summer, I learned dad was right. But she was worse then what dad thought. I tried to tell him but he couldn't comprehend it.

"She could go out in the sunlight unlike most vampires. And she was good at everything. I'm mean like superhuman good. She knew things, before they happened and when she moved- the way she moved, sometimes it was so surreal. She would do things before she should have. I've never seen anything like her."

Asher knew this already from what he knew of Emie. Knew what James felt. He himself had felt it too. He wanted to know more about what dad had done though.

"And so you and dad…?" He left the question hanging in the air for James. He couldn't believe what James had done to Jesse. He could see the deceit that had been done all these years now. They, meaning his father and James, had discovered the truth, and they had done something. Probably something they could never take back. Something worse than what the Whitby's had done to his family.

"She fell in love with me easily, just like dad wanted her to. She was still getting over Jesse and accepted all the attention I was giving her. I kept telling her lies about Jesse, and she believed them. Dad told me to marry her so we could keep her close and watch her."

Asher felt sick at his stomach. His father had orchestrated this whole thing because of his fears. Frank could have handled this differently, but he chose to do it this way.

"I made sure she believed I loved her, and that Jesse didn't, couldn't love her like I could. Then I married her that summer."

Asher remembered. He remembered Jesse, the heartbroken boy he had been sitting at James' wedding, drunk out of his mind. He remembered the years his mother had worried about Jesse. How much Jesse had loved Luna. Asher had often wondered how James had done it. But the 'why' had always plagued him.

Asher sighed out loud. He needed to end this conversation. This was a matter between his brothers.

"You listened to the ramblings of an old, jealous man-"

"No, Asher." James pleaded with Asher now, scooting closer to the desk in his chair. "Dad was right. She really is a vampire. And so are the Whitby's. You know-"

Asher raised his hand and interrupted James sternly. He was so upset with James he didn't even care about the conversation they were having any more. "There is no such thing as vampires James."

"Then how do you explain what the hell is going on-"

Asher almost stood up then. He sat there wiping the anger off his lips. He knew his face was heated and knew James could see it from the way James stopped talking.

He couldn't believe James had just confessed all this to him about Jesse and he didn't even feel bad about it. He couldn't understand how James had been married to such a sweet woman like Luna and not fall in love with her like Jesse had.

Was there no good left in James? Had his father corrupted him so much?

"How could you do that to your brother, James?"

James looked at his brother. Really looked at him. Wondering what he could say to convince him that they were sick, twisted and evil. "Asher, are you listening to me man? They are-"

Jeremy chose that moment to walk in. Scaring the hell out of James.

Asher took a deep unpleasant breath as James almost jumped out of his own skin. Jeremy was lucky James didn't pack a gun like Jesse did. Or was it Asher who was lucky?

Jeremy winked at Asher at his thoughts. He reminded him that he was faster than a speedy bullet.

Asher looked at Jeremy directly and he wondered if they would ever trust him to handle things on his own.

Jeremy spoke before James could, who had just stood and looked pleadingly at Asher. "Asher, I need to show you something outside. Alone." He flashed a grin at Asher when James wasn't looking.

The domineering man Jeremy was, Asher could see why his father and James believed they were all vampires. Just by looking at Jeremy you could see he wasn't normal.

Asher knew this was all a ploy to scare James for what he had done. Jeremy just wanted to show off that Asher was his, in some sick twisted vampire humor. Asher played along though. There was a seriousness to Jeremy that Asher found compelling.

"You can't go outside Asher!" James pleaded with his brother grabbing the desk in front of him. He looked like he was having a panic attack right there in front of them.

"Shut up, James. I don't want to talk about this anymore. Understand?" He commanded him. He stood to his full height, grabbed his keys, cell phone and radio, and attached them to his sides. He started to walk around his desk when James grabbed his arm.

"You can't Asher."

Asher looked at his little brother. He didn't know what to say to him to make him understand this. "That's enough James."

James turned to Jeremy then. He grunted stubbornly under his breath and walked out of Asher's office.

Jeremy looked after James in wonder. He looked back at Asher then and asked "They're twins?"

Asher nodded in agreement to Jeremy. Jeremy was also a twin who looked just like his own brother.

"You could have waited five more minutes." Asher told Jeremy as they both stared after James walking out into the meeting room.

Jeremy turned slightly, looking crookedly at Asher, flashing his fangs as he smiled. "He threatened my sister. What'd you expect me do?" He found it fun and entertaining that Asher knew how to play along with them.

Asher sighed at that. "I'm surprised you didn't pee on me to show him who was alpha."

Jeremy chuckled at Asher's jest. "I'll see if I can get Luna to do it for me."

He stood to his full height and straightened up. Emie was in his head again and he needed to finish this with Asher. "We really do need to go upstairs though. I wasn't just trying to scare James."

Asher followed Jeremy up the back steps up to the roof. Jeremy motioned off the roof to the streets. Asher watched as mad, raving vampires, roamed the streets under them. They were running in all directions.

"They can't see you. Emie is using her powers to distract them from the department." Jeremy could see Asher's fears. He was afraid to get too close to the ledge.

Jeremy hoped he could give Asher some comfort. "When Jesse gets here safely with Luna, I'll go and do what I can, but I can't take them all on."

"We have to protect this department and the people in it." Asher told him hopelessly.

Asher bent his head over the ledge. He watched as the men ran and disappeared down the streets into the darkness. He could smell fire in the distance. It was the first time he couldn't respond to the city in distress.

"Do you have everyone here you need Asher?"

"There's so many people still here in the city." Asher grabbed the ledge. He wanted to break it, throw it at the demons ruining his city.

Jeremy put his hands on the ledge looking where Asher was. "Your brother was right about one thing. You can't go outside anymore."

They stood there for some time watching. Not being able to do anything.

Jeremy looked down and leaped over the edge when he saw Luna running with Jesse who was firing at one of the vampires.

Asher ran down the back stairs to the front door. He prayed Jeremy could save his brother.

Jesse walked through the red door of the fire hall and closed it firmly behind him. He had to leave Luna standing outside the door and it was killing him to do it. Vampires were running wild on the streets.

Would she be safe?

Asher grabbed his shoulder then and Jesse almost raised his gun. When he saw his brothers worried face he sighed heavily in relief.

Asher grabbed his brother and shook him.

"What the hell were you thinking?"

Looking at Jesse seriously Asher admitted he couldn't scold his solemn brother any longer. Jesse had that look that said he would have risked it all for the woman he loved. And in that moment, Asher knew how Jesse felt.

He wrapped his brother in a tight embrace and held him. They both had lost so much already, and now their world was turning upside down.

"Come on. It's time."

Jesse spent the entire next day and night sitting under the bay floor in the darkness with everyone. He watched as the hours past. They all waited and listened. For what, they didn't know.

Jesse worried. He wanted to pace the floor. He felt like he was in a sinking ship. He wanted to scream, fight, call out for help. He wanted Luna, here with him, safe. But he knew she couldn't. She had to free herself from them. She had to find her mother.

The only peace he found in the hours he waited in, was when Emie would look at him and tell him Luna was still ok. She was safe with Jeremy.

It wasn't until the next day that Asher stirred him and woke him. It was almost evening again.

"Some of the men and I are going out."

Jesse started to rise and get to his feet. He was going with them.

"I need you to stay here Jesse."

Jesse looked at Asher like he had lost his damn mind. "But you don't have a gun. Are you crazy? You can't go out there alone Asher!"

Asher hushed him from waking anyone else up. He looked over at Emie and nodded his head towards her. "I won't be alone Jesse."

Jesse took a deep breath as the truth hit him. Asher would be safe with Emie.

Asher whispered to Jesse so no one else could hear. "Jeremy is still upstairs. He's going to stay here and protect you guys from up above. I need you to stay here and protect everyone from down here."

Jesse hated this. He wanted to find Luna. He wanted out of here. But Asher was right. He had to stay here with his family.

Jesse saw, through the darkness in the bay, as Asher reached his fist out for Jesse to bump. Jesse stood then making Asher do the same. When Asher stuck his fist out again for Jesse, Jesse grabbed it in his hand and wrapped his big brother in a hug.

"Just stay safe, brother. Please."

Asher returned Jesse's embrace and patted his back in a brotherly hug. "Just stay put, ok? Do as I say, please Jesse."

Jesse was always good at obeying Asher. He'd never questioned his authority before. Asher took a step back and looked at his brother for reassurance.

Obedience. Their father had drilled it into their heads for years. It was the one thing Asher was grateful for now. Listen, obey, follow orders, don't question or people will die.

"No matter what happens, stay here, protect everyone." Asher looked around then. "I don't trust James to do it Jesse."

It was what Jesse was trained to do. What they were all trained to do. At all cost. Protect and serve.

"I know. I got it." Jesse begged him lightly, trying to lighten the mood. He didn't trust James either. "Just don't die, ok?"

Asher bumped his shoulder and reminded him. "I'm superman, remember?"

Jesse chuckled and nodded his head at Asher. He would stay here. Right here.

But what he really wanted was Luna.

Night turned into day. It wasn't until James opened the hatch of the bay that Jesse realized something was going on.

Jesse looked up from his cot that was wedged amongst many and took out his head phones in his ears. He had been drowning out dreams of Luna he longed to come true with dark music. He got up and started walking over to James who was looking up to the hatch door and watched as James looked expectantly up the ladder.

Ken and some of the other men who had left with James and Asher came down the ladder, shutting the door firmly behind them.

Jesse looked for Asher and Emie. They weren't with the group that had returned.

Jesse jumped forward and had to grab James by the shoulders when he tried to lunge at Ken.

James started hollering at Ken trying to break Jesse's hold on him. "What the hell do you mean he's gone? You were supposed to be protecting him!"

Ken's eyes were wide looking at James' anger. He was so scared of his own shadow he couldn't even begin to explain what all had happened up there.

Jesse took a firm hold on James then. Something had went very wrong out there and James was making the situation worse. "Shut up James! Let them talk!"

It was little Katie who had walked up to the men in their midst that brought them all back down. She reached up for her kitty bear in Ken's hand and took it from him.

"Daddy, where's Uncle Asher?"

Ken looked at James, and silently asked for his patience. He looked tenderly down at his little daughter and knelt down to talk to her.

"Honey, he's-"

Katie put her fingers on Ken's lips to hush him from telling her what she didn't want to hear. "No daddy! Don't say it!" Tears were welling in her eyes she couldn't control.

She looked down at her kitty then and held her tight against her heart. "It's all my fault daddy!" She exclaimed, holding her kitty tight and throwing her arms around Ken crying.

Ken embraced her and hushed her soothingly. "No. It's not your fault sweetie."

"It is! I asked him to save my kitty for me. The zom-pires got him didn't they?" Katie cried more, uncontrollably, begging Ken for answers.

Miranda came closer and took Katie from Ken. They shared a knowing look and she carried Katie away from them consoling her.

Ken stood then and looked at James who was demanding an answer now and gulped down his fear wiping away tears of his own. He looked at Jesse instead as he spoke.

"He's gone guys. He's gone. I'm so sorry."

Jesse let go of James when he fell to his knees. James demanded the answers Ken couldn't give them.

Ken put his shaking hands on his hips and looked down at the floor below him. "Asher and Emie left us at my house. He was going to get Cookie and Emie was going with him. We thought they were ok together. He had her-"

Ken kept his head lowered. Jesse wondered if in that moment Ken knew what Emie was. The way he had said that Asher had her, he said it like Emie was the only weapon he needed.

"After we all made the rounds to everyone's house," Ken gulped for air taking a deep breath so he could continue. "we were on our way to his house when we heard Emie screaming."

The look on Ken's face said it all. It would haunt Jesse forever.

Ken looked at James then, apologizing for the details he couldn't give him. "We all ran to Asher's house, man. We ran like hell, but we were too late."

Ken looked at Jesse then, because he couldn't say it James. Tears were spilling out of his eyes blinding him. "The Whitby's, they murdered him. I'm sorry, we were too late. There was nothing we could do."

The look on Ken's face said that Asher was his best friend and there was nothing he could have done to save him.

Jesse took a step back. He couldn't do this. He couldn't handle this. He looked around for someone to explain it to him, but he couldn't talk to anyone down here.

Ken was wrong. Jesse didn't know what it was, but he was wrong. The Whitby's said they wouldn't kill any of them! There was no way Luna would have let this happen.

Unless- No. Jesse couldn't lose faith in the only thing that was keeping him alive.

James was going on and on like his father had. Instilling fear in every one about the Whitby's. Ken couldn't confirm or deny it. He didn't want to say what he had seen at Asher's house. He couldn't relive it.

The truth, even though Jesse didn't believe it, was the Whitby's had killed Asher.

Jesse was the only one who knew the truth about them. Or so he thought he knew the truth.

Jesse climbed the stairs against everyone's wishes. He ran through the department screaming for Jeremy. He had to find him.

When he reached the roof and the sunlight hit him, he ran for the ledge and waited. For what he didn't know. He just needed the fresh air and a moment alone.

Shaking, he knew he was safe in the sunlight. It was the only place he knew he could be safe.

There was a pack of smokes lying there on the ledge. They were Asher's. Jesse hadn't smoked with Asher since high school. He picked up Asher's smokes and lit one up letting the burn of the nicotine seep into his lungs. He took hit after hit until it was gone, then threw the butt over the ledge. He braced his hands on the ledge and gripped it, squeezing the ledge, digging his fingernails in the cement.

He kept seeing Asher in his mind, dying. But it couldn't be. It couldn't!

He couldn't face reality. He couldn't think about it. It couldn't be true!

"Jesse."

Jesse closed his eyes at the sound of Luna's voice. Her still, small, perfect voice behind him sent shivers up his stone cold body. He spun around on her, anger raging inside his heart.

Luna almost lost it right then. The way Jesse was looking at her like he was afraid of her. Like she had killed his brother. There were huge tears welling in his eyes and his heart was breaking, it was racing, pounding out of his chest.

"Jesse, baby, please." Luna begged. She wanted to hide herself, plead with his heart not to hate her for the monster she was in his eyes now.

Jesse leaned his back against the ledge defeated. He couldn't hate her even if he wanted too. He picked up his hands and put them back down in surrender at her. The tears he was holding back fell down his cheeks and pooled in his mouth. He was broken, barely holding on.

"Curtis, my father, now Ash-" He lost it when he started to say his big brothers name. He slid down the edge of the ledge and sat on the roof below him.

Luna followed him to the ground. She nudged up under his chin and molded her body into his protectively. She wanted to use her powers and vanish with Jesse, to take him somewhere safe. Anywhere but here.

"Ooh Jesse." Luna cried and held him. She wrapped her hands behind his head and pressed him into her shoulder. "I swear it to you Jesse, I swear it on my life, I didn't do this. I had no part in this. I tried to save him Baby."

Luna wept with Jesse there on the roof for Asher.

She had tried to make it to Asher in time, but she was too late. They had already killed Asher. When she had watched the men take off with Emie, she tried to follow them. Remembering it all hurt like hell.

She had no idea who those rogues were, or where they were going. She knew the Whitby boys knew though. She had come back here now only because of Jesse. Then she was going to the Whitby's to find out what she could do.

"Help me understand Babe." He grabbed her hips and shook her in his hands. "Make me understand Luna!" He demanded of her, burying his face in her chest, trying to regain his composure.

Luna bit her lip and broke her promises to herself not to reveal too much to him. She swore she would give him whatever he wanted in this moment.

"Tell me what you need to know?"

Jesse was trembling now. He feared the worst. "Ken said the Whitby's killed Asher. Why?" He demanded, shaking her in a cry that scared Luna when he hollered it out loud.

Luna took his face in her hands. His tears and sopping crushed her as she tried to wipe them off his face. She made him look at her though so she could calm him down. She was confused by what he had said.

"Jesse, it wasn't the Whitby's, Baby. It was rogue vampires after Emie." She looked in each of his eyes. Begging him to believe her. "Asher was just in the wrong place at the wrong time." She couldn't tell him the rest though. She couldn't tell him what she had witnessed.

When Jesse looked away from her, Luna let her fingers slide away from Jesse's worn face. He was so unsteady it burdened her.

"So it's true then?" Jesse questioned her. "He's gone?"

Luna knew now she needed to stay here with him and stop being so foolish. She put away all her selfish ideas and was determined now to stay.

"I'll stay. I'll fight now, Jesse, I'll find out what happened-"

"No!" Jesse grabbed her hands. "I can't lose you too. Luna," Jesse took her face in his hands then. "I can't Babe. Please- Luna-"

Luna hushed him with her lips. Kissing the tears off his cheeks she looked at the heavens through the skies above them, pleading with God to stop his anguish.

Luna brushed her cheek with his and placed her forehead on his with her hands. "You won't, I swear it Jesse. I'm right here."

She crawled up further on his lap and wrapped her arms around his neck and kissed Jesse. He had been begging her for it in his dreams and now she showered him in them.

Jesse took from Luna's lips everything he needed. The world be damned. He reached his hands in her hair and kissed her like he could save her.

It was the gasp that wasn't theirs that stopped them. Stilled them. When they turned to look at the stairs to see who was behind them, Luna almost hissed at James.

James could see the blood in Luna's eyes. The blood that was running down her cheeks. It confirmed what he thought her to be all along.

Dark, demanding clouds hovered and formed above them, drowning out the bright sunshine that had been keeping them all safe.

James was sickened by everything he was seeing in that moment there on the fire department roof top.

All these years he had known she had loved Jesse more then him. It was always there between them. And here she was, he thought to himself, caught in her own sins.

Luna stared at James, stood quickly and walked over to him hauntingly. She wanted to slap him. "How dare you judge me like that."

Jesse got up and made it to his feet. He had seen what she could do to Jeremy. Quietly he stood there behind her, knowing she wouldn't need him. So not to disturb her from what she was about to unleash, he stilled himself.

Sometimes she was heavenly, and other times she was hell fire. He would finally be able to witness the destruction of the pain in his existence.

James confronted her. Face to face. "How dare I? Look at you! Can you honestly blame me?" This last he said more to his brother than to her. He was so angry by what he had just witnessed. He couldn't believe Jesse like Asher, knew what she was and still he was up here with her.

"She's a monster Jesse! What the hell are you doing! They murdered Ash-"

Luna stared him down then. Anger and anguish fueled her on. James was lying and he knew it.

If he wanted a monster, she would show him just how scary she could be. She was going to use her words like a two edged sword and slice his soul to pieces.

She used all her powers to bend him, to bring him to his knees. Jeremy had revealed the truth to her last night while they were hunting. She didn't have to hide who she was to James anymore.

"It takes a monster to know one James." She almost smiled at him when he took the set down as a slap to his pride there on his knees.

"Let's get the story straight shall we? First: it wasn't me that ruined our marriage, it's was you. You and your father sought me out to destroy me! You stole from me the truth and used it against me. You've lied about me and lied to me!

"I trusted you! For years! And you've ruined me with your jealousy!"

James wanted to fight back. He could have, but he honestly didn't know what to do. She was making him not only see the truth, but feel it also. There was no denying her.

He was almost awed by her powers, but he hated her so much more now than ever before. He couldn't believe she could hold him down like this. He balled his fists at his sides and tried to fight her.

Luna pointed her finger at him and continued. "Secondly: what you didn't know about me, was I couldn't read your mind, but I could read your heart. You accused me time after time of cheating on you and not loving you. But no matter how damn hard I tried, you never wanted me James."

She felt it inside of him when he finally admitted it.

"And then, and this is the kicker all your family will finally see; I found your phone! Your emails! I read all those sick, twisted messages you were sending that girl, James! You were cheating on me, for years!

"And where is she now?" Luna really didn't want to know, but she asked anyways. "Is she here? With our family?"

Luna reveled in the way he bent down in reverence and looked up at her. The surprised look on his face as she revealed the truth he couldn't hide anymore brought her back to life. But the sick truth was that girl wasn't here with him. James hadn't even went and looked for her. He'd saved his own life and abandoned her.

And then, there was something else he was hiding. "What else are you hiding James?" Luna edged closer to him and cocked her head at him looking inside of him as the skies above them darkened still. Thunder roared from above as she looked for it.

James seen it as she dug for it in his mind. "No." He begged.

Luna reached for it harder inside of him. When she found it she regretted it immediately.

"There were others?" She spoke softly aloud, astonished by his secrets.

James swore when she found it. "You fucking bitch."

Luna covered her astonished gasp when she found it. There were other women in his life. They were like her, vampires. He was addicted to it.

All those nights she'd spent alone wondering where he was, trying to fix their marriage and to give him his space. He'd been with them.

She had to look away from him then. It tore her heart open when she learned the truth and she couldn't hide the tears anymore. What was so wrong with her, that he had resorted to it all?

"You stupid, fucking whore! You don't get to cast stones at me like this when you've been whoring around with my brother!"

Jesse cut James off before he could say more by stepping between the both of them. James could be colorful with his words that no woman deserved.

"Shut the hell up, James! She never, cheated on you."

Jesse turned and reached for Luna's hand then. She was still crying, breaking inside because of James' words against her and what he had done to her. The rain poured around them.

He pulled her fingers that were at her side into his hand stopping her from the raging storm above them she was about to use on James.

Jesse knew Luna could kill James with just a look, and God help her he didn't know how she hadn't done it all these years.

When she turned and she looked at Jesse, blood dripping from her bright red eyes, he could see the hurt there like it had been before in front of James. She showed Jesse everything in his mind in the space of few heart beats.

Jesse could see all the reasons she had left James that she had never told anyone about. Not even him.

He essentially knew it had been bad by the way James treated Luna in public, but he never dreamed James could be so cruel at home. Her trust had been shattered by James to the point she had been afraid to trust even Jesse.

The screaming, the yelling, James never let Luna do anything without making her think she wasn't good enough. He had condemned her every move with his angry words, haunted her days with it and his judgment she carried with her that would have belittled even the strongest of human women. No matter how perfect Luna tried to do things, it was never good enough for James.

That's why she had run so far away. Jesse wanted to kick himself for not seeing it sooner. She had run away from the face that had emotionally tormented and abused her soul and defeated her heart.

Rain softly started falling from the darkened sky above them; the raging storm moved passed them now. Jesse almost smiled at the calm he felt when she relaxed at his touch knowing he knew everything now.

Luna looked back at James pulling out of Jesse's grasp. "You don't deserve to know me or the truth about who I really am." She had shown James everything she was showing Jesse now.

James interrupted her with renewed anger, hating that she could hold him on his knees like she was still. "You deserve to die, you fucking bitch! You're going to die! You and your whole blood sucking family, all of you!"

James looked at Jesse then when he said that last. Jesse would die too, like Asher had.

Luna saw red. She was flaming with hatred now. The darkness in her took over.

She walked daringly close to him on his knees. "You want to see a monster James, you sorely underestimated me and my family. I'll show you a monster!"

This time she screamed at him. Loud enough that she echoed in the storm she was brewing.

She was a predator. A restless machine. She was a vampire, a werewolf. She became who she was meant to be and rained hell upon him.

"I will swallow you whole! You bastard!"

Jesse grabbed her then. He had to stop her before she did something she would regret out of anger. Not that James didn't deserve it, but he couldn't let her kill him.

So he did what she couldn't do.

In her blowing rain, Jesse stepped in front of Luna. In her breaking thunder, he breathed in her rage and used it as his strength picking James up off his knees. In her cracking lightning, he threw his fist into James's face. He knocked James off his ass and picked him up to his feet again and threw him back into the stairwell.

Jesse took James by surprise. James tried to stand up and regain control. He wiped the blood off his cheek that was now broken. "She killed our brother Jesse! Both of them. What the hell is wrong with you? How can you defend her like this?"

Before Jesse shut the door on James, he pulled out his gun and raised it to James head. He reveled in the moment that James finally registered the severity in the moment. "No, she didn't! You have no idea what the hell you're talking about or the hell you put her through! Or who she is! Damn It, James! You wasted any chance of ever knowing the truth!"

Jesse lowered his gun ashamed of his brother then.

"Get your ass back down stairs. Go take care of what's left of our family while I take care of what's mine." And with that Jesse slammed the door on him.

Luna watched Jesse in stunned disbelief. She hadn't wanted him to do it but she watched and couldn't believe Jesse was being her hero. Again.

He had always been in her past, but to finally see him be able to be what she had always needed him to be, it made her heart break in joy.

He had saved her.

Luna looked at her hands. Had she honestly almost killed James?

Jeremy entered her mind then. I would have. He's on my list.

Luna smirked at him in her mind, but thanked him for being here with her. He was close, she could feel his protection over them.

Jesse turned then and cocked his head at her in question. So many thoughts running through his head now. "James has known, all along? You knew he knew?"

Luna looked away from him then. She couldn't look at him when she told him the truth. It hurt just to remember the years she spent alone with this. "I didn't know he knew everything. I just recently found out the truth.

"Jeremy told me last night." She whispered to herself. She looked up into the passing storm she released and continued. "I almost didn't believe it myself. I thought I was just going insane all those years at home. Trying to be someone I wasn't."

She tripped on her own words as she spoke them aloud. "I couldn't read his mind sometimes. He knew how to hide things from me. But sometimes he would wonder. It would cross his mind and I would try to act more human. I'd act sick, or like something only a human girl could posses."

Luna shrugged then, defeated by her past. "Sometimes it worked, sometimes it didn't."

Jesse remembered when she would do it. She would take off work and fake a cold. He would come over with chicken noodle soup his mom had made for her and play along, just so he could visit with her. He was a sucker and useless fool when it came to loving Luna.

Luna turned back again to face him, he was standing there in the cloudy sunlight, wearing clothes he had been in for days. He was still in his uniform pants and gun belt, but now he had on a fire department t-shirt tucked in to his pants. He was holding his hands on his belt, resting them on his hips.

Jesse had always been neat and clean, a perfectionist at heart. It almost made her smile knowing he was like that because he had wanted to impress her.

She looked at Jesse who looked worn. He had just lost his big brother to vampires like her, and yet here he was still trying to love her. She didn't deserve his love.

"I was so blinded by it all though Jesse. By his lies, and mine. All I was trying to do was be close to you."

Jesse almost screamed at her then, but he stilled himself. "You should have trusted me! I went fucking crazy just trying to be with you Babe. You should have known that I, out of everyone, would have moved heaven and hell to love you."

Luna walked up to him then. She placed her hands on his heart. She bit her lips too hard worriedly. The storm was still raging inside of her. When she looked up into his eyes she knew she had to leave him soon and bless his heart she didn't know how to do it.

"That was exactly why I couldn't trust you."

Jesse grabbed her wrists on his chest confused. "What?"

Luna smiled into Jesse's innocent eyes. She spoke to his broken heart then. Tears, she had been longing to shed for him for years finally fell. She could finally tell him the truth.

"You saved me the day you fell in love with me Jesse. I was so alone before you came into my life. I was... so bored." She told him honestly, laughing. She truly had been bored before Jesse.

"You were the first person to ever walk into my life and stay there, who didn't have too. You wanted to be with me, hell you enjoyed being with me."

The reality of what she had allowed to happen between them, hit her though. The consequence of their love she was now paying for also, troubled her.

"I wasn't good for you Jesse." This she said slowly, catching the tears that were falling on her lips. "I was a danger to you. To your existence."

And with that, it started to rain again. Luna was hurting again.

Jesse felt her truth then. Somehow he had always known it. He lifted his face up in the rain and tried not to let her see it on his face.

She reached up and touched his face and cried. "I couldn't let my life destroy you Jesse. When I thought Collin was going to kill you Baby, I almost killed him. I almost killed Joseph." She let him go then, backed away from him and turned around again.

"I am a monster Jesse." She let the rain cover her, trying to hide herself in it.

Luna turned around then. Faced him. "Do you understand Jesse. I could have killed them. I would have destroyed anyone or anything that harmed you, including myself, because I loved you too much."

Jesse closed his eyes. The rain tasted like tears. He sighed greatly as his life played out before him like a puzzle coming together.

"I didn't leave you for James that summer. I went to James hoping you would leave me. Hate me." She started to turn around, she still couldn't look at him. "I was trying to protect you, but I selfishly wanted to be close to you. Being with James was as close to you as I could get.

"But every time I looked at him,"

Jesse stuffed his hands into his pockets then thinking she was going to say that James looked just like him, like everyone always said. But she didn't.

"He wasn't you." She whispered to him honestly.

The thunder rolled as she held her face in her hands. James never loved her. It hurt because she had needed him too. She had needed someone to love her. Someone to hold her.

Jesse walked the few steps between them. He reached for her hand and took it in his turning her to face him. He kissed it and smiled at her when the rain let up.

Everything made sense now.

Luna moved into Jesse then. She wrapped her arms under his and held him. "I'm sorry. I should've done everything differently-"

"No." Jesse kissed the top of her head and hushed her. "Everything happens for a reason, Babe. I'll never understand why, but I believe it now."

Just before he could tell her that Ken had told him this at Curtis' funeral and explain more to her, Jeremy jumped over the ledge.

"I need you Luna, right now."

Luna looked at Jeremy, seen the seriousness in his face. She looked at Jesse then and begged him to understand.

Jesse closed his eyes the moment Luna softly kissed his cheek. Even though he wanted to hate Jeremy, he knew when he opened his eyes, she would no longer be in his arms. No matter how tight he held her.

Jesse opened his eyes. He felt like a steel pipe wedged itself in his gut. She had left him, and all he could do was pray for her. Pray she came back to him like she had promised him.

It was time for him to go back down and see his family. Be the shoulder they needed right now.

Asher, his brother was gone now. Jesse took a moment to himself to remind himself of Luna's words, it wasn't the Whitby's fault. He was going to take that truth with him. Then he sighed deeply and headed back into the fire hall.

~ Seven ~

Be still, learn the truths that are hard to see

Luna found herself following Jeremy into the cold, dark dungeon of the Whitby mansion suspended by time. She truly hated it here.

She didn't know how to deal with what she was seeing in front of her now as she stepped of the stairs down into the dungeons main room. When she finally found her voice she rounded on Joseph.

"What have you done?" Luna cried aloud, slowly, deafeningly looking at each of the Whitby men accusingly.

Joseph stepped forward, humbly with his head bowed towards her respectfully. She could kill him for this. She wouldn't win against his brothers, but she would kill him.

"Luna, listen-"

Luna stopped him and looked at him. "Listen… to you?" Had he lost his mind? She wondered to herself.

"How?" She questioned him simply. Not wanting him to answer, only truly wanting him to suffer trying to find the right words.

She looked at him wide eyed with hurt in her eyes when he couldn't and begged Joseph. "Why, Joseph? Just tell me why have you done this?"

Joseph looked at his brothers, he couldn't explain this the way she needed him too.

Luna looked at Asher, withering on the floor in pain. He was slowly turning into one of them. She looked at Curtis, who had been presumed dead by her entire family for a year now, standing solemnly next to a woman Luna didn't know, clearly already turned. Then she looked at Izzy who was clinging to Jordy, the one who had turned her into a vampire, and Luna almost screamed. She had to cover the hate dripping from her lips.

Luna whispered softly aloud to them all in righteous anger. "Their family, thinks you have murdered them. All of them. Premeditated it, I might add!"

Their thoughts betrayed them all then. Everyone of them. Luna read it in their thoughts.

Luna looked directly at Joseph then when the truth finally hit her. "You have! Oh my God! Joseph!

"They will never forgive you for this Joseph. Ever."

She looked at him astonished then. Realizing the truth of what he had done to her family. "Oh God! This was your plan all along? This is what you've been hiding from me!"

Luna remembered their conversation a few days ago. He had known all along she had loved Jesse and he never told her his plans for his family. Was this Joseph's punishment for her? For deceiving him?

Luna fell. She fell to her knees and pleaded with God to forgive them all.

Joseph heard her prayers. It caused him to sigh greatly.

He heard inside her heart how for years she had believed the Whitby's to be death angels. He realized now why she had stayed so far away from them for so many years. She thought they just killed humans at random for sport. And how she thought now they were playing games, turning Asher and his siblings for the hell of it. That he was doing this to her to hurt her.

Joseph reached for Luna's shoulder quietly without her knowing and placed his hand there. He used his powers and showed her everything he couldn't voice to her aloud. He let God's words flow through him so she would understand.

He should have done this along time ago, he told himself.

In those moments Luna saw everything. She saw the beginning of time when God created the heavens and the earth. She saw God's plan for all his creations and how it was destroyed by sin. How God had turned his back on everything because of it, but then how his Son had stepped forward and pleaded for the lives of the innocent. Why He had created vampires, the Whitby's, why he had created her.

He showed her what had happened at Asher's house. The rogues that had showed up. Who they were and what their purpose was in all of this. They were there for Emie, not Asher.

It wasn't the Whitby's that had taken Asher's life. Asher had taken his own life to protect Emie from those men who sought to use him against her.

God spoke to her heart then and showed her those he wanted to save from the evil that was happening all around them. How all along that had been what he had been doing.

When Joseph was done, when he removed his hand from her shoulder, Luna bent forward and put her hands on the cold stone floor. She tried to breathe. She tried to gasp for air under her tears. Her heart felt like it was breaking.

Luna turned to Joseph then. "All these years Joseph... I didn't know."

Luna had ran away from him when he had turned her. Joseph hadn't a chance to raise her, to teach her or train her. Now looking at her, Joseph knew everything happened for a reason like Jesse had said.

Joseph smiled down at the creation that was Luna. He tucked his hands safely in his pockets. "Now you know."

Luna looked at Asher, Curtis and Izzy. She understood now. The Whitby's had saved them when their lives would have been lost. Luna turned then to Joseph again. She was about to beg for Jesse's life, to show him all this. Give him back his family, when Joseph looked at her sternly.

Joseph took her hand then and helped her stand. He prayed she'd understand this. He even asked Jordy to guide his words carefully. He needed to say this just right to Luna.

"We will protect the Stone family and all those down at the fire hall. You have my most fervent vow, Luna. I need you to believe me when I say right now is not Jesse's time." Joseph lowered his head, knowing his next words were true. "His family needs him down there right now."

Joseph could only imagine the pain Asher's family was going through right now. Looking at Asher, withering, but thriving, the guy Joseph had come to know who had brought fun and laughter back to the Whitby's, Joseph wished he could go down to the department and tell them Asher was still alive.

He looked at Curtis, the strong man he was. He had been a leader in his family that they all needed now.

He looked at young Izzy and could see her mother in her eyes.

Joseph felt the pain Cyndy was sure to be feeling right now at the loss of so many in her family.

He looked at Luna. "What happens next, and this is very important Luna; we have to do this quickly. For them. You asked me before what you were supposed to do. We need your help.

"Emie has been kidnapped, like Linda. We think she is with the same men who have your mother."

Luna listened to Joseph's heart and agreed with him. "I followed them south when they took Emie, but I lost them just inside of Ohio." She turned to Jeremy then who had told her about the caves in Tennessee. She looked at Jordy then. "Can you tell me for sure if they are in those caverns?"

Jordy nodded to her assuredly. "They are." He looked to Joseph before he spoke again. "They keep moving Emie, but I think they are headed there. I don't see them going anywhere else."

Luna looked at Asher. She looked to Curtis who couldn't look at her. She didn't know how to leave them now. How was she supposed to leave Jesse when she had promised to protect him? He needed answers she couldn't give him now.

Joseph spoke to Luna making her turn back towards him. "We will protect them. Go, find your mother, find Emie. Bring them back so we can reunite them with this family. And we will destroy this evil together."

"I need Jeremy." Luna told him honestly. "I need his help finding them and knowing what to do before I do it." She looked at Jordy, then at Jeremy. The strong brothers she would need.

She looked at Joseph then whose strength matched her own. She would need him to survive. "I need your strength to fight them. I need all of you!" She thought helplessly, honestly out loud in almost a plea. She looked at each one of them knowing who she really needed, and wondered who she could do without to stay here.

Joseph looked back at his family. At Asher and his family. He didn't know either.

"They murdered our brother, Jesse!"

Jesse was standing in the pits with his family and friends, in shock of his brother James. He really wanted to murder his own brother right now. In the span of a few minutes while he had been with Luna, James had turned everyone in the pits against the Whitby's and him. He had even told everyone about Luna. Everything!

But the way he had said it all, it was so twisted and wrong, Jesse told himself quietly, thoroughly defeated.

Jesse stood taller then against his brother. Asher didn't trust James, and neither should anyone else. "They protected us James. They are the ones who got us down here to safety." He had to convince everyone that it wasn't the Whitby's.

But looking around at everyone, James had them all so scared right now, they wouldn't even listen to him.

James looked away and started to pace. He was angry with the Whitby's, scared of losing Jesse like he had lost Asher. But apart of him hated Jesse. Jesse was still in love with his wife.

"They probably set us up down here just so they could take him! Can't you see that?" James rounded on Jesse, pointing his finger at him. "They are probably planning to do the same thing with all of us! One by one," he started looking at everyone slowly, getting their attention. "they are going to kill us all!"

Jesse had to rub his headache away at the sound of James rambling on and stroking the flames of hysteria in everyone. James didn't know the Whitby's, he didn't know Luna.

"They are probably waiting for us right now!"

At the audible gasps of their frantic family and friends Jesse realized his headache would never go away. Ever. He could never forgive James for this.

"Seriously James!" Jesse needed to think. He needed to shut James up for just one minute so he could think. "After everything that just happened up there with Luna, do you really-"

Cyndy Stone, Jesse's mother, touched Jesse's arm softly and tried to get his attention before he could continue on.

Jesse turned at his mother's gentle touch. "Mom?"

"Is what he's said true? About Luna?"

Jesse sighed deeply. "What did James say about her before I got down here?" Jesse held his anger at bay, but knew it would soon overpower him. He prayed his friends would stop him before he killed James.

"James said Luna was a monster like those rogues that are destroying our city. She was the one causing all the storms. That she's always been one, Jesse. And that you knew! Did you deceive us all? Because you loved your brothers wife?"

Jesse could hear her ashamed question in her last statement as she grabbed his arms and shook him. James had done the worst damage he possibly could have tonight.

"She's not his wife mom-"

Again, ashamed of her son, she interrupted him. "You've known all along that she was one of them?"

Jesse watched as everyone stopped listening to James, and turned to look at Cyndy. Even James stopped to listen to her next words.

"Emie? Luna? That man who helped Asher with the party? His brother who opened the pits for us and knows where we are! How could you do this to us?" She shook her sons arms again in fear.

Jesse looked at James in anger. Then back at his mother. "She is not a monster mom. None of them are monsters!" He looked at everyone then, pleading with them to believe him.

James spoke up, louder than before. "They murdered your brother Jesse! Ken saw it happen. They probably murdered dad, and Curtis too. And Izzy has never come back home. No ones even heard from her!"

Jesse bent his head lower and rubbed it. His head was pounding now. He looked back at his brother, his friends, his family. What could he say to them to make them understand? Asher was the leader in this family, not Jesse.

Jesse looked at James. Heat raged inside of his body. He was thoroughly pissed at the man who had carelessly thrown away Luna. Cast her loving heart on the floor so many times Jesse had lost count. James never loved her, but Jesse had. He knew Luna was coming back. The Whitby's would come back. They would help and protect everyone down here with their own lives. Jesse didn't understand what had happened with Asher, but he trusted Luna to figure it out.

Jesse took a deep breath and let Luna's love fill him. He was going to fight for her now, like he should have done so many years ago.

A woman's scream interrupted the family quarreling. The silence of everyone waiting on Jesse's reply to his brother James was split and raptured into complete and utter panic. The hatch above the pits was trying to be opened from the other side. Jerry and James reacted by pulling their guns out and aiming them at the hatch, waiting for whatever was about to come through.

Jesse hurriedly reached up towards their guns to stop them. "Don't!" Just as the hatch came open. Nothing happened. Everyone held their breath.

Jerry used his body to maneuver in every direction to look past the opening to see who was out there. When he heard the screams of the monster that jumped into the pit, Jerry didn't hesitate to shoot.

More screams followed the monsters body down to the floor as panic took over everyone's emotions. Jesse knelt and searched the body on the floor, worried it was a Whitby or worse, Luna. He held his breath until he discovered the truth. The body of the 'monster', or so everyone was calling them now, Jesse noticed was the teenager that did yard work around the city. The kid even had other kids who worked for him to keep up with the demand.

Jesse had watched the kid grow up everyday on his shift at the department. He'd watched him get on the bus every morning for school, excited to be free when he returned home.

Jesse looked up at Jerry as he spoke. "It's Zach Jerry. He was just a kid."

Jerry looked at the body of the kid. He knew the boy also. Jerry looked at his gun and couldn't believe he had fired on him. It was only the second time Jerry had fired his gun, and the first time Jerry had ever killed anyone.

Jesse looked down at the boy. He looked as if he was sleeping now. At peace. If it wasn't for the blood around his lips, you wouldn't have thought him to be a monster.

Jesse checked him for a pulse, and silently laughed to himself. The boy hadn't had a pulse before he got shot. Jesse secretly lifted up the lips of the boy's mouth to reveal his teeth. Jesse didn't know whether he hoped the boy had fangs or not, either way the boy had been condemned to die. When Jesse saw the fangs he let his lips fall quickly back.

Zach had been turned. But he didn't have to die. He could have been saved.

Jesse stood then and turned on everyone, determined to set everyone straight. "What would you have him do Jesse? Question him before he shot him?" James shook his head at Jesse and walked away from him ashamed. "You're probably one of them too."

Jesse stood there dumbfounded. James had just sealed his fate. No one would listen to Jesse now. Jerry had even walked up to

Jesse and made him kneel, he placed handcuffs on Jesse and made him walk to the back of the pits away from everyone.

Jerry left him there and walked back over to the crowd that was now surrounding James. They were all talking at once and Jesse knew what they were planning. They were going hunting. Jesse sighed. He felt like a monster. He wanted so many things right now and none of them were considered righteous.

Luna looked back at the fire hall in her rear view mirror as she drove over the overpass of the interstate and descended on the other side away from the city. She looked away from the city and ahead to her purpose, headed south. Luna placed her elbow on the window and ran her fingers in her hair as she thought of turning around and going back for Jesse. Her throat felt tight, like it was closing up on her.

She needed more blood. She reached beside her to the cooler and opened a bottle of blood Joseph had packed for her. She drank from it heavily, letting the thick, cold liquid run down her throat and ease the pain there. It wasn't bloody meat, like her inner wolf craved, but worked all the same.

Her heart still ached. She wanted this all to be over. She just wanted to be with Jesse. What would she tell him if she went back though? "I'm sorry, yes, your brother is a monster now. But I had nothing to do with it. Please hold me." Luna shook her head. She wasn't that weak girl in her mind. She had never been that girl. Luna was independent, she was strong. She was a loner. A werewolf and a vampire! So why did she want to be that girl in her mind that gets to cuddle up under the man she loves and just let him hold her?

Luna knew she was making the right decision. She couldn't go back to him yet. She had work to do. She had to find her mother and Emie. Luna worried now about James. He was probably very angry with her and Jesse. They all thought that the Whitby's had killed Asher. They were sure to all be very frightened down there like caged animals ready to strike. She wouldn't be surprised if James had broke his silence now and revealed everything to them all.

Curtis leaned forward then from the back seat. Luna had to smile in the mirror at him. She couldn't begin to describe how happy she was that he was still alive.

"You know, you could have brought him with us."

Luna looked back at him confused. "Can you read minds also?"

Curtis scooted further forward awkwardly. He felt like he was sitting on top of Shelley and Cristina back here in Joseph's SUV.

"No. I wasn't lucky enough to be blessed with that annoying habit."

He whispered sarcastically for Luna. Luna smiled at him in the mirror. His main goal in the jest was to tease Shelley, and he could see by the look on her face as she turned to look out her window better, that it had indeed hit it's mark.

"Thank God. I can't imagine hearing voices in my head all the time. It's bad enough having to listen to people talk out loud."

Joseph turned then and looked back at Curtis interrupting them. He let him see his disapproval in Curtis' sarcasm.

Luna was thinking about what Curtis had said. Could she have brought Jesse with her? No. He needed to be with his family right now. Sure, she could have went there and told them all the truth. But what proof did she have? She could have taken Joseph with her and he could have shown them. But even then, would they have believed him?

"It's too soon."

Luna looked over at Joseph who had spoken. He was leaning his head up against the window with his eyes closed looking like he was resting. To look at him like that, you wouldn't think he looked like a vampire.

"What do you mean?"

Joseph sighed and opened his eyes. He looked up straight and looked at the interstate in front of them. Luna had to drive slow to maneuver around vehicles left abandoned. They weren't even to Ohio yet.

"They believe we murdered Asher in cold blood. More than likely James is trying to piece things together and placing blame on all of us like his father had done."

"Piecing what together?"

Joseph looked out his window next to him. He tried not to believe the truth that was staring him right in the face. Destruction was all around them in the night outside his window. Alongside the road and in the vacant vehicles that were abandoned. Bodies were everywhere, littering the ground, lying in their own cold blood.

"There have been a lot of murders and arsons in Luna Pier over the last year Luna. Before all this." He motioned out the window. "Jerry and Jesse have been investigating them. Jerry and James have been filling Jesse's head with stories of vampires committing them. Jesse had been trying to deny it, but there is only so much he could do when the truth was there in the way the bodies were discovered. They were murdered by vampires. Sucked dry and left to be found that way.

"In truth, it was a set up all along, but we did not do this Luna. James is bound to have assumed it was us with the help of Frank, who has been feeding him lies about us. Horror stories."

"Frank did know then?" She questioned, already knowing the answer. "How did he find out?"

"Yes." Joseph told her honestly.

Joseph remembered the night he had caused Frank to get into an accident. He let Luna see it in her mind. He showed her how he had saved Asher instead of his twin brother, Axel, from the icy channel off Summit Street. He showed her how he tried like hell to save Asher, knowing who he would become, and how he didn't have time to save Axel.

"There was nothing I could do for Axel. It was too late for him. He was just a baby. He wouldn't have survived. Asher barely survived."

Joseph sat in silence then knowing Luna was processing it all. He let her see how Frank had argued with him over his decision at the accident. How for years Frank knew who Joseph was because of that night. How Frank treated Asher because of it. And then when Asher fell in love with Emie, how Frank hated her, instead of seeing her for who she really was.

"I see now, how it looked to Frank. I should have done things differently." Joseph thought about Asher then. The last time they had spoke, Asher had been so angry with Joseph. He hated him for what all his father had revealed to him on his deathbed. He wouldn't be able to forgive Joseph for what he had done. All the secrets Joseph had kept to protect his identity were revealed in a way that no one would ever understand.

Joseph looked at his hands then. He had never felt guilt like he did now. "Because of it, I've lost Emie."

Luna reached for Joseph's hand then. She heard his thoughts and read his heart. "We are going to find Emie, Joseph. And then we will show them who we are, together. They will accept it because of Asher and Curtis. Jesse will make them see. He knows the truth about us. He will show them. I promise."

"I just hope we aren't too late." Joseph questioned even his own best intentions now. He had to trust Jeremy and Jordy with the lives of everything Asher and Emie held dear. He prayed they could do it.

Luna spent hours winding around traffic. Vehicles had just stopped on the road. There was signs all around them why people had just abandon the safety of the vehicles. They had been trying to run away thinking they could outrun the rogues on foot, not knowing that even their own vehicles couldn't outrun them.

It reminded Luna of an apocalypse the way the roads were littered with vehicles and bodies. Some roads were eerily empty. It reminded her of a time when she was younger and these same monsters had done this to her tribe. They had run through this land and destroyed everything, again.

Luna had to keep watch every minute to make sure they weren't attacked. She made a decision at some point in the night that it would be safer to drive during the daylight hours.

When the sun finally rose the scenes of the night were worse somehow in the light of day. Luna had to keep her eyes fixed on her destination and away from the pain she saw in the lives lost.

When day turned into night again, the group hid out in an abandoned steel building. It was just an empty warehouse. It was one level and had an open floor plan which made it less likely to become a trap for them.

Joseph took inventory of their bags, making sure their weapons were all intact and ready for a fight. It would be easier to have a hands on battle, but he hoped at least they could take down as many as they could first with their automatic weapons.

Joseph watched as Curtis kept watch from the windows above. He looked at Shelley and Cristina who were in a deep discussion. Then he found Luna. She was distraught sitting on the steps that led to the upper floor where Curtis was.

Luna was tired, if it was possible. She had been running for days now trying to save what she could, not knowing who to save first. Joseph could tell. When all she really wanted was for this all to end so she could finally be with the man she loved. It was so unfair, the way her life turned out. If it wasn't for Joseph she could have had the life she dreamed of now.

Joseph shook the thoughts from his head. He had to figure out how to get to Emie faster. He was going to slaughter the men who had done this to them.

Jesse had waited longer than he could for Luna. Luna had not come back yesterday. As far as he could tell now, she wasn't coming back today either.

Even if she came back tonight, James would kill her.

No matter how he called to her in his mind, she wouldn't answer him.

Jesse hung his head as he watched the night fall on the fire hall below him. He was sitting on the rooftop, letting his legs hang off the wall ledge, defeated smoking what was left of Asher's smokes. He looked at the one that was almost gone watching the smoke disappear in the air around him. He remembered the times he had seen Asher up here doing just this. Thinking. Or trying to anyways.

Jesse blew out his smoke and looked into the clouds that were now turning colors in the sky. Asher would know what to do, he told himself. Asher would have said some great speech from his heart and would have convinced everyone that the Whitby's were good, honest people.

Jesse laughed at that. The Whitby's were vampires. They did kill people. Jesse shook his head. Even he didn't believe in them any more.

Jesse sighed, trying to picture what could have happened at Asher's house. He could hear Luna in his mind telling him that she had tried to save him. But Ken had said it was the Whitby's.

Why would the Whitby's have killed him? They had sworn to protect him. Jesse tried to figure out in his mind now. Where had Jeremy taken her to? Had he killed her too?

Jesse felt for her one more time. "Talk to me Luna." He pleaded with her.

Jesse tried not to lose faith in Luna. He tried to shake the feelings that James stirred up in him that she was one of them and was just waiting for the right moment to strike. He couldn't help but wonder if she had tried to come back and heard all of James' hatred for her. Would she have turned and ran away again from it all?

Would she come back for him? Jesse wondered.

James hated them all now. He hated the Whitby's and believed them all to be bloodsucking murders. Because Luna was one of them, he hated her also. It didn't matter that he had been married to her for years and he knew her. No, James only saw what his mind had made up. The lies their father had told them about her.

Jesse wished Luna would have listened to him. Wished she had turned him so he could have helped everyone. So he could be with her right now.

And then the answer he had been looking for was there in Jesse's mind. He couldn't believe it! It was the only thing that made sense. They had probably turned Asher! Not murdered him. That's what Ken had seen. Asher probably had wanted it so he could help like Jesse had wanted to. They hadn't murdered him. Asher was still alive! Jesse could feel it. He believed it. Jesse was so excited he almost got up to go and tell James. But then he remembered who James was.

Jesse sat back down. He had to figure this out better. James wouldn't believe the truth unless Asher was standing in front of him. Jesse had to figure out how to convince James to go and look for Asher. He had to get him to see that Asher might still be alive. He had to make him believe. Or make James think it was his own idea. Sometimes that was the only way to get James to do anything, to see reason.

Jesse wished he was more like Luna. Had her abilities right now. He needed them. He needed her.

Jesse inhaled another smoke deeply. He could see Luna in his mind. If he closed his eyes he could see her body perfectly. If he tried real hard he could remember her touch. The way her hands felt running up his arm, across his tattooed arms she liked so much. The way she would find a path to his chest, not looking at him, ashamed of what she was doing, what she was feeling.

Jesse's heart lurched at the thought she wasn't married to James any more. The thoughts hardened his heart towards his brother. Why hadn't James told him they were divorced? If Jesse had known sooner he would have done things so much differently with her. He wouldn't have wasted so much time without her.

Knowing now how she felt about him, he knew he could love her openly now. His soul felt free now to be with her. He just had to be still and wait for her.

"Come back to me, Luna." He said her name like a whispered prayer, looking up at the moon.

"Jesse?"

Jesse turned around at the sound of her voice next to him. He could feel her the moment she wrapped her arms around from behind him. But he couldn't see her.

Jesse knew it was only in his mind. He closed his eyes and held tight to her as she clung to him. She had connected to his mind, finally, from wherever she was.

Jesse kissed her arm that was resting across his shoulders. He intertwined his hand in her delicate fingers, picked up her hand in his and kissed the back of it. He let his lips linger there.

Luna was reeling in her mind. She wanted to transform where he was. Be there in his presence. She had to stay grounded where she was though. She beckoned to his mind, pleaded with him to not ask her any questions. To just leave it be and let them be in the moment.

Jesse chuckled at her thoughts. He wanted the same thing.

He closed his eyes and remembered a moment in time. A place they could slip away to, if only for the night. "Remember that night, I held you on the couch?"

Luma remembered. They had laid on her couch, watching a superhero movie he had wanted to see.

James had been at work. They had fought so bad about the divorce papers she had filed before he had left for work, that she started planning to leave him. Jesse showed up and interrupted her plans though.

Jesse sighed and rested his forehead on her arm, listening to her thoughts.

"I knew about the fight." He whispered to her mind. James had went to work that day, reeling about Luna and how he hated her. Jesse couldn't understand him. He had left the fire department, off shift that night, and planned an evening to spend with her.

Luna smiled at his thoughts. He had been so sweet that night. She had needed him, and somehow he had sensed it.

He had slipped into her house, scared her when he had come up on her in the kitchen while she was staring out her back window. She had been so lost in her anger towards James.

Jesse had jumped up on her countertop next to her, set down a DVD on the sink and given her a flirtatious smile. It was a movie they had both wanted to see.

Luna let her mind go back as she rested her head on Jesse's shoulder up there on the roof. She could smell him even though he was hundreds of miles away from her.

Jesse had walked over to the edge of her sofa and sat down, trying to relax his body after working twenty four hours at the department. He had stretched out and rested his legs on the ottoman in front of him. After she had put the dvd in, she had snuggled up next to him, resting her head on his leg.

Innocently, they had laid there next to each. Both too shy to touch each other, but the desire had been there for most of the movie. They couldn't concentrate. Luna had felt it and kept it to herself the best she could, until Jesse had rested his arm on hers.

Luna giggled remembering. "Your arm had been so cold from holding it up on the back of the couch for so long."

"It hurt!" Jesse remembered, laughing a little. He had been afraid to touch her. He had left it up there until he couldn't feel it anymore.

But the moment his bare skin on his arm touched hers, it had come alive.

Luna couldn't remember what happened in the movie after that moment, she could remember the way his fingers felt when they started tracing outlines on her upper arm. The way he ran his fingers softly up her arm and back down again in a sensual caress.

She had been wearing a spaghetti strap tank top, with short gym shorts that drove Jesse's mind crazy looking at them. Her soft legs were tucked under each other teasing him. He had to look at them just so he could take his eyes of her breast he could see peeking out of her top.

At some point he had drug the back of his fingernails across her bare back to the top of her shoulder strap, moving it slightly down her arm, revealing more of his desire.

Luna remembered what it did to her. She had been letting his touch heal her wounds from James. Sooth them like a sweet balm that felt too good to let end. Just to pay him back for what he was doing, she let him feel everything he was doing to her.

Jesse let the back of his fingers drag down the underside of her arm that was resting on her side. He had to stop for a second when he twitched inside of his shorts.

Luna smiled shamelessly at the memories. He had been so turned on by just sitting there with her.

Jesse's smile widen to himself remembering it all. He had been so devilishly mean to her back then.

Her hand had been resting on her hip. He had ran his finger around the edges of her pinky finger first, then slowly around each finger, inside of them, killing her softly with his caress. When he had made it to outer edges of her thumb, he ever so softly tucked his finger inside the bottom of her palm on top of her thigh, and knew when she raised her thumb a little that he had her in his spell, slowly unwinding her piece by shattered piece.

"I couldn't breathe, Jesse!" She sensually remembered.

Jesse laughed out loud at that. "You didn't need to breathe." He reminded her behind him.

Then he drug his finger over her wrist and down to her bare hip that was peeking out from under her top where he lifted it up a little so he could look at her hip he was so attracted too, guiding his fingers along the edges of her shorts.

His heart felt like a freight train was bounding down the tracks of his veins through his body. When he finally reached for her bare thigh, he could've sworn she was going to stop him. But she hadn't. She had let him linger, drawing soft circles on her skin all the way down to the back of her knee.

When she thought he would keep using one finger, he had spread them all out and touched the back of her leg with all of his fingers. He ran them softly, daringly back up her leg to her knee. Dipping them over the edge, stopping at the edges of her thigh.

He had to make a decision. Stop there and just hold the top of her thigh, letting his fingers play with the skin above her knee. Dip forward. Or dip backwards.

The waiting almost killed her. She could read it in his mind all the things he wanted to do under her shorts. It had been enough just to see it in his mind. Her skin, her body could feel it all even though he wasn't doing it to her.

The skin revealed to him by her shoulder, under her ear, caught his attention. He wanted her to know what it felt like when he touched her there. He moved her hair gently off her shoulder that was in his way, letting it slide off her tenderly. He nudged that spot with his knuckle. Then he extended his finger and drug it slowly up her neck to her ear, where he took her ear lobe between his thumb and finger. There he squeezed gently, like he was milking her.

Luna let him feel the chills he had sent up her body. He stopped when he knew it had worked on her. He was stiff and hard next to her face. She knew it too.

I did. She whispered to his mind.

The movie had ended before they wanted it too. They were out of excuses to lay there any longer. Luna had placed her hand on his thigh, almost touching his hard on that was resting there.

She had picked herself up slowly off the couch onto her knees in front of him, letting him see her hardened nipples through her tank, drawing his attention there in his mind. She kissed his cheek slowly thanking him for coming over.

Jesse's eyes were still tightly shut remembering the night. He didn't want this night to end though.

"Go back to your cot." She whispered softly behind him. "Don't forget about me, baby. I'll see you soon."

Jesse sighed as her arms, her presence dissipated like smoke into the night that had fallen upon him. He had to go back to his family. He had a job to do.

But first he had to find Ken, he thought, as he slipped off the edge of the wall.

August

The Department of NSA, Washington D.C.

Sitting at a round table surrounded by all that was left of the American Intelligence Agency, Darryl found himself feeling like they were all wasting his time.

These men were dressed in their tight, crisp clean, military commander uniforms like they had to be even though there was a apocalypse going on around them, while Darryl was dressed in his special ops black t-shirt and tight military cargo pants ready for war.

These new military commanders, who had only been given the new position they were now in because someone above them had recently died making the position now theirs until they died, or quit, were looking to Darryl for answers he didn't have. Lead scientists and technologists who didn't have clue why they were here, were only here because the new military commanders thought they were intelligent enough to here.

They all assumed they were here under some kind of protection the military could provide them with if they came up with fresh ideas to fight this enemy with.

Truth be told, Darryl thought to himself looking around the room, everyone who should be here, was either dead, or presumed dead. These men, were next.

His Commander-in-Chief, the President of the United States, was facing Darryl. Now across the divided table of people Darryl didn't know anymore, the President stretched out his folded hands in a plea towards Darryl and his men like they were the saviors of this war.

Darryl knew his men and teams of special ops had always been the outcasts to this agency, the last resorts. They had been at the bottom of this military totem pole these last few years. Intel gave them little information and used them like they were expendable, all the time.

Darryl was fed up with all the bull shit they had fed him. Nothing they had been commanded to do these last years had done anything of worth other then get a lot of his men killed.

Now, all these inexperienced, undignified men in the room surrounding Darryl wanted his help. Wanted a solution, like the President had just said to him.

You could hear the silence in the room sweep over them. No one was moving. They were all waiting for Darryl to answer him.

Darryl sighed greatly and looked at the reports again sitting in front of him. Folders were scattered there that had been tossed over the table by one of the young buck commanders, who like the President, wanted answers. Gruesome pictures fell out of those folders in front of Darryl. Men and women, the top officials in the United States Government had been brutally murdered at the hands of the enemy that was now taking over the world.

Darryl knew things these new commanders didn't. He knew what this enemy was capable of. Darryl looked at the young bucks who were waiting for his answer.

"The men and women in these pictures, as brutal and gruesome as they may look to you, are the lucky ones. My men and I have seen far worse fates. These, are just tragic losses."

When one of the young bucks Darryl was eyeing down started to speak up, the president silenced him. "Darryl. You've commanded this army, training the special task force units that have been fighting these- What do you call them?"

"Vampires, sir. Demons, if you will." Darryl gave him.

"Vampires." The President stated awkwardly. He let Darryl see he didn't particularly like the word, but he continued anyways. "You must know what can be done to stop them."

Darryl braced his hands on the table and stood up to face his commander. He looked the President dead in the eyes. "Mr. President, sir. It's too late. We've lost this war sir."

The President stood and matched Darryl's stance, bracing himself on the table to steady himself. "There must be something else we can do! The people of the world depend on us to do something. We can't just give up and surrender, Darryl."

Darryl chuckled a little, looking away from the president. He looked back and eyed the old man sideways. "Surrender isn't an option sir. Neither is fighting back. Right now, all those people can do is hide."

The president sat back down in his chair in disbelief. Darryl could read his mind. It showed on his face as clear as day.

No one else in the room commented either. There honestly wasn't another move to be made.

Darryl turned his head at the opening of the door next to him. The General commander of the US Army, who Darryl had spent his childhood idolizing, walked into the office he was now in.

Everyone in the room stood and saluted the man, including Darryl and his men.

Bartley, Darryl's second in command edged closer to Darryl and whispered to him addressing him. "Who is that?" As the General held the attention of the room walking over to his seat next to the President and the Chief of Staff.

Darryl looked at Bartley and raised his hand to cover his jest. "He's the head MF in charge."

Bartley stepped back away knowingly at Darryl's jest. "Ah. I see."

Darryl knew no one would listen to him now. There would be no report to the people or emergency radio broadcast that informed everyone what to do. What they should be doing. No. The Army wasn't going to stop now until everyone was dead or dying. It was the military way.

Darryl sat down when everyone else did. He looked to the man who he hoped he could still idolize after this meeting with faith in his rugged heart. He even slicked his tight military cut hair back in hopes he looked somewhat worthy to be here.

The General of the Army looked and addressed the President first, then looked directly at Darryl and addressed him cordially.

Darryl stood then to attention. It was what he was trained to do when spoken to.

"Lieutenant Colonel Krause. We have a new mission for you."

Darryl felt his heart sink in his chest. He stood straight back though in front of them all. Not letting them see his most recent fear. A fear so great, he almost wanted to defy them all and retreat out of the room.

"You've been re-commissioned by this agency and the Presidency of the United States to Lieutenant General Commander of the United States Army. Second only to myself."

Darryl wanted to chuckle out loud as he lowered his head. The last Lieutenant General must be in that stack of photos somewhere on the table in front of him.

As the General continued on describing Darryl's new mission, Darryl looked around at the the men who didn't understand what was out there. They were protected here on the base they traveled in by men and women like Darryl and his men. They hadn't fought hand to hand battle with this new enemy. They hadn't been wounded by one, or rattled to their cores by just the sound of a demon creeping up on them they couldn't see.

No. These men were just paid to sit at their desks and come up with ideas. Ideas that proved to be nothing for the people Darryl had sworn his life to protect.

"I'm sorry-"

Shit. Darryl thought to himself regretting his wandering thoughts. The man he had waited his whole life to meet had been talking to him, and he'd accidentally, selfishly ignored him.

"Is there something you would like to add, Lieutenant?" The General asked Darryl in all seriousness.

Darryl stood straighter, and nodded at the General in apology. "No sir. Forgive me, sir. Please continue."

"We believe this man,"

Darryl took the new folder that was handed to him, with the picture of a vampire royal paper clipped on the front of it.

"Victor, is the leader of this war."

Darryl couldn't stop the jest that left his lips. This man was a brutal, angelic killer. Darryl could see it just by looking at the vampire. "No last name?"

The General looked more directly at Darryl, clearly offended.

Darryl wondered if he seen resentment in the man's eyes. Surely he knew Darryl couldn't stop Victor let alone kill him.

The General handed Darryl another photo. "This is Axel. Victor's second in command. They own the trade center and have taken control of New York City."

Darryl looked at the photos of this new enemy. Axel looked like someone he knew but he couldn't place him. The picture was distorted. Axel was standing afar off on a darkened street in New York. Darryl could tell just by looking at the size of the vampire that he would be impossible to defeat.

"We believe they have set up ground control there. Their men, are responsible for the loss of the city."

Darryl noticed the way he said 'men'. The General was using the word metaphorically.

Darryl looked at Bartley and handed him the photos. Bartley passed the photos to Jimmy. Jimmy was Darryl's lead intel advisor on missions. Jimmy would store the pictures and the data in the folders to their tablets for later investigations.

Darryl looked back at the General and waited for further orders stuffing his hands defiantly in his pockets. Apparently he and his men were going to New York.

"Your team is the last of the UN's Special Ops Task Force left to us."

This new information to Darryl struck him and threatened to knock him off his feet. He knew they had lost his British Ops team earlier this year in London. It had been a loss Darryl's team was still recovering from. But he hadn't known his US team had been lost. "What do you mean the last team? What the hell happened to my other team?"

The General, who was clearly displeased with Darryl at his choice of words and looked to the President for permission to reveal this information to Darryl. When the President gave it to him, the General continued. "After we used them to secure the President, we lost contact with them when the White House went down. We've just recently learned that all the men have been accounted for.

"They all died." The General stated reluctantly.

Darryl had to brace his hand on the table in front of him. More of his men had died? Darryl had been the man in charge of training these teams of special ops. They weren't tools to be used for the military and their own personal gain. They were his men.

He knew them all by name. They had families, like Darryl's. He could see each member of the team in his mind now.

"You commanded my men to die," Darryl paused and had to swallow the bile that was rising in his throat now. "protecting one man?"

Darryl wanted to shout at the General, but he kept his voice steady and calm.

"They were my men! Not the Army's." He almost spat at the General.

He looked at his President now angered that he had lost Darryl's men. "What do you expect me to do now?"

The General, now thoroughly put in his place, finished addressing Darryl after the President commanded it. "We need your team to go into New York and find these men. Send us ground intel on their movements and report back to Fort Bragg.

"I'd like you to meet Chief Warrant Officer Williams here. He will be your men's eyes and ears in the sky." He turned to Williams, one of the young bucks Darryl did not want to meet, to introduce him to Darryl.

Darryl pointed his finger at the General and the President. Darryl had enough. "You both honestly think that I am going to take this new rank, sit here on my ass and send my men to the front of this war without out me?"

The entire building shook and debris started falling around them all.

Darryl and his men immediately looked up. It was what they had learned to do in field. The enemy always attacked from above now.

Pieces of the ceiling and roof above them started peeling back. Darryl and his men knew it was time to leave now while the other men in the room started raising their guns they had probably never shot before.

These kinds of men never screamed. Darryl knew their screams would be the last sounds they heard before he turned and left the room.

"Run!" Darryl ordered his men, without looking back.

Bartley wanted to argue. Darryl read it on his face as he pushed him out of the room. They should stay and fight, protect their commanders.

"This is their fight now. It was lost before it began Bartley." Darryl instructed his second as they walked through the halls firing their guns on the enemies.

The only way he could save the people they were all trying to protect now was to complete their mission. It was time to go to New York.

~ Eight ~

Be still and seek what you have lost

Months later...

Asher could feel the days and months slipping by as he paced around the forgotten city at midnight. It was all disappearing from his grasp forever. He had lost more than his life. He had lost everyone.

He was left with the two men he couldn't stand. Well, truth be told, Jeremy and Jordy were becoming his friends, but their jokes and antics about their way of life only made Asher hate what he had become.

Asher couldn't stop thinking of the night he had lost Emie. He finally had Emie in his hands and then she had slipped away from his grasp like sand.

She had been alive. Well, not really, Asher reminded himself. It was just, her love was so alive with a newness that Asher craved every day.

Asher jumped on the ledge of the fire hall and sat next to his smokes Jesse kept stealing. He lit up and continued thinking about Emie. He believed if he kept remembering her, she would magically come back to him, like she had before.

He missed her essences. The way time stood still when she was in his presence. It wasn't her smile that lighted up her face that he missed, it was the light in her being that made her body react in a way that caused Asher's to come to life.

When she moved, Asher could feel her in his soul. When she looked at him and shared her deepest thoughts with him, Asher thought life as he knew it could disappear and he wouldn't have noticed, he was so taken with Emie.

He could feel her now as he dreamt of her, from where he was sitting on top of the fire hall where he could finally be alone from her prying brothers. The sound of silence all around him felt like the calm before a raging storm and he could have cared less what came. He was so pissed he could take on the world if he had too.

Emie was there before him in his mind. Her body, her light, everything she was. She was there before him calling for him.

"Asher?"

Asher snapped out of his dream. He turned his head to look over his shoulder at the human who had snuck up on him.

It was Ken.

Asher looked at him. His best friend. Seen the way Ken was looking at him. He just stood there, stone cold, scared out his mind, not knowing whether to run or stay still, like a deer blinded in headlights.

Asher sighed, inhaled more of his smoke and turned his head back around to look over the ledge at the moon.

He hated the way he looked now. He knew what he looked like to Ken. The monster he was now. He thought about standing up and greeting his friend but thought better of it knowing what all Ken would see.

"Dude!" Ken stepped closer to Asher not believing his eyes. "You're ..." Words escaped him.

"A freak?" Asher questioned him jokingly, casting him a glance when Ken couldn't finish his sentence.

Ken thought about that. He almost called him a monster like James had called them. Asher had been his best friend. Asher wasn't- well, he couldn't be-

Ken was lost for words again. As much as he didn't want Asher to be a monster, he truly looked like one.

Asher was a mess. His natural shaggy blonde hair, was longer now and looked wet, dirty. His face looked smeared with dirt and blood.. It was so unlike Asher it confused Ken.

"You're alive Asher." Ken said finishing his earlier thought.

Asher grinned at that and turned to look back out over the city. He breathed in another long drag of his smoke. "I'm not alive anymore Ken."

It was the only thing he was sure of. Death had taken him. He had awakened to a fate worse than hell.

"Katie calls you guys zompires." Ken tried to reach for normalcy with Asher. He hoped it would work.

Asher chuckled at that. Ken was trying to act calm, but the pace of his heart beat told Asher he was afraid. Asher could smell his fear.

He remembered what little Katie had said to him the night he had died. She was right. He was the walking dead now. Just like a zombie, but he was worse, he was a vampire now. There was no denying it, there was no bringing him back to life.

"You should run for your life Ken." Asher told him softly as he flicked out his smoke over the ledge.

Ken seriously thought about running away.

Asher smelled the air again. Ken's skin was sweating in the cool night air. Asher had to close his own eyes and remember Ken's wife Miranda, little Katie and Gabby. All the reasons why he couldn't kill Ken.

Ken stood his ground. Took in a deep breath and reminded himself that Asher was his friend. Jesse believed there was still good in them, so Ken wanted to try his best to believe it also.

He looked at Asher bent over the ledge. Asher looked defeated. Different, but yet still himself.

"What are you doing here Asher? What happened?" He had to know both those questions before he sat down, before he got too comfortable. He wasn't sure if he really wanted to know. Just that he needed to know.

Asher raised his head and sighed into the night. He didn't know why he sighed, there was no reason to breathe anymore. He did it now out of habit. It felt so unnatural now.

He thought of Ken's question then. He didn't know why he came every night. He didn't know why he fought against the darkness and the evil. It was like fighting against his own soul. There was something left inside his soul though that made him fight. Like the fires he had fought when he had been alive, he was trying to protect the city he had sworn to die for.

"I can't go home."

It was all he had to say. Ken understood. Every firefighter felt the same way. The department was their home when they had no other place to go. He may not be alive, but he was still a firefighter.

Asher got angry again. He tried to reel it in when he told Ken what had happened. "We were ambushed, Emie and I. They tried to use me to get to her."

"Who?" Ken questioned him, coming closer to his friend. He wanted to help Asher. Jesse had said the Whitby's hadn't killed Asher. If not them, then who?

A cool breeze whipped around Asher causing him to have to wipe the venom that was dripping from his mouth away. The closer Ken got to him the more powerful his scent got. Asher could taste Ken's scent on his tongue. It was so enticing.

Asher lit up another smoke. He needed to feel the hot burn of the fire in his lungs mixed with the sweet nicotine to distract him from Ken. He needed to feel something other than death.

Asher was still confused by the events of that night. "I can't remember much." He kept seeing himself in the eyes of the man who took Emie and he didn't understand why. "The change, between life to death, it's still fresh Ken. It's sucking the life out of me still. It's taking all my strength, to hold onto what's left of me."

Ken looked down at his hands worriedly remembering the night with him. "I was there Asher. When it happened. It was Jeremy."

Asher looked at Ken then, swung his head so fast that it made Ken look at him. "What?" He asked Ken hungrily.

"I saw Jeremy. It was Jeremy Asher."

"No, wait,". Asher stood then with one hand raised begging Ken to explain himself. He could see the look in Ken's eyes when he did it, but he couldn't worry about that now. "You were there? Did you see anyone else?"

Ken had been afraid of Asher the moment he seen his appearance tonight. Just looking at Asher, the change in his physic, he looked like a rock solid God. All reddish tan, bulging out of his Fire Department issued t-shirt. He was almost unreal.

It was how dirty Asher looked now. The mess. He could see the dirt and blood better now like Asher had just been on an accident scene and a house fire back to back.

When he had watched Asher light his smoke with his finger earlier, Ken thought he was missing something. Then, Asher stood up, and Ken almost forgot how to breathe. Asher had smoke rising all around him like he was on fire. His skin was redder than before.

Ken could see the desperation in Asher's red blood eyes. Ken started to back up, he was truly afraid Asher was going to grab him now. Or worse, shake him. Ken put his hand up towards Asher in surrender, or was it fear? He looked down, submissive, trying not to look at Asher. "No. I didn't I swear Asher, I only saw Jeremy there."

Ken chanced a look at Asher. He looked like he wanted more answers so Ken went on. "When we heard Emie screaming from blocks away, we knew something was wrong."

Asher turned around and put his hands on his head trying to regain his composure from what Ken had said, so Ken could continue.

"I ran man, faster than I've ever ran before when I heard her screaming. I tried to get there. I tried-".

Ken stopped when he couldn't breathe and his voice cracked. He remembered running. He remembered hearing Emie screaming. It echoed throughout the whole city.

Ken knew Emie was Asher's life, his love. He knew what she meant to Asher. Ken had run, trying to reach her, trying to save her from whatever was making her scream like that.

"When I got to your house, the door was wide open." Ken remembered the feelings that had caused him. It scared him still. "We came in slowly, guns drawn, ready for a fight.

"I heard Jeremy talking to the others, his brothers, like they were arguing. Then we heard them all leave. So I crawled up your steps...".

Asher rounded on Ken when he stopped talking. He had to stop breathing. He had to let Ken finish. He could see the distant look in his friends face like he was reliving those moments. He needed to know what Ken had seen.

Ken looked up at Asher and made eye contact. "Jeremy was still there. He was-". Ken didn't know if he could finish. He had to swallow the bile rising in his mouth. He had to look away from Asher in order to finish.

"He looked like he was eating your neck. He looked up at me, your blood dripping from his mouth!" Hate and anger were dripping from Ken's voice now. "He told me to go away. "Go away Ken." That's what he said to me."

Ken looked at Asher then. "I didn't want to man."

Asher saw the tears welling in his friends eyes. He could see in them what Ken saw. They had been friends since they were kids. Asher couldn't imagine what he would have done if he would of seen Jeremy doing that to Ken.

"But I ran." Ken lowered his eyes away from his friend, ashamed. Tears dripping off his cheeks he couldn't stop. His mouth was dripping with hot saliva. He shakily told Asher, "I ran away, and I shouldn't have." He looked at Asher then again. "I should have stayed and done something. I'm so sorry man."

Asher huffed out the breath he had been holding trying not to breathe in the smell of Ken's fears and turned away from him. He knew Ken could see the smoke now. He grabbed the ledge and tried not to break it.

Ken was his best friend. He couldn't fault him for what he'd done. Ken had no idea what was going on. Hell, he'd just witnessed his best friend dying.

"No. You did the right thing Ken." Asher told him, shaking the hold he had on the ledge.

Asher already knew it was Jeremy who had turned him. But he had no idea what had happened to Emie. He was hoping Ken knew something they didn't.

"Jeremy didn't kill me." Hate started to drip from Asher's mouth. "When those evil bastards tried to take Emie from me, they were going to use me, break me the human I was, make her watch and force her to do their will."

Asher started breathing fire then. He hated these men. He wanted to destroy them, slowly. Watch them burn in his hands.

They had taken everything from him! He thought loudly within himself, pacing the wall.

Asher could see Emie in his mind that night up in his rooms. Trying to tear apart the men who were holding her. She knew what they were going to do to him.

"She would never have been able to escape them. I was hoping Jeremy would have gotten there sooner." It hurt Asher still that he hadn't made it in time.

Asher knew what it felt like to cry, this felt worse. It was like breaking open from the inside out and bleeding, but never being able to fix it.

Asher looked at Ken. "I killed myself." He watched as Ken gasped and took a step back. Realization hit Ken and Asher knew in that moment Ken would have done the same thing for Miranda.

"Jeremy saved me afterwards by turning me Ken. He didn't kill me.

"By taking myself out of the equation, she would be able to free herself. I just have no idea how to help her now. I have no idea where they took her."

"Asher. I'm sorry man. I didn't know."

Asher looked at Ken. He could see the serenity in his eyes.

Ken looked away from Asher processing this new information. "We thought they murdered you. The Whitby's. James, he's keeping everyone safe, but they have different guns now. Steel bullets."

Ken looked at Asher wondering how much to reveal. "James kept talking about your Luna and your father and how he knew about the Whitby's all along. How he had plans to defend us against them. Weapons Asher.

"Asher, you'll never be able to convince him of this. I mean, if I talk to-"

Asher interrupted him. Looked at him. "No. It's fine man. I know my fate now."

Ken knew that look. "No. Let me help you Asher. Don't do that. Don't- don't push me away man, I just got you back, Asher." Ken begged his friend.

Asher looked away and tucked his hands in his pockets. "You can't help me Ken." Asher hung his head and reigned in the monster he was one last time. He wasn't strong enough for this, to be here yet.

Asher's eyes opened wide at the sound he heard below him. There was rouges wandering the street. He needed this fight. He needed it like he had needed a fire call. Asher growled, cursing at them and jumped over the ledge.

Ken grabbed the ledge and watched as his friend took down two of the 'zompires' walking on the streets below in front of the fire department. He shook off his fears knowing Asher would protect them all. Even though he couldn't be around them, he would protect them.

Ken turned and walked back into the fire department. He could sleep better tonight knowing Asher was alive and out there. First though, he had to find Jesse.

New York City

Emie looked out her cell window from the bed she was chained too. It was night again. She could finally stand up without having to hide from the sunlight.

She thought better of it when she heard the unmistakable sounds of her captor headed towards her cell. She closed her eyes instead and buried her face in her pillow.

Anguish rose up inside of her soul. It felt like it was choking her. She wanted to beat her pillow, tear it to shreds. When the door opened to her cell all she could do was pray Axel would leave her alone instead of trying to tempt her like he and Victor had been doing for days.

Victor assumed Emie would do her bidding. He mistakenly underestimated her in ways she inwardly congratulated herself for. She would never assist him in this war, no matter how strong the pull of their blood connected them. He may be her creator, but she would never bow to him.

As for Axel, he was a sorry excuse for a mate. Victor was insane with power that he thought he could use on Emie to make her bend to his will. He was in for a rude awakening if Emie ever got out of these steel chains he was binding her with.

"You realize Victor built this tower with you in mind? When he destroyed the first ones trying to get rid of Asher, he built this one planning on destroying everything in Asher's life, but the fool born idiot finished the job for us."

Axel was leaning up against the inside of her cell door, waiting for the moment she would lash out at him and fight back. It was always the highlight of his nights. The only entertainment he got in this god-forsaken life now.

Emie felt everything within her dissipate. Venom dripped on her tongue. She stole a peek out of her pillow out to the skyline above her window. This unknown city she was being held captive in was New York City? She questioned herself.

Emie looked at Axel then dead on off her pillow. "What?" Her voice was weak and cracked. She hadn't spoken in weeks.

Axel smirked at her with evilness in his eyes. Finally, he thought to himself, he'd gotten the bitches attention. "You didn't know where you were?"

Emie jumped out of bed and padded bare foot on the stone cold floor, dragging her chains over to her window. She looked at the buildings around her in wonder. She had not been to New York in over a hundred years. Not since she had come to America.

She let her eyes search for anything in the distance she could see that would give her a clue to where she was. In the distance she saw it.

Lady Liberty was standing proudly on the water. It was a beacon for those traveling across the great divide to the freedom, that once, could only be found in America. Now she was torn apart. Her arms were broken, disfigured.

"I did that." Axel stated proudly from behind her.

Emie shivered at his nearness. She despised him in ways she couldn't explain.

"Those travelers now will see a deterrent. We have conquered this land. Taken it back." He moved Emie's hair off her shoulder as he spoke, smiling at her.

Emie closed her eyes. He was close enough now to strike at. She knew though, if she did, it would only scratch the surface of his pride. She wanted to cut him deeper.

She turned her face towards his and tried not to gasp at the sight of him. He looked like a mirror of Asher. She couldn't let him see how it affected her.

When she spoke, she let her words seep into his evil soul where he couldn't deny them. She pushed him to the point of truth where he had to see her revelation and couldn't escape it.

"You can cross oceans, tread upon the weak, conquer lands. But you, will never have me." She walked away from him with that last. She knew she hit her mark when he left the room forgetting to take the treats he was going to tempt her with.

All Emie could do was pray, and drink what little bit of life that he allowed her to have.

Jesse was standing in the morning sun light that was creating a bright, twinkling path on the water right up to his feet on the southern beach in the pier. He was waiting in the sand for the moment Luna would materialize in front of him.

He knew he was playing Russian roulette with his life, but it was worth it. He had to know the truth. And this was the only way to make her do it.

The night before, Ken had come to him and revealed what happened with Asher. Jesse had waited till morning, waited for the sun to rise on the cool, crisp fall morning. Standing there in the sand knowing the sunshine would protect him from his enemies, he waited for Luna.

When it happened, down the beach from where he stood, he saw her walking towards him through the sand like she had just magically stepped off the water.

She was dressed in a long sleeved, shimmery gray dress shirt, that was open along her arms, neatly tied at her wrists, baring her delicate Indian toned skin to the sunlight. She was wearing tight designer blue jeans and her little bare feet were sinking in the sand. Her long, ravin hair was flowing behind her in the breeze.

She was all beauty and beast wrapped in the lovely essence of a woman he craved.

"This isn't a game Jesse." She warned him playfully. "You shouldn't be here."

Jesse looked away from her, back out over the sparkling lake in the morning light and sighed heavily. He could see his breath in the sun as he exhaled the cold air he had taken into his lungs. He was shivering now in the cool morning air as it rose away from him off the lake in waves of mist that sent chills all over his body.

"I know." He whispered to her into the distance between them. "But I needed to."

Luna walked up beside him. She could see his arms were trembling that held his hands tucked deep inside of his jean pockets, mostly in fear, and because of his body temperature. His short sleeved police t-shirt did nothing to protect his upper body from the wind.

Luna looked up to his face then. He looked rugged and untamed now in his unshaven apocalyptic state. Hiding under the fire hall must be driving him crazy, she thought.

His hair was longer than she had ever seen it. Long enough to run her fingers through and pull. She teased him with the thought and winked at him when he glanced at her sideways.

Jesse looked down at his booted foot in the sand. He was digging into his boot print, kicking the sand. He needed to talk to her. He needed to tell her why he was here. But he was robbed of speech in the presence of her beauty. She was shining brighter than the sunlight that was blinding him now in front of him. She was glowing with excitement he didn't deserve for her to feel.

They hadn't been together like this in months. They shouldn't be here. There was so much that needed to be done. Taken care of.

Luna made the first move. She could sense his unease, like so many times before. This time, he didn't have to feel like that. They would have a future together, just like this, the one they had dreamed of even if she had to move mountains to make it so, she would find all the faith she needed and then some.

She brushed his arm with her cool fingers and ran them up his tattooed path under the edge of his shirt sleeve. She watched as the bumps appeared on his arm and danced around, appearing everywhere she touched. His veins in his arms filled with warm blood she knew was boiling inside of him now. She could hear his heart thudding, trying to keep pace with his wandering thoughts.

Jesse lowered his head and watched her fingers closely. Watched her fingers trace his tattoos. Watched her long hair move sensually around her body in the breeze. Watched the sunlight as it danced on her skin.

Luna always put her hands wherever she wanted to on his body, like she owned him. No other woman had ever dared to do that to him. Jesse loved that about her.

"Why are we here Jesse?" She breathed, looking up at him unable to contain her pleasure in the moment.

Jesse turned in all seriousness. He kept his hands tucked into his pockets. He couldn't touch her yet. "Is Asher alive?"

It was the one of the many questions he feared asking her. But he had to know now.

Luna tilted her head and read his mind. She dug inside and needed to know what had happened. When she found what Ken had told him, she was relieved. She wouldn't have to keep it a secret now. She looked out into the sunlight and watched as the diamonds sparkled on the lake.

"Is it Ken you don't trust, or is it me?"

Jesse looked at her confused. He watched as she turned back to him, tucking her hair behind her ear. When her big golden eyes looked in his, he forgot how to breathe. He forgot what they were talking about.

Luna grinned at his bashful thoughts that made him blush. She helped him out then. "Remember when you found that lost dog?" She crossed her arms and turned towards him fully.

Jesse remembered, but had no idea where she was going with this.

"She was so adorable and sweet." Luna remembered the day like it was yesterday that Jesse had walked into the shop with her. "You stayed mad at me for weeks when I took her to the vet to see if she was chipped to help find her owners."

Jesse looked away from her stubbornly. He had wanted to keep that dog. But Luna wanted to find the owners.

Luna had to hold her hair now, the wind had brazenly picked up. She glanced at Jesse playfully who was pouting now, pretending like he could keep his eyes off her, when really he couldn't. "I asked you to trust me."

Jesse sighed and kicked around some sand. She had been right. The dog belong to a little boy who needed her. She was a therapy dog.

Luna was right now. He needed to trust her. Especially now.

Luna nudged his shoulder and tipped him sideways. "You promised you would trust me." The poor guy had stray dog syndrome. He couldn't leave well enough alone to save his life.

"Alright. I'll trust you." He relented, grinning into the sunrise.

"Why are we really here Jesse?" She asked him again. Because time was running out, and she would trade a million lifetimes to just run away with him right now.

"Because this is the only thing keeping me alive." There was no other way for him to explain it. It was true. He needed her in the moments they stole like this.

Jesse reached inside his pocket and turned towards her. "I got something for you." He placed a bushel of lily of the valley bells he had found growing outside the fire department on his way here in her hair. Luna loved to put them in her hair like she did with feathers and clips.

It reminded her of her heritage. A song her mother would sing to her.

"Not even Solomon, in all his glory, was arrayed like one of these." He quoted for her, looking down at his handy work.

Luna regretted not wanting to come here with him now. Jesse was so endearing and sweet to her. She couldn't believe he remembered this from their past.

Jesse grinned at her sideways, daring her playfully. "I just, wanted to run away with you." He shrugged knowingly at her.

Jesse backed away from her playfully, spreading out his arms daring her to catch him.

His heart pounded proudly for her when her smile took up her whole face as she ran after him. Jesse couldn't help it, he ran up to her and caught her in his arms, spinning her around against his body. He had to feel her there, next to his heart.

She shrieked out loud and kissed his neck and danced with him when he set her down on the sand.

When she bent back to look at him and shook out her hair behind her, Jesse couldn't stop looking at her. He had to capture every moment with her so it could last him until he saw her again.

Like magic he had to have, she bursted with it, making him high off her fumes.

Luna placed her hands on his chest when he wrapped his arms around her hips. She continued to follow his steps like he was leading her through the last strands of a love song.

She could hear it, the song their hearts sang. It wasn't the lonely heartbreaking song of their tragic past love they couldn't have. No. It was the song of reflection. Of the love that was going to blossom into a beautiful story they couldn't wait to live in.

"I love you Luna."

Luna didn't know what she loved more about him. His heart, or his soul.

She looked into his eyes and spoke to his mind in her native language what meant more than just love and waited for his response. "Gvgeyu'i."

It was his soul that responded to her. It was his soul that felt the love she spoke to him. It would be there, in his soul that she would dwell forever.

Jesse didn't know how she did it, he only knew that he felt her words more than he understood them. She loved him more than life itself.

Jesse leaned in. He kissed Luna and devoured her lips until he couldn't breathe. He deepened his kiss and picked her up, wrapping her neatly around his waist. Holding her neck, he pressed her deep into his kiss. He was only a few stumbled steps away from the cylinders that lined the pier.

He bumped into one, passionately still kissing her, setting her down he walked between her legs till he was seductively pressed up against her. He smoothed her hair behind her and crushed her with his ecstasy he couldn't control now.

Luna greedily growled when he started kissing down her neck. He leaned her back and left a trail with his moistened tongue between her cleavage that made her shiver. Jesse always had her at a disadvantage. He knew how to make love to her in ways she had never dreamed possible. What she needed to learn from him was what his body desired. So she dug. She tore into his mind and found the spot where his pleasure burned.

She reached inside of him, even though her hand was only touching the back of his hair by his neck, and stirred it intoxicatingly. Bringing him to the point he couldn't deny it. Jesse felt it when she did it. He had to pull back ever so slightly and eye her curiously. Luna, for all her sweet innocence she tried to maintain, when she was with him, she did bad things well.

"That," he laughed out loud and put his forehead on hers, "yeah, Babe I don't know what that was. But,"

Luna bit her lip and waited. There was always a 'but' left in Jesse.

"But?" She asked him patiently.

"But I liked it." He told her, helplessly lost in her playfulness.

Luna smirked at him. She had learned a long time ago in counseling that communication was key to any relationship. And she loved it when Jesse communicated with her. Luna looked into both his deep blue eyes. She had used up all her time here. She had to go back. She gently kissed his lips breaking the sensuality between them.

Jesse sighed heartbreakingly placing his forehead back on hers. Pulling her body back against his. "Times up?"

Luna bit her lip. She didn't want to show her sadness. Clouds would form and she would put his life in danger at shielding the sun for the rogues that were waiting in the distance for the chance to strike.

Jesse looked down at her body he needed more time to explore again, slowly. He wanted her so bad he had to straighten up and walk away from her. He was busting out of his jeans just being close to her.

Luna watched as he stood towering over her, looking away from her with hands on his hips. He wasn't ready. She hopped off the cylinder and walked around him. She stood in front of him and backed up into him, making him hold her.

Jesse stuffed his hands inside his pockets stubbornly. He knew if he wrapped his arms around her she would transport him back to the department and she would disappear. For longer than he could bare again.

Luna closed her eyes at his thoughts. He knew her too well sometimes. She looked back up at him and nodded. "It's time Jesse."

Jesse wanted to hold her. He could see it in her eyes that she wanted it too. He looked at her arm through the shirt where her skin was peeking through. He followed his gaze up her arm to her shoulder. He touched her neck with his nose sliding it up, then down. "One more minute." He whispered.

Luna could feel the clouds behind her rolling in. She could feel her heartbreaking the way he was loving her. She could sense the danger behind them, but she gave him his minute.

Jesse touched his palms to her hips and guided her back against him. His lips he barely brushed against her skin on her neck. Kissing her softly. He pressed into her, behind her, letting her feel his pleasure he felt against her. He knew she craved this. Wanting to know what made him feel pleasure. So he showed her.

Luna closed her eyes, she picked him up behind her and carried him through space and time, lingering in the wake of the spiritual firmament between reality and heaven. She found the pleasure where he showed her it was in his body and took it from him like she was stroking it out of his essence.

Jesse found himself standing naked under cold running water, gasping for air in the men's shower at the fire department. Leave it to Luna to get back at him and she knew just where to hit him harder than was fair.

New York City
Battery Park at Pier A, North River

Darryl could feel the demon behind him, that had been following him down the street, breathing down his back as it flew above him. Bartley kept trying to turn around in front of Darryl while he was running to fire at it, but he kept losing his balance, tripping and slowing Darryl down.

"Don't stop. We are almost there. Just keep going." Darryl instructed him.

Cain was at his side getting tired. Darryl could only hope that his dog could make it to the Pier before the demon got the both of them.

They were pulling up the rear, running from the trade center tower. Darryl could still see it looming behind them when he looked back for the demon who had just swooped up and away from Darryl's men who had made it to the pier ready to fire on it.

"Just go!" He commanded them all. The pier doors were being held open by Pat and Johnny for them to run into. The demons wouldn't follow into the buildings without their vampire recruits. And right now their vampires were lying out on the streets with their heads in their hands. Darryl had made sure of it.

Jimmy confronted Darryl when Darryl slid into the doorway on his knees, praying they could get the doors shut before the demons flew in. Luckily, Pat got a shot at one of them that may have been fatal to it.

Darryl told the men to head for the back of the building towards the bar where there were better windows to see their surroundings before they looked at the footage Jimmy had recorded inside the tower.

He stayed there on his knees to catch his breath with Cain, who was also panting. Cain stood and started to pace around Darryl. When he shook out his fur like he was shaking off the fear he had just experienced running for their lives, Darryl laughed at him looking up at the white walled ceiling above them.

"We are getting too old for this Cain." He told his partner breathless.

Cain huffed what looked like his acknowledgement to Darryl.

Darryl got to his feet and walked slowly down the main hall that led to the bar where his men were at. The scene that unfolded before him looked like something out of a comic strip. His men, his soldiers, dressed in full steel armor where kicking back in the stools drinking heavily from bottles that lined the bar, sharing stories of the events that they had just encountered.

Darryl sat in between Bartley and Jimmy who were ready to give their report. He let his other men have their moment. It wasn't often they got to do this after a run.

Jimmy started showing Darryl the footage on his tablet that was streaming a live feed from back at the tower. Victor and Axel were having a conversation in one of the halls where the drone was set up.

Darryl watched as Victor paced around cussing up a storm over the fact that Darryl's men had been caught in the basement. Darryl was trying to listen to see if Victor sent any other vampires out in search of his men. He hoped they could rest here for just another minute before they had to run again.

Jimmy had enough drones set up in the tower now that they could remotely set up on an island until their mission was complete.

"I can't believe this. You lost how many outside? To humans?" Victor condemned Axel with a vicious set down.

Axel was shaking his head trying to prove his point. "These are not just humans-"

"Well of course they are." Victor ranted on. "You will be responsible for recruiting more. I'm tired of losing vampires because you are too distracted with her to train them appropriately."

"Yes sir." Axel facetiously saluted to Victor in a manner that displayed his narcissism to the whole situation.

"I'm serious Axel. Go find more human recruits we can use to help the swingers get the job done. I will not let these arrogant assholes, who think they can break in here for the hell of it, get off this damned island."

Darryl looked at Bartley then. "Times up. Let's go."

Bartley and Jimmy rounded the men. They had their proof now that the drones worked inside the building. Jimmy reassured him as they packed up that the other drones were online now.

Darryl looked back out the front doors he had slid into and grinned wickedly. He looked at the tower he could see from the windows in front of him and flipped off Victor from the distance between them. "These arrogant assholes just intercepted your balls, mother-"

"Darryl. Come on, man." Bartley beckoned from behind the bar.

Darryl smiled in the win he knew he had and ran with his partner at his side out to the waiting submersible that would take them under the North River to the Jersey shores of Liberty State park. There, Darryl and his men would hide out until they had the information they needed to report back to Fort Bragg.

Then Darryl was going home. He was done with this war no one was going to win.

Luna looked at her watch again. She had checked the time twice now in the last hour. It still wasn't dusk yet. She closed her eyes and prayed the time would speed up. Every day seemed to go like this. It was almost winter now. Months had passed since she had left Jesse arms. The days were getting shorter as winter crept closer. The nights took forever to end and the days never lasted long enough.

It had taken until November to reach Tennessee. They had to double back so many times it was drove her insane. Now it was almost December.

Luna squeezed her eyes shut tighter at the knowledge. She could see Jesse waiting for her on the roof of the fire hall. She could see him down in the pits with their family. Probably still going insane, she told herself.

Jesse wasn't good at sitting around, she thought, making herself smile. He had proved it to her when he had made her come back. Unlike Asher and Curtis who craved time to sit around and do nothing, Jesse hated being idle. He used to fill his days at work with cleaning the police station, cleaning and polishing his police SUV, or driving around the city seeking what he could do. His nights were filled with taking care of his condo or working on his boat. Or entertaining her.

Luna sighed at her thoughts. She had longed to just stop and be with Jesse in his mind, but her time was always taken with trying to figure out their next moves. Looking for blood seemed to consume her days. She would have to travel out alone and find enough to feed everyone. She made a quick decision to speak with Joseph about that. They needed to hunt at night together. She wasn't going out alone anymore risking her own life.

Luna looked around one more time. She couldn't see anything coming in any direction from her perch above the burnt out police department where she was keeping watch.

Joseph had chosen this place to hide out during the day so they could load up on more ammunition and weapons. His luck was wearing out though. The more Luna tried to explain to him that the vampires were setting fire to everything the humans left behind and there was nothing left, the more he argued with her. He would have to see for himself before he believed and that suited Luna just fine. She hoped he hadn't found anything today.

Finally she relaxed. She had too. She needed to do something other than what she had been doing all this time. She needed to just forget, for a moment.

Luna looked around once more. Just to be sure. No one was coming. There was no threat or danger around them.

Butterflies started rising inside of her. She wanted to be with Jesse, just for a moment. She let her eyes stare off and she pictured Jesse, calling to him.

Luna reached through space and time, something she only did with him. She called to his mind and found him right where she had thought he would be. He was laying down, trying to sleep. But sleep was eluding him.

Luna took his hand in his mind. She offered him a dream he couldn't resist.

It wasn't just any day, it was the day Luna cherished most. A memory.

Jesse had been standing on his jet ski, making waves in the lake. She had been on the shore laying in the hot sand sunning. The sun was warming her body through and it felt amazing.

"Come on Babe! Jump in!" Jesse had called to her.

Luna had tipped her sunglasses down and watched him playing in the water. She only had a few more hours of sunlight left and she wanted nothing more then to enjoy it. Except Jesse.

She had spent all day that day wasting away grooming at work. She had longed to be out here on the beach in the summer sun. But watching Jesse, spinning in the waves, beckoning her to come and play, she couldn't resist him.

The thought of what she had been contemplating that day still gave her chills. Still gave her butterflies. Luna remembered the way the sand felt on her feet as she walked out towards the lake. Towards Jesse. It was warm between her toes.

She remembered the way the water felt when she walked out to Jesse, taking off her tank top, letting it fly carelessly back in the wind to her blanket as she left the world behind, she walked out to Jesse in her bikini.

Jesse had moved out to deeper water teasing her. He looked so handsome in his dark sunglasses and hot, tanned skin. His swim trunks were still dry and Luna wanted to see him get wet.

"You know the rules babe. If you can't jump on the jet ski in the deep water you can't ride." He was grinning down at her now as she held onto the back.

"You said you only say that to the girls so you watch their boobs as they try to climb up behind you."

Jesse let his sunglasses fall down his nose as he looked down at Luna. "Yep." He told her, unashamed of his wandering eyes on her.

Luna gave him her best smirk at his jest watching his wandering eyes. She tried to give him a show as she bobbed in and out of the water, but there were kids and families swimming nearby. She couldn't just shoot out of the water and land on the ski like she knew she could do.

"Come on vampire. Let me see what you got."

He had winked at her quietly. He wanted to tease her in the worst way and Luna knew it.

Luna judged the way up onto the ski. She tried to put her foot up on it and jump for his outstretched hand but her foot slipped on the slippery surface. Vampire or not, this was harder than it looked. She tried again and once she had his hand, her foot slipped again and she pulled them both into the water.

At first Luna let herself fall, and then she felt Jesse's arms around her. She turned in his arms and looked at him. He pulled them both up, using all his might. It flattered her because he didn't need too.

When they breached the surface, she watched as he gulped for air. It made her chuckle at the way humans did that. She watched as he shook the water out on his hair playfully and reached for her in the water.

When his hands found her hips he pulled her closer to him. "If you can't get up Babe you can't ride."

"Ride or die, remember?" She reminded him of what he always told her.

"That's right Babe. Ride or die." He stated for her, proud of her determination.

Jesse had looked so intently at Luna that she almost let go of him. She read his thoughts and saw the way he was picturing their bodies coming together in the water. It wasn't a part of the memories. Jesse was awake now trying to control the dream.

Luna let herself revile in the way she had felt the heat from his hot, tanned body. She felt his shoulders and traced the outline of his tattoos in the way she had wanted to then. But when she looked at his face her memories took over.

"Watch me." She winked at him, trying to get out of his grasp splashing water on him. If she hadn't she would have let Jesse have whatever he wanted there in the water.

She could see in his mind as he watched her turn and reach for the back of the ski. She watched as he watched her climb up, and she felt what he felt when he touched her hips and helped her climb up, even though she didn't need his help.

The way his eyes and hands had studied her body there in the water. Luna wondered why it hadn't effected her then the way it did now.

She would never forget the way he climbed up behind her with such force and speed like a vampire would. Jesse had lived in that lake his whole life. His body was built for fighting fires and taking down bad guys, but he was also built for the water. He knew things that not a lot of guys knew or even understood about the water that seemed to amaze her.

He started the engine and whispered in her ear as the rumbling of the engine vibrated under her legs. He was sending shivers across her shoulder all the way down to her core with his breath.

"Just in case you were wondering Babe, I like it better when you're in front of me."

Luna closed her eyes at the memory. Of Jesse pressed up against her. The way his strong arms wrapped around her hanging on to her as she drove the ski through the waves around them. Every bump in waves they took, Jesse would lose his mind pulling her back to him. His hands felt like they were all over her. Every time he lost his grip he found it again.

When they got lost in the water, far enough out there where no one could see them, it was the one place they could really be alone. She got to be a vampire, and it didn't matter that he was only human. Nothing ever happened of course. It was just the rush they enjoyed.

Luna could dive in the water, deep enough to find trinkets. She could pull him under with her and they could swim together for hours. They would get lost on the empty islands that lined the shores of Lake Erie exploring. And there was no one around to tell them they couldn't.

Luna took over her memories, pictured herself slowing the ski down and coming to a stop out in the middle of the lake where no one could see them, turning around, wrapping her body around his, even though that didn't happen that day. She could feel the way his mouth opened when he kissed her through the space and time she held still for them. The feel of his lips touching hers. The way he deepened his kiss. The way his tongue tasted on hers. The way his-

Luna opened her eyes at the sound of footsteps outside the window. She cussed aloud at the sight of a vampire below her sneaking a look through the window.

It was almost dusk now. The rogues were out. Luna had dreamed the rest of the day away remembering Jesse and the day they had stole together. Obsessing with his presence and the feel of his body. She had replayed the memories slowly, over and over so many times she had lost track of time.

Just as she was about to stand up a hand wrapped around her face and covered up her mouth. She closed her eyes wishing she had brought Jordy instead of Joseph. He would have seen this. She called out to Joseph in her mind, but the pain in her mouth prevented her from finishing her thought.

Whoever had covered up her lips had stuffed a steel mesh in her mouth that caused her to chomp down on it. The steel hurt her teeth and her tongue and felt odd. She tried to twist out of the hold the vampire had on her, but it didn't work. He was stronger than her.

Luna tried to reach for her powers, she tried to make it storm, make it lighting, but all she could do was fight the steel in her mouth. It burned like hell. Her mind started to lose hold of reality. For the first time in her life Luna felt weak. Tired.

She felt herself slipping away and it felt amazing. There was no more pain, no more feelings. Luna closed her eyes. She could have sworn she felt a smile on her lips. Peace. Freedom. She had searched her life for it and there it was. She slipped into the oblivion.

~ *Nine* ~

Be Still and have mercy

Two days before Christmas.

"Are you going to talk now?" James barked at Jeremy angrily. "Where is the rest of your blood sucking family?"

Jesse was standing in the Whitby dungeon looking down at what James had done to Jeremy. The dungeon looked like something out of a gothic novel in medieval times his sister Izzy loved to read about.

He was filled with so much regret about coming here, but mostly, he was overflowing with anger towards James.

This was the first time James had brought him here. Jesse had no idea what James did when he left the department during the day and went hunting with their friends. Only that when he returned, he'd gotten more people killed than he had saved.

Jeremy was pinned down by a steel cage with spikes through his body; his head, his shoulders, arms and legs. There was no way he could move let alone escape. Even his powers were held at bay by the steel that was crushing him.

Jesse sighed out loud, racking his whole body in a tremble of shivers he felt all over his cold skin. He had no idea how Jeremy was still alive.

James spoke up, startling Jesse from his thoughts.

"Well, maybe she will tell us what we want to know." James had his hands on his hips dominating over Jeremy.

He bent down on his knees and whispered to Jeremy so only he could hear. "You think what I've done to you is bad." James chuckled at that. "You have no idea what bad is yet man. I will be fucking brutal to her."

Jesse heard that last bit. Jeremy hadn't answered James, so James planned his attack on the woman they had followed into Luna Pier who was somewhere in the mansion. He assumed Jeremy had brought her here to rescue him.

Jeremy was going to kill James if he got out of there. Jesse knew this and he had only known Jeremy for a brief time. He hoped Jeremy could hear his thoughts now. This wasn't his doing.

Jesse promised Jeremy then. I'll get you out of there man, I promise. He had no idea how to do it of course, but he would do it. Somehow.

James turned to Jesse, seeing the look on his face. He started begging him then trying to get him to see the need to capture Jeremy's woman. "We have to go find her. She's a vampire Jesse! She's one of them."

He pleaded with Jesse again before he could back out of his plans.

"Look at Izzy! I told you they turned her!" James handed Jesse a loaded gun with steel bullets and slammed it into his chest. "We have to finish this."

Jesse looked at the guns James handed him. He had been trying to help James capture the Whitby brothers in hopes that they would lead them to Asher. If not, James planned on killing them all.

But this... Jesse hadn't thought James would take it this far.

It had been a month since Jesse's nightmare. A month since he had lost contact with Luna. Something had happened, and he needed answers. But this, he looked at Jeremy and almost lost his ability to stand, this was not going to help him find her.

Jesse looked at the steel cell along the wall where Jordy was being held by James that looked like a jail cell the Whitby's had down here. Their sister, Izzy was in there with Jordy. She was one of them.

Jesse closed his eyes at the reality that hit him. He had to trust Luna.

He had to remind himself that Izzy was ok. She was like Luna now. She wasn't the monster that James thought she was. He had to save her. Before James got his hands on her.

He had to concentrate on breathing so he could pay attention to getting this over with James, but the scent of blood caught his attention and threatened to overpower his best intentions.

As they started to walk out of the room and head for the stairwell, something caught his eye. He moved his flashlight over the pool of liquid he found on the floor. Years at the police academy studying crime scenes investigations made him shudder at the scene unfolding around him.

There was blood on the floor and wine bottles turned over with blood spilling out of them on a table nearby. Jesse looked to the wall where he had seen more wine bottles lining the walls on shelves. Jesse had no idea what the Whitby's did down here, but it was a surreal sight to behold.

There were chains on the floor and the walls. Old, forgotten rotten blood smeared the walls where the chains were. He had to shake his frightened momentum and keep walking.

Jesse sighed as they walked back up into the main floors of the mansion. He was astonished at what James had pulled off. The attacks on the city had stopped weeks ago. James had stalked the Whitby brothers, watching them pass through walls here in the mansion. Their powers seemed limitless. Jesse had no idea how James had done this to three vampires.

James and Jerry, and some of the men down at the department had used some of the ideas their father Frank had told James about to do all this. He had left papers in his desk at the fire hall and at his home that gave the men something to use against the Whitby's. They had made weapons of steel, like the cage on the floor. Even the guns they carried now had steel bullets in them.

Jesse wanted to fear that James was going to get himself killed, but truth be told, after seeing that James was capable of killing and premeditated murder, Jesse couldn't bring himself to do it. He feared for their family and friends instead. Praying that the rest of the Whitby's wouldn't try to hurt his family because of James.

Jesse followed James through out the mansion in stunned silence searching for the woman they had followed here. Secretly he was searching for evidence of Luna.

He had to control his temper whenever James would get scared by a noise searching the halls and draw his gun unsteadily, ready to fire his weapon at nothing. Jesse remembered similar feelings of anxiety when he first started the force, but James was careless with his guns. He was always pointing them where he shouldn't, even when he wasn't hunting. Jesse had worried more than once down in the pits for everyone when James had his guns.

Jesse watched James as he jumped around corners, not even checking where he was going with his flashlight, or covering his own back. Jesse used all his training and tried to protect himself the best he could.

He remembered the fire scenes he had been on with James. The excited mess he would become put everyone in danger. Jesse had sworn long ago he would never go into a fire with James again. He wondered now, what in the hell he was doing with him here.

In the kitchen they found another bloodbath. Jesse stood there, stunned, lowering his own gun and flashlight, looking around the makeshift kitchen.

Jesse didn't want to know what had happened. From what he knew of Luna, they drank blood from the surrounding medical facilities. But this… Jesse shook his head and tried to regain his composure. This looked like someone had been feeding on dead bodies. Leaving bones, unwanted meat and blood everywhere like the scene of a savage murder on television.

In all his years on the department he had never seen anything like it. In all his years with Luna, knowing what she was, he never pictured this.

Vampires had no need for a kitchen. He wondered why it was even here. For show maybe? To unsuspecting humans. Or for what he was looking at now. To kill, and feed. He didn't even want to know what was in the cupboards.

There was no sign of the woman they had followed here. She had either fled in fear for her life, or she was hiding somewhere. Jesse knew this mansion was too big to be searched without getting themselves lost or killed.

Years of experience that James didn't have kicked into full gear for Jesse and scared the hell out of him. If the other Whitby's were coming, they would kill them for what they had done to Jeremy. He suddenly felt very vulnerable here and he didn't trust James to have his six.

"James, we should go."

They were both still standing in the kitchen looking around at all the blood on the counters and the floor in awe. Neither one had looked at the other.

"What the hell happened in here?" James demanded to know in a voice so loud Jesse almost jumped him to shut him up.

Jesse grabbed James by the shoulder. "We should go!" He demanded.

James shook off his brothers hold on him. "No! We are going to finish this." James wasn't looking at Jesse. He was disgusted looking around. He couldn't believe what he was seeing. "We have them right where we need them now. With or without that woman."

Jesse sighed as his brother walked away from him and walked back down to the dungeon through the hall just outside of the kitchen. He followed James hoping he could protect Jeremy from whatever happened next.

Jesse had spent months listening to his brother. They had lost many brothers and sisters on the department fighting against an enemy they sometimes couldn't see. Many more in the city had died because they had failed to protect them.

Jesse let James believe the lies he told everyone and prayed no one suspected his own personal treachery. Some days, a small part of him was beginning to believe it himself. He tried not to think about the kitchen as he followed James, feeling like the walls were closing in on him.

As he walked down the circle stairwell down to the dungeon Jesse tried to remember how long it had been since this had all started. It was late December now. Almost Christmas. This would be the first year his family wouldn't spend it together. They were torn apart, separated by death and destruction that was all around them.

Jesse needed to find Asher. He knew Asher was alive, well, sort of. Jesse grinned thinking about the kitchen; it looked like a mess Asher would have made. One thing the Stone boys had in common, when they were angry, they made a mess.

It really wasn't funny, but somehow it was. Jesse never understood some of Luna's vampire humor, he wondered what she would say about all this.

Jesse and James entered the dungeon. They were swept off their feet and dragged into the cell where they had held Jordy. Jordy, Izzy and Jeremy were standing on the other side of the cell doors. They had escaped.

Jesse sat in the cell, throwing himself down defeated. Now they were being held captive. "Nice James." He spat at his brother. He didn't even have his guns anymore.

Jordy was emptying the steel bullets into a drain. He broke the guns eyeing James carefully, letting him see what he was doing. They were useless to anyone now. Jesse sat there resting his elbows on his knees, holding his head, while James tried to fight with them. Jesse had known all along this plan wouldn't work. He had feared what would happen if it didn't. Listening to the way Jordy was talking to James who was arguing with him, Jesse knew they would be ok.

If Jeremy had wanted to kill them, he would have done it already, Jesse told himself looking over at Jeremy. Jeremy was angry. He was heaving, trying to control the healing that was happening in his body. It shook Jesse and scared the hell out of him.

Jeremy acknowledged Jesse with a look and a nod of his head as Jordy and James continued to argue. Asher will be here soon. He silently told Jesse. You're safe, for now.

Jesse saw the angry look on Jeremy's face. Whoever that woman was, she meant something to Jeremy. It must have taken a miracle for Jeremy to get out of there. Jesse knew if it had been Luna that James was threatening to hurt, he would have done the same thing Jeremy was doing now.

Watching James shake the bars of the cell and curse at the vampire brothers, Jesse knew James didn't deserve to know the truth about what was going to happen to them. His hatred for them was too deep.

Jesse shuttered as he watched Jeremy pick up the cage on the floor they had used against him and he threw it at the stone wall next to the cell shattering it into a million pieces. He watched again as they walked out of the dungeon. Jeremy was having trouble walking. Jesse shook his head worried then. They were either in for a beating, or something worse when Asher got here.

James didn't see the way Izzy looked at him before she followed Jeremy and Jordy. He didn't see the truth right in front of him. The Whitby's weren't monsters. They were just trying to survive in a world were they weren't accepted.

Jesse sighed and rested his head against the wall of the cell and waited. He remembered how Ken had described Asher. The hot mess he was now. He knew Asher would come now that they couldn't hunt him anymore. Jordy had their guns and their weapons. Asher was coming, and with him, so was hell.

Emie didn't know what she was feeling from her cell in the tower. Something had changed in the times and space of reality. Something was going to happen and the pull of anxiety she felt caused her to toss in her seclusion.

Asher. She reached for his essence she had lost. She clung to the hope that God had him now and was going to bring him back to life.

Her family was out there somewhere. His family was still alive, she could feel it. They were still fighting for the right and life that was theirs to have in this war that was destroying the world.

Emie's captors were absent enough to give her a reprieve from their evilness. Her hatred towards them built inside her making her strong enough to continue her frozen bitterness, so cold and ever present in her being to bring them to their knees in the face of her resistance.

She clung to hope she had given to Asher. She restored her faith. She hung on to the reality of righteousness in her God given abilities as a warrior, an angelic vampire who was strong enough to withstand the injustice of evil. She didn't know how, but she knew God would win. He would take this world back. He would defend His people. He would give back all that had been taken by His enemies in this war.

One day, one day she would be free. One day she would have the love she was meant to have. Emie smiled into her pillow and willed the energy she felt in the change and welcomed it.

Asher had made his brothers wait before he had come to them. He stood at the double doors of the dungeon and tried to regain his composure. He hadn't been in this room since Jeremy had turned him.

As Asher held the long handles of the wooden dungeon doors he closed his eyes trying not to remember his death. The memories were crushing. The pain, the hate, they overpowered him still.

Asher had to step back. He pushed his hands in his pockets and stood there for a moment. He was so angry with his brothers in this moment he wanted to strangle the life out of them.

Why had they tried to kill Jeremy and Jordy? Their own sister!

Both brothers had waged war amongst themselves for years over Luna. Jesse had a valid reason to hate James. What Asher couldn't understand now was why Jesse had chosen to follow James here, to capture the boys and try to kill them.

Jesse wasn't like James. He didn't have a vengeful bone in his body. Jesse carried himself with an air of sophistication in his career. He was all about justice and sympathetic gestures.

He was neat and calculated. It was one of the reasons the police department had suited him better then the fire department. Jesse had more control over situations there. He had more time to plan. Unlike James, who tore through life without thinking, without planning. James lived to the beat of his own drum.

Asher walked into the dungeon more relaxed now that he had reminded himself who his brothers were. He couldn't kill them no matter how bad his desires and hate wanted him too. He planned to find out what they were up to and judge them based on that truth.

When he sat at the table in front of the cell he drank heavily from the bottle that sat there. The blood was old, like a fine aged bottle of whiskey.

Jesse stood and walked up next to James who had also looked out of the cell as Asher walked down the stairs into the dungeon and sat at the table in front of them. He couldn't believe his own eyes. Asher was, a walking, hot mess.

His hair was longer and looked wet hanging off his massive shoulders. His skin looked red, like he was sunburned. There was determination in his gait, the way he carried himself. His strength was astounding.

Massive didn't quite explain the sight of Asher, Jessie thought to himself. Asher was clothed in a fire department issued t-shirt and a ripped pair of holy jeans that didn't fit his body anymore. He was dirty and bloody.

Jesse almost smiled to himself again. The mess in the kitchen had been Asher's.

There was no escaping the man- Jesse corrected himself, the vampire in front of them. He watched as smoke raised from around Asher sitting at the table drinking what he knew was blood from a bottle. Jesse could tell from the way Asher was hunched with his arms on his thighs that he was raging inside. He was angry, and heaven help him, Jesse was glad someone finally was.

"You're one of them now?" James asked unsteady, even though he already knew the answer. "You can't touch us inside of here Asher. The cell is made of-"

Asher stood then and grinned walking over to his brothers in the cell. Silencing James. Finally. "You think this can stop me?" As he placed a hand on the steel bars in front of them, Asher looked at his hand, grinning evilly.

James and Jesse watched as Asher's hand on the bars started to heat and turned the bar red hot, melting it. His hand was on fire now. They backed up, mesmerized at his power.

Asher let go, looking sternly at James. He knew he had made his point.

"But?" Jesse asked incoherently, disbelieving what he was seeing. He hadn't expected this. Fire could destroy vampires. Couldn't it? He looked to James for help who was staring just as astonished at Asher as he was.

"What are you going to do now Asher, kill us?" James tried, thinking guile would help him.

Asher laughed in a deep growl as he walked back over to the table and sat his heavy body down. "I'm not going to kill you James." He looked at him then from under his brow resting his arms again on his legs. "My job now is judgement." He cocked his head looking at his brother daringly. "I judge the lost, and save the chosen ones. I'm here to judge you based on your sins."

Asher cocked his head to the side looking at him. "What are your sins James?"

James backed up to the walls behind him.

Jesse stepped forward then. "You know why I'm here."

Asher nodded in agreement to Jesse and hung his head as he spoke. "Yes. You are here because of Luna."

James silently called Jesse out. "Trader! You would choose her over your own flesh and blood?"

Jesse ignored him, waiting for Asher's answer. He needed Asher to find her.

Asher looked at Jesse more intently. "Either you join us, in the search for what you seek, or it will destroy you."

Jesse wanted nothing more. He nodded his head to Asher, praying his brother wouldn't deceive him. "What's the plan?"

James stepped forward then, ready to argue with the both of them.

Asher stood and walked quickly up to the cell. He met James there.

Jesse backed up, fearing what was about to happen. Asher was raging hatred.

"Let go of your hatred for your brother!" Asher bellowed at James. "You don't know what you're doing!

"You never wanted Luna! You never loved her! Why are you so persistent in punishing him for it?"

Asher pointed at him and gritted the words through his teeth as he spoke them. "Our father instilled an unholy hate so deep in you that it's blinding you." He hated his brother now, almost as much as he had hated his father. Both of them had caused everything to go so out of control Asher feared he'd never regain a strong hold.

"You can't see past it can you? You can't see what's right in front of you!"

Jesse agreed wholeheartedly with Asher, looking at James ashamed of him.

Asher backed away from the cell, sickened just by the scent of James. "I've been watching you James. I've always been watching you. It was my job as your brother. And I've seen what you've done James.

"You've deceived everyone!" Asher looked more pointedly at James then. "Except me." He stated matter of factly.

Asher turned his back and paced in front of the cell. "You tried to outcast your own brother in your prejudice hatred for something you knew nothing about. You stole from him, you belittle him. You used him to get what you wanted. And then you accused him of things he couldn't control, because he was just trying to clean up your mess."

James wanted to argue his point. He wanted to argue that Jesse wouldn't leave Luna alone. The truth was that James didn't love Luna, or want her all those years. The hatred he had always tried to feel for Jesse was never real in that.

Asher stopped in front of James and looked at him directly, making him see his own anger and how real it was. "Now, people need you James. You got a young boy killed who needed help James! Instead of seeing the need to save people like I taught you, you carelessly hid down there and used our family and friends to accomplish your will."

He started pacing again. He tried to control his anger in doing so. "When I came back, I was going to save you, try to save everyone, but you had instilled an unrighteous fear in all of them and armed them against an enemy they were helpless to fight against!"

"You are the enemy Asher! You are exactly what I was defending them from."

Asher stopped pacing and put his head down. He put his hand on the bar in front of James. He wished it was his throat. "How many died James? How many of our friends did we lose because you wanted to hunt us?"

Asher looked up at him then for an answer. "How many of MY men did you loose James?" Asher demanded answers he almost broke through the steel bars to have.

"You weren't defending them! You were using them! You wanted the truth!"

Jesse spoke up then. He had to know what Asher meant. "What truth? About what?"

Asher locked eyes with James, sickened by it. "He wanted the power."

Asher looked at Jesse and explained it. Wanting to know if the truth was there with him too. "Growing up dad told him I was different. That Joseph Whitby was a vampire with enormous powers. And that Joseph had given them to me. James wanted those powers for himself."

Jesse felt like the bottom dropped out from under him. Everything made sense now. That was why James had married Luna. That was why James hated her so much. Because she couldn't love him and because she wouldn't tell him the truth.

Jesse stepped back not wanting to look at either brother.

Asher looked at James, finally seeing the truth in his eyes. James had so much hatred in his heart. But it was the jealousy for Luna that was eating at him that was so clear. Asher wondered now if what he had seen in his father's eyes all his life had been the same thing.

"Joseph had saved me during a crash father had gotten mom and me into."

Asher looked away from them, ashamed of the truth. "I was a twin also. My brother and I were in the car together when it crashed. Joseph was there when it happened. He saved mom, then dad, and came back for us.

"He chose me because he knew there was good in me when he realized my brother couldn't be saved. But father had wanted him to save my brother instead. The oldest." Asher turned his head away knowing the ugly truth.

There was no good in Axel. Axel was the one who had taken Emie from him. Axel was the evil that was destroying this world.

Asher didn't reveal that truth though. He didn't want James to know.

"Joseph could have saved us both and dad knew this. Dad had wanted Axel over me.

"He believed for years after that Joseph had somehow deceived him and given me that same power Joseph had. All the years I excelled above everyone else, dad believed that I too was some sort of monster. That he had lost the wrong son.

"He hadn't lost the wrong son. He was just too busy watching Joseph and judging him with a jealousy that was blinding him from the real me."

Asher looked back at James then. "You've been watching also. Wanting what dad so wrongfully had judged me for.

"I didn't have any special powers James. Joseph did nothing to me that night except save my life and our parents. I am who I am, and I was who I was. Me."

Asher looked at Jesse, getting his attention. Making it clear to him why James had been with Luna. "He watched Luna and craved her powers, thinking she could make him better than me. He wanted it for himself. And when she wouldn't reveal the truth to him, when she couldn't love him because of the monster he was; he turned his jealousy towards you and blamed you for it."

Jesse looked at James. He suddenly needed out of the cell. He was going to be sick.

"You don't know a damn thing, Asher!" James bellowed aloud disgustedly.

Asher laughed at that. "Admit it James." He accused him. "You hated her, you wanted her only because you wanted to use her. When you thought she was deliberately deceiving you, instead of seeing the hurt you had caused her, you pushed her aside, leaving her alone, without anything. All because you wanted what she had."

Asher looked into James's soul daringly, eyeing him closely by the bars he was standing next to. "And why is that James? What on earth do want with this power?"

Asher could feel Emie's presence. He could feel her calming him. Somehow, he didn't know how or could explain it even, but he could feel her seeping into his soul trying to save the man she loved. It calmed his raging storm.

Asher straightened his neck, declaring himself the leader he was always meant to be. The one Emie promised him he was. "I am going to save our family and our friends. I am going to bring them here and protect them with the help of the Whitby's who have sworn their lives trying to save them with me. You can either join us, or you can rot in here for the rest of your God forsaken life!"

Asher was shaking. He steadied himself in front of James. "Either way, I am going to restore this family, this city, with or without you."

Jesse stood up taller, proud of his brother Asher. He knew Asher could stop him. One second he was standing next to James in the cell, the next he was outside the cell, standing next to his older brother Curtis who was holding him steady.

Jesse forgot how to breathe. Curtis was alive, looking at him with a grin on his face only Curtis could master. All of Jesse's composure fell to the dungeon floor below him.

"Curtis." He whispered in a breath he couldn't contain any longer.

Curtis bumped his brother Jesse on the shoulder letting him stand there on his own. "Yeah, I'm one of them too." He told him flashing his fangs for everyone to see.

"But how-". Jesse looked around then trying to understand how he had gotten out of the cell.

Curtis looked at his brother James. James was standing there holding onto the bars of the cell not believing what he was seeing. Curtis had never been more ashamed of James than he was now.

Curtis looked back at Jesse. He held out his fist for Jesse to bump. "Join us?" He asked in a honest, simple question.

Jesse looked at Curtis' fist. He had missed this. Missed his brothers camaraderie. He bumped his brothers fist and looked to Asher who was awaiting his answer. "I never-" he didn't know how to say he didn't want what James had wanted. The thought had never even crossed his mind. "I'm in." And he hoped that would say enough.

Asher watched as Curtis and Jesse walked out of the dungeon together. He looked at James who was watching also, still holding unto the bars that caged him, angry, hatred dripping from his lips. "One day, you will see. One day you will understand. And it will be your choice whether I save you or destroy you."

James waited until his brothers had left him behind. He whispered aloud to the darkness he was now surrounded in. "Never."

Townsend, Tennessee

Luna opened her eyes. She couldn't figure out what had jolted her back to life.

Her mouth still held the steel mesh that was blinding her from her abilities. She found the will to reach through the blindness and look around her.

Cold, dark, rock walls lined the hall she was being drug through. Ancient writings she couldn't read were strewn across the caves like graffiti. Voices were chanting an unholy song that filled her soul with fear.

Luna felt the drug high that stilled her as she swallowed her venom mixed with blood and a substance she couldn't describe that burned her throat from the steel wedged inside her cheeks. She lost feeling again in her weakened state.

Crying out inside of her mind she longed for Jesse's presence. She needed his arms, his strength. She needed to feel his energy.

Luna took a breath and created a shield around her soul. It was the protection she could wield with her powers. She had to protect herself against the evil that was being created. She had to find some way-

Powerless she felt when her energy left her with the slamming of the steel cage doors that would now be her hell.

Luna peeked out her eyelids she was trying to keep closed in her fear that was making her tremble. There were demons surrounding her. They were tearing at her making her scream with an empty voice she didn't have any longer. Ripping her body with their claws, leaving their mark upon her.

Jeremy and Jordy's visions were coming true.

~ *Ten* ~

Be still, find peace

Jesse found himself standing in the spotlessly clean kitchen where just last night he had seen the most horrific sight. And he'd seen a lot in his life.

Now the kitchen looked like he had just imagined the whole thing.

He watched as his brothers, Curtis and Asher stood amongst the Whitby men, cracking jokes and making plans. They were going to move everyone down at the fire department with the fire trucks and bring them here to the Whitby mansion.

"What do you think Jesse? Think it will work?"

Jesse looked at Asher who questioned him standing next to him now. He nodded at Asher and sighed deeply as he put his hands in his pockets. "It's a good plan. I think it will work just fine."

Asher looked at his brother worried. "But?" He knew there was a 'but' inside of Jesse. There was always a 'but'. It was a Stone trait.

Jesse looked around at the family. They were about to bring everyone Jesse cared about back here. But there was one person who wasn't here.

Why wasn't she here with them? He wondered to himself. Where was she?

Jesse looked at Asher directly. "Luna's been gone a long time Asher. She promised she wouldn't, but she never came back."

Asher sighed heavily. Jesse always worried about Luna. He motioned over to Jeremy. Jeremy would know where she was.

Jeremy walked away from Juliet. Jesse hadn't had a chance to meet her and apologize to her. He made a mental note to make sure he did that soon. He read Asher's mind and caught himself up on the conversation they were having.

Jeremy remembered Luna's righteous anger that had scared every one of them down in the dungeon the day he turned Asher. Jesse now knew exactly what had happened that day Asher had died. What had happened to Emie, so he understood why Jeremy had done it.

He told Jesse now how Luna and Joseph had left with Curtis, Shelley, and Cristina to go in search of Luna's mother, hoping they would find Emie.

Jesse listened, but he was waiting for the answers to his question as he looked around the room. Why wasn't she here with them now then?

Everyone in the room was silent. They had read Jesse's mind.

Jesse looked at Jeremy when he stopped talking to him. He tipped his head to the side and almost lost it right there in front of them all. Something had happened to her. He could feel it now. He hadn't heard her or felt her in a long time.

Jesse lost feeling in his entire body.

Joseph stepped closer to Jesse then. He got his attention with his gaze. "Let me show you." He looked at Asher then for permission.

Asher gave it to him. It was time Jesse learned everything.

Jesse looked at the hand Joseph extended to him. He had to know where Luna was. If he was going to do this, join them, this had to be done. He could see it in the way Joseph was looking at him.

Jesse extended his hand to Joseph in a gentleman's handshake and took it. But when Joseph took his hand, Jesse wished he could take it back.

Everything went black in Jesse's mind. He was no longer standing in the kitchen of the Whitby mansion. He was standing on the precipice of time and space.

Joseph watched in his own mind what was happening. He was no longer in control. He let go of Jesse's hand in awe. Jesse's soul was no longer in his body.

Jesse went down to the floor on his knees where he was now. He could hear Curtis and Asher pleading with Joseph for an answer to what was happening, from somewhere Jesse couldn't explain he wasn't anymore. He was thankful when Joseph told them to leave him alone. Jesse knew this moment in time was the most important moment of his life and he welcomed it.

God was there before him in his souls midst.

Jesse's life played out before him like a movie on a screen. He had believed in God his entire life. He wasn't a saint. Jesse had sins, regrets, he had seen things he couldn't unsee. But he had believed. In the Father, the Son, and the Holy Spirit.

Jesse at a young age had been dragged to church with his mother sleepily on Sunday mornings just like his brothers and sisters. He'd forgone the youth ministry to sit with his mother.

Sitting in the adult church made him seem older. He didn't struggle with feeling childish. His mother had never let him feel like that. She had always accepted him at her side, glad that he was there.

Jesse had listened to the pastors messages. He'd learned the Bible stories and knew God's plan. Knew as long as he trusted God, begged honest forgiveness for his sins, accepted God's Son and what he had done on the cross for the sins of the world, that he was saved from the hell fires.

Jesse made the commitment to God One Sunday night on his knees. Jesse knew there was no sin that could separate him from God. No demon, no hell bent servant, and no wrong way could take that away from him. He had lived his life in this hope, walking by faith, and showing others the way when they needed it. Especially in his line of work. So many people Jesse had showed the way to. Some had taken his advice, others had turned away from it.

Jesse knelt before his God in His presence at the end. He bowed low not even looking at his feet.

"My son." God reached for the man he had created and comforted him.

Jesse couldn't believe that God's voice didn't sound like thunder, rather it was a calm, gentle manner in which He spoke. Jesse waited patiently for whatever God wanted. He would do anything for Him.

"But?" God already knew the answer to His question. He asked Jesse anyways to prove a point.

Jesse almost laughed out loud at God's jest. "Please forgive my-" Jesse reached for the right words, but couldn't find them.

"Stubbornness?" God gave him.

Jesse laid his forehead on the darkness floor. He felt the shame God wanted him to feel. He had been stubborn for years. Wanting something he couldn't have. "You know me Lord. No one knows me like you do."

Jesse wanted to ball his fist together though.

"But you love her."

Jesse heard God sigh when He said it. He waited for God's condemnation. He knew if it came to his own salvation though he wouldn't know how to let go of Luna. "I love her Lord."

"Jesse, my son, I have never wanted you to let her go. What I have brought together, no one can separate."

Jesse almost rose up to look at God. That was the last thing he expected to hear. He wasn't married to Luna, James had been.

"I never wanted Luna and James to marry. When two people come together before me, in true sincerity, and ask to be blessed by me in holy matrimony, I give it to them.

"But..."

Jesse knew what God's 'but' meant. Luna and James didn't do that. They both married under the wrong pretenses. Making false promises to God neither one wanted to make.

Jesse could feel God's smile when Jesse understood the truth.

"What would you have me do now Lord?"

In a moment, God revealed everything to Jesse. The beginning, the middle, the present, but not the end.

He showed Jesse who the Whitby's were, who his brothers were now, how they were His created, chosen angels, doing His will. He showed Jesse what His plan was for them, how He was going to use them to save everyone.

He showed Jesse who Luna was. How His creation of her astounded even Him. He showed him what all had wrongly happened to her in her life. He showed Jesse what had happened to her while she had been away all this time and how Joseph was using her now to find Emie.

God wasn't finished. He wasn't showing Jesse what he wanted to know though.

Jesse wanted to know so bad he interrupted God.

"Where is she now? Is she ok? Make me like them Lord, so I can go save her." Jesse begged God's forgiveness on his humble, reverent, bended knees and balled up fists as he pleaded for the answers. Surly that was why God had brought him here. Right?

Jesse felt the moment God knelt next to him. He trembled at the breath of God upon him when He whispered to him.

"Be still, my son, and know that I am God. I love her more."

Jesse was very still and waited for more answers. When nothing came, he looked up and found himself in the Whitby kitchen surrounded by his brothers again.

Joseph was leaning against the counter in front of Jesse when he came too. He watched as Curtis and Asher stood him on his feet. Joseph was always impressed with how God did that. He never knew when it would happen, but it always happened when God wanted it too.

Jesse looked at Joseph when he spoke.

"Did you get your answers?"

Jesse shook off his brothers who were steadying him. He was stronger somehow now that God had touched him. He lunged at Joseph, throwing his fist at him and had to be caught by Asher and Curtis both. He hoped they were strong enough now to hold him back.

"How dare you!" Jesse yelled at him accusing him.

Asher was just as stunned as everyone in the room. Joseph had a lot to be sorry for, but he couldn't figure out how Jesse thought he could take him on as a human.

"Jesse!" Asher tried to correct him and struggled to hold him. Jesse was all righteous anger now. "Stop this man, you're going to get yourself killed."

"No." Joseph said looking in their direction, never letting his gaze fall from Jesse's eyes. "Not yet." Joseph knew when that would be. It was in Jesse's light now.

Asher looked at both men confused. "Jesse, what is it?" He let him go then, trusting Joseph, but he kept his hand on Jesse's chest.

"He let them take her! He is using her to find Emie!" Jesse told Asher looking at him for help.

Joseph was not surprised by this Stone brother. Jesse needed to learn restraint like his siblings. Joseph was willing to show it to him, but he had to let Asher do it.

Joseph understood now why God had chosen to leave him out of the conversation. He needed Joseph out of the way so He could explain it to Jesse without clouding his meaning. Jesse had misunderstood that part.

Joseph had cowardly let it happen, yes, to Luna, hoping her captors would lead them to Emie, but then Jeremy was taken by James and he had to give up the search for her.

Joseph asked God's forgiveness. He probably should have sought out His will first. Joseph forgot to do that a lot lately.

Asher turned towards Joseph, stunned at what Jesse had said. "You what?"

Joseph told everyone in the room what had happened the night Luna had been kidnapped. He watched as Jesse tried to fight his way towards him again and how Asher and Curtis had a hard time holding onto him.

Truly impressed now, Joseph knew Jesse was going to be something powerful when he changed him.

"The night it happened, she was keeping watch out the windows." Joseph shook his head knowing she had been right. He should have done things her way. "She was protecting us. But she got caught up in a moment, took the moment to herself, got lost in her own head."

Joseph looked at Jesse then.

Asher let go of Jesse when Joseph let everyone see in their minds what she had been doing. She had been with Jesse in his mind and had let her guard down.

Jesse shook off Curtis then. He bowed his head defeated. That was the night Luna had come to him in his dreams. They were sharing a memory together. When it had stopped suddenly, Jesse had just thought she had ended it, not understanding why.

He wanted to kill Joseph for this. "You should have saved her." He looked at Joseph then. "You were supposed to be protecting her!"

Asher and Curtis grabbed their brother again and stopped him when he lunged at Joseph.

Asher looked at Joseph and made him continue. "Where is she?"

"When they took her, we followed them. For whatever reason, they didn't want us. Just her."

Jeremy spoke up. "You know why they wanted her! You know what she is. How could you let them take her Joseph? What's wrong with you! Do you know what they are going to do to her?"

Joseph looked at Jeremy angry at his words. He looked at Jesse who was looking at them both in disbelief.

Joseph continued. His reasons on the tip of his tongue. "We gave chase and followed them through the mountains. We made it to the cave entrance and were about to go in, when you're brother" He pointed at Jesse then. "took my brother and tried to kill him!" Joseph said, with renewed anger and audacity towards Jesse. "I won't apologize for this."

Jeremy spoke up then, silencing everyone, even Jesse. "Nah, but he will never forget what you did to her. You used her man. And for that you owe him more than an apology."

Jesse looked heavenward and asked God again what he was supposed to do. He wanted vengeance he couldn't have.

He listened to the words God had spoken to him before.

Be still.

Asher was standing outside the fire department. He had been longing for this moment when he could be reunited with his family. He only hoped they would accept him now.

"At least you changed your shirt." Jeremy jested at him bumping his shoulder as he walked past him into the meeting room.

Asher looked down at his shirt. He had changed, into the exact same shirt, like he always did. He had hundreds of them at home. But at least this one was clean. He'd even showered.

Jesse looked to his brother as they walked into the meeting room of the fire hall using Jeremy's abilities to walk through walls. No one knew they were here yet.

"How do you want to do this Asher?" Jesse asked defeated still over losing Luna. Luna still wasn't present in his mind. She was lost to him. He almost didn't know how to function now.

Asher thought he had planned this out so perfectly. But he had forgotten to figure out how to open that door to the pits and not get shot.

"I need you to go down there first."

Well, that was a given, Jesse thought to himself. "But they're going to want to know where James is."

Jesse hadn't spoken to any of them in a few days. This was going to be hard to get Asher to understand now. He didn't know the depths of James' deception yet. Jesse had taken to himself and just wanted to be alone for months now. He'd be lucky if anyone believed him. He had no idea how Asher planned to do this. And right now, Asher seemed just as unsure as Jesse felt.

"I need you to go to Ken first. Tell him I sent you. He will follow you and defend you. Miranda and the girls will too. Then go to mom."

"But what do I tell them Asher?"

Asher hated this about Jesse. Jesse's mind worked just like his. He had to know every detail. He was right though. Asher turned to Jeremy for help.

Jeremy read their future. "Asher's right. They will listen to you."

Jesse sighed exasperated. They weren't understanding. He closed his eyes and tried to get them to hear him. "Asher, you're the talker in the family. Not me. No one down there wants to listen to me. What do I tell them?" Jesse hated that he had to admit that.

Asher thought about that. It was true. Jesse had separated himself from the family because no one believed him when it came to Luna. No one had helped him. All this time he thought Jesse had just been sulking, but inside the guy was dying. He knew her secrets and could tell no one. He had fought their father and James a hell of lot more than he had. Now, the poor guy didn't know his own place in the world anymore. He had also lived in this unknown world longer than Asher had. Asher couldn't imagine loving Emie for that long and not be able to be with her like Jesse had with Luna.

Jesse needed his help now. Not just to walk down there, but to be strong in the face of their family and win them over. It was his turn to shine, and the oaf didn't even know it yet. Asher smiled at his little brother. "You don't have to say anything Jesse.

"Sometimes the act of saving people isn't enough. You have to show them compassion in the face of their worst fears. That's what real heroes do.

"Right now, everyone down there has been sitting in fear for months. They don't have the same information you've had. They don't know what's out here. Or what to expect if they leave the safety of the sanctuary we built for them.

"You have to go down there, humble, ready to save them, believing in yourself.

"When you get down there, look at mom. You'll know what to do if you just look at her."

Jeremy looked at the brothers. He chuckled to himself. Asher didn't know what it was like to be the outcast brother in the family. "Just tell them the place is on fire, Jesse. They will all run up here real quick."

Jesse laughed at that. He had no intention of doing it, but it helped him relax and made him go. He walked into the truck bay where the engines were. The sights and smells that always took him off guard and brought his senses alive overtook him. This was his home. This is where he had spent his entire life. Down here with his family. Whether it was fighting fires, waiting for them to come home safe from one, or just here gathered together being family. His family was waiting down there for him. For answers. For the truth.

Jesse knelt down next to the door that was hidden in the floor. Under the coat rack of the fire men's bunker gear. He knocked three times like James had instructed everyone who left to do. He moved the coat rack and waited for someone to open the door. At the bottom of the steps he was greeted by Jerry who started searching him like a criminal. And with that Jesse knew no one trusted him still. He took a deep steady breath when Jerry backed off him.

"Where is James?" Jerry questioned him when he was done.

Jesse looked to Ken. He still had no idea what to say to everyone. Everyone was looking at him now for answers he didn't have.

Ken walked up to him. "Jerry give him some space."

Ken grabbed Jesse by the arm. When Jerry tried to press issue, Ken gave him a look. "Not your man." Which told Jerry what he needed to know.

There was separation in the departments that Jesse was in the middle of. Sometimes he was a cop, sometimes he was a firefighter. Right now, Jesse was a firefighter, and Ken knew it.

Jerry backed off.

Ken pulled Jesse aside. "What's wrong man."

Jesse looked around making sure everyone was ok. He looked at Ken, worried he wouldn't get this right. "I found him. Well, he found us."

Ken took a deep breath in. This could be a good thing or a bad thing.

He turned his body so no one could see him mouth the word 'Asher' to Jesse.

Jesse nodded his head at Ken.

"Oh thank God." Ken exclaimed. He sighed out the breath he had been holding and turned to Miranda who was now beside him. He whispered in her ear what was going on.

Miranda covered her lips and looked at Jesse. "Luna?" She whispered to Jesse gently.

Jesse knew they had been friends and she had been worried about Luna. She had always wanted and encouraged Jesse to go after Luna all these years. She knew they belonged together.

Jesse lowered his head and looked away from Miranda. He didn't know how to tell her what had happened. "Not yet." He told her.

Jesse looked for his mom. Sure enough, just like Asher said, just seeing her, he knew what needed to be said. He looked back at Ken. "Will you go up there with Miranda? He's waiting for you."

Ken nodded his head at Jesse in agreement.

Jesse grabbed his arm and got his attention before he left. "Ken, he's worried everyone is going to hate the way he looks." Jesse smiled then jokingly. "Make sure you tease him about it."

Ken winked back at him in jest. Miranda even grinned at him. They were both so excited they hurried up the stairs.

As Jesse made his way to his mother, Jerry wanted to know where Ken was going. No one was supposed to leave without weapons.

Jesse excused himself and told Jerry to go up and see without telling him anything else.

Cyndy looked at her son walking towards her. She was worried for James. "James?"

"James is ok mom. There is someone you need to meet upstairs though. He's gonna rescue us."

Cyndy looked at her son confused. When she saw the smile on his face, she looked over to where Ken had just went. Ken would only have left like that for his... best friend, she told herself.

"Asher?" She cried aloud, looking at Jesse in disbelief.

Cyndy was his mother, and when his mother cried, God help him, he didn't know how to be brave. All he knew was he was going to be giving her back the one- well, three things, counting Curtis and Izzy, that she wanted most of all.

Jesse couldn't help the tears he had to wipe from his cheeks. He nodded towards the stairs and encouraged her to go. He stood taller when she ran away from him. He stuffed his hands in his pockets and watched as everyone else wanted to know what was going on. He motioned for them all to go and see.

When Jerry stood next him, he took up the same stance next to Jesse. "What's up there?"

Jesse grinned, not wanting to give the surprise away.

"I don't know how you do it man."

Jesse turned his head and looked at Jerry. "Do what?"

"You have a charisma about you man. Even when no one understands you, they all fall for that charming smile of yours."

Jesse watched as everyone headed out of the pits. For some it was the first time they had dared leave. "It's a Stone thing. You wouldn't understand."

Jesse walked away from him. He and Jerry would have words one day about all that had happened, for now, he hoped the put down was enough to punish him.

Jesse was standing in the meeting room again. He watched as everyone was huddled around Asher. He was explaining everything to them. What he was now, who the Whitby's were, and what had happened to Emie. Joseph was there helping him.

Their mother had her arms wrapped around Curtis and wouldn't let go of him. Curtis was returning the embrace. It was a happy reunion for all of them.

Just in time for Christmas, Jesse reminded himself.

Just give me a sign Lord, he prayed. Wishing he knew what to do about Luna.

Jesse looked towards the shadow he saw out of the corner of his eye by the door to the Chief's room. Asher's room. He noticed the small little head of Katie peeking out from behind the door. What was she doing, he wondered curiously.

Jesse walked over to her, hushing her as he approached her. She disappeared back in the darkness of the room, so he knelt down next to the door and called out to her.

"Katie Bear." He called to her gently.

Little Katie Kruse, like her father, was braver than she thought. But something was scaring her now and that was odd. When she didn't come out at first, Jesse looked around the meeting room wondering what it was she was afraid of. He caught sight of Asher who was looking at him. When Asher started to walk towards him worried, Jesse knew what she was afraid of and held up his hand staying Asher.

Jesse looked in the room from his knees. He tried to think of what to say to bring her out here. Asher was like her uncle. She had loved Asher like no one else.

Asher must look like the monster everyone had said he was to her, Jesse wondered. "Katie, where is Kitty?" He asked, wanting to make sure she had her comfort bear, knowing she would come out to talk about kitty.

Katie stood up in the darkness from under the desk, holding tightly to her kitty, playing with her long tail. She gulped loudly. "She's right here."

Jesse tried not to let his emotions get the better of him. He had to wipe his grin off his face as she walked up to him. He knew this was the only thing that would work. Sometimes little Katie could be so sweet.

"Who got that Kitty for you?"

Afraid, she told him honestly, "I don't know."

Jesse leaned his head to the side, trying to earn her trust. "It was Asher."

Katie's eyes got real big and then she put her face on her Kitty's head. "That is not my Uncle Asher out there." She told him in a still, small voice.

Jesse had to give her that. Asher didn't look like Asher anymore.

"I bet Kitty would know if it was Asher." He told her, whispering, like it was a secret only they could figure out.

Katie perked up. She peeked out and looked out the door. She looked back at Jesse and whispered back to him, holding her little hand over her lips so only he could hear. "She would!"

Jesse smiled at her. He envied her innocence.

Katie looked at him in confidence. "Will you take her to him so we can find out?"

Jesse reached for the Kitty when she handed it to him. He put his finger up to his lips secretly and they shared a knowing glance. He stood up and was about to turn around when she grabbed his pant leg and pulled him back.

Jesse looked down at her in question.

"What if it's not him?" She was wringing her hands now worried.

Jesse looked at his brother Asher. He knew the truth, but he had to prove this to her in a way she would understand. He turned back to her and told her secretly, "Well,". He even kneeled back down so she could hear him. "I'll let Kitty tear his eyes out so I can save you."

Katie looked at him covering up a laugh.

Jesse winked at her and stood back up. He looked at Asher who was watching him walk over to him. He watched as Asher never took his eyes off Kitty. Asher knew what he was doing.

Jesse reached Asher and gently handed him Kitty. He watched as Asher looked at her. Took her just as gently. It was honestly one of the harder things in life to do. To pretend with a child, to earn their trust. To never break that trust once it was given. Never hurt them.

Asher looked at the doorway where little Katie Bear stood shaking, worried about her Kitty. It shook Asher to his core that she was afraid of him. He hated it. He needed her to trust him so he could protect her.

Asher knew the dangers and the evil that was out there, that could harm her. He swore to never let anything hurt her. Katie was like a daughter to him. He remembered the day Miranda and Ken had her and placed her in his arms. He held that little girl and promised her the world.

Asher spent money he didn't have on that little girl. Her Kitty was a gift from him he had bought for her when she was a year old because Ken had insisted she not have a pacifier any longer. Asher had wanted her to have something of comfort. Never guessing Katie would carry that Kitty with her everywhere.

Asher felt like everyone in the room had stopped talking. Like all eyes were on him now. They knew the relationship he had with Ken and his family. They all knew who that Kitty was. They had all been there on her first birthday when Asher had given it her.

Asher looked at Kitty and stepped closer towards the room where Katie was, but not too close. "Hey Kitty." He grinned at Katie's bear, pretending he was talking to her. The kind of grin he always gave to Katie, knowing she was watching him. She was waiting to learn the truth about him.

He knelt down and paused. Praying, hoping any second now his little Katie would come running out of the dark where she was hiding. This had been the longest time he had ever been away from her. Damn, he thought to himself as he looked at Kitty. He loved that little girl so much.

"Have you seen my little Katie Bear?"

Even the vampire he was, he struggled with the words. He couldn't cry now!

"I can't find her anywhere. And she promised me she would wait for me-"

Asher felt the moment Katie gasped. He looked to the door and when he saw her come running out of his room headed right for him, he almost dropped Kitty in his haste to catch her. She wrapped her little arms around his big arms and held him tighter than he deserved.

"Oh, Uncle Asher!" She cried shakily.

Asher had to bite his lips to stop the blood tears he couldn't let her see. Just the sound of her voice brought a joy to him he hadn't felt since he had died.

"Oh, my Katie Bear." He whispered to her resting his head on hers. He vowed, and he prayed. He knelt there with her in his arms and begged God to restore everything to him. And to never let any harm come to his little Katie.

Jesse looked around the room. He could see the reaction everyone had to the moment with Katie. She had sealed their fate for all of them. Seeing Asher hold her the way he was erased all their doubts and fears that James had instilled in them.

Asher wasn't a monster, Jesse thought to himself. Jesse nodded at heaven then. Everything happens for a reason, Ken had told him. He promised to be still now. He would wait and know who was God.

~ *Eleven* ~

Be still, rest

Months later.

    Jesse woke from dreams he had been chasing, trying to hold onto. He opened his eyes and forgot where he was for a moment.

    After the Whitby mansion had been taken over and destroyed, by demons and rogue vampires, Asher had set the place ablaze. With the help of the Whitby's, Asher had rebuilt the fire department and turned it into a house for everyone. Apartments now lined the outer walls that were now lined in steel casings. They were currently working on plans to rebuild the city. But first, Asher had to find Emie.

    Everything was almost perfect for Jesse.

    Jesse tried not to remember the things that had happened. In the destruction of the Whitby mansion, they had lost more members of his family and friends. James had disappeared. He was lost to them now.

    Jesse rolled over in his bed and pulled the pillows tighter to him trying to return to his dreams. Luna's voice was calling to him.

    "Jesse."

    Jesse squeezed his eyes tighter at the heavenly sound of Luna's voice. He had been hearing her voice all night in his dreams. He rolled over and let go of the pillow in his arms. They weren't pillows anymore. He opened his eyes and looked into the face of his angel. Luna was there in the bed with him. She was finally here with him again. Luna brushed his hair gently and smiled for him.

    Jesse blinked at least a hundred times trying to adjust his sleepy eye sight. "Are you really here?" He beckoned her, touching her face everywhere. It had been so long since she had done this. He had worried she had been lost to him forever because of it.

    "Not really." Luna whispered to him in the night.

    Jesse raised up on his arm next to her looking around his bedroom. "I feel like I'm awake." It felt different somehow. This definitely wasn't a memory.

    Luna touched his cheek and let her hand linger there when he looked back down at her. Jesse closed his eyes at her touch. It felt different too. More real than ever before.

    Jesse had been longing for this moment. The moment he would have her in front of him again to tell her everything he never got the chance to tell her. He reached forward and touched her face like she was doing to him. He could feel her on his hand like the times before, he could see her now in the darkness. She felt so damn real. "Is this real, or am I just imagining this?"

Luna rose up and laid him down while she laid beside him on the bed and looked down at him. "You are here." She looked down at his shirt and looked away from his eyes. "I am not here with you though, but I am." Then she looked back up into his eyes hauntingly.

Jesse didn't understand. Her words felt like a dream. He ran his hands up in her hair along her cheeks. He could care less about what she said, he told himself. He watched as she closed her eyes and leaned into his touch.

"Where are you Luna? Tell me so I can save you."

Luna opened her eyes and looked at Jesse. She touched his hands with hers and cupped it closer to her cheek. "I am where Jeremy said I would find my mother. Do you remember? In the caverns of the smoky mountains. Jesse," She pleaded with him, moving her body closer to his under the covers. "Baby, you can't come here. You can't save me."

Jesse rolled her over gently so he could be on top of her. She hadn't called him baby in forever. He interrupted her words with his kiss that he let linger. He stopped quickly, short of breath and placed his forehead on hers. He had to tell her. He had to make sure she knew he was coming for her.

"Listen to me Luna. I am going to move hell to save you. Nothing can stop me-"

"Shhh." Luna hushed him sweetly with her lips.

"I'll bring Jeremy-" he interrupted her.

"Jeremy can't-"

"He can pass through walls, damn it!" Jesse tried to explain. More to himself than to her. "I know he can pass through the mountains with his abilities. He can find you." Jesse said as he stared her down.

Luna started playing with his shirt. Teasingly lifting it up. Jesse ripped it off for her, he needed her to listen to him. The moment she touched his chest he became hard as a rock pressed up against her side. She started tracing the outlines on his shoulder of his tattoo.

"Neither Jeremy, nor Jordy could survive these demons in these caves with me."

Jesse moved the covers down her body and almost closed his eyes at the sight of bare body for his eyes to gaze upon. "I'll bring Joseph and Cristina. She can shift into bat and find you in the caves. Joseph, he's strong enough-"

Her fingers were drawing a path down his middle teasing him. He couldn't think anymore. Luna waited for him to drag his eyes off her body and look back up at her before she spoke again. "Not even them."

"Asher then?" He questioned more loudly. "Asher, everything he touches turns to fire. And Curtis-"

Luna kissed Jesse making him forget about all the reasons he couldn't save her. She took over his mind and controlled him, stirring his passion for her. They would all die trying to save her. He had to understand.

Jesse ripped off his pants she was fumbling with. He knew what she was doing. He wanted it, but he didn't. But he was helpless to her touch. He reached for her face when he was ready and kissed her like his life depended on it. He deepened their kiss and clung to her lips. Promising her he was going to come and save her.

Jesse rose up on top of her, let her wrap her body around his as he held her body, pulling her up into him. He drove himself deep inside of her and reveled in the way she accepted him.

He wondered if this would be the way she felt in reality. When she assured him it was, he didn't stop making love to her. He lifted her off the bed on his knees and placed her down on his lap, driving into her deeper and deeper still, clinging to her body. The way she moaned and cried out to him as he barreled inside of her drove him higher.

"Don't let me wake up Luna." he begged her kissing her bare neck.

Luna called out his name like she was howling at the moon for her soul mate. She beckoned his heart to love her forever.

"Please Baby, don't stop."

Jesse could only fall backwards down on the bed and let her take over. He was lost in the spell she was holding over him. She had her hands on his chest, her head was thrown back. He drove himself mad, deep inside of her body. Feeling her sway and rock, he watched the way her body looked lifting off his, he could only hold onto her hips and beg her for more.

He drank in the picture of her, the way she took from him all the pleasure she had sought from him for so long. She was falling and lost in the paradise of his body. As much as he wanted to take over, he couldn't stop her ecstasy in those moments. So he held her through it.

Reaching up her body he pulled himself up and held her in his arms, letting her have her way with him. Finally, he couldn't hold back any longer. He picked her up and laid her down. When she wrapped around him again he felt the moment he couldn't stop. He gave into her and let her milk him. He let go and held her in his hands, lost in a sea of her enchanted pleasure.

Jesse woke up in his bed again. Alone. He almost tore apart the pillows he had been holding onto looking for her. The dream felt so real last night. She had felt so real. He couldn't tell what time it was, he didn't have windows in here to keep out the dead. He sighed, knowing he needed to get up and go check on things. Asher was gone now in New York, trying to find Emie based on a lead he had come up with Darryl.

Jesse rolled out of bed and stretched his body. He almost laughed at the fact that he was naked. He never slept naked and he hadn't went to bed naked. He turned and looked into the covers and found his clothes there.

Well, it was either a really good dream or she had really been there last night he told himself as he found his night cum there on the sheets and knew it had just been a wet dream. But the power emanating from her she had used on him he had shared with her had been enough to state them both.

Jesse got dressed and walked through the new halls of the upstairs apartments in the fire house. He made his way over to the stairs that would take him down to the meeting room.

Jesse stopped when he heard screams coming from the roof down the hall. Talia, Darryl's guardian angel who was living with them now, was on the roof. Screaming.

Jesse broke out in a run faster than his legs had ever run before. He could hear demons screeching and Talia screaming. When he made it to the roof door he opened it slowly, guns drawn.

Damn it! He thought quickly, as he watched her try to fight them off. He started shooting at the flying demons around her, trying to pull her off the ledge. One got her and another one came flying full fledged towards him, screeching so loudly it hurt Jesse's ears. He missed his mark the first shot, then he amid for the demons head and shot both guns until he blew holes in the demon's head, not before it slashed at Jesse's neck.

Jesse tried to stand up, holding the wound on his neck and look out over the empty roof. Talia was gone.

He quickly turned once the demon was dead and tried to run back into the hallway, but he was bleeding heavily from the wound in his neck. It burned with a fire so badly he couldn't stand on his feet any longer.

Everything went black.

Luna was trying to wake up from a groggy sleep. Time slipped past her, softly, she couldn't fight it.

Finally, waves rushed over her. She fought them from carrying her away again into the heavy abyss of dreams. When she was able, she looked around the cave through sleepy eyes. The dripping damp, cold stone she was laying on wracked her body through with a chill that caused her to tremble.

Luna closed her eyes blocking out the reality of the unknown. She hated the cold. Her body would shiver to no end. She longed for the warmth she could only find in the arms of Jesse.

Jesse. Thoughts of his presence she had just shared with him, filled her with fear. Where was he? She had begged him not to come here in her dreams. Had he listened to her?

Luna rose up off the floor and looked around. She was in a cell of some type in a cave. The unknown of her whereabouts became real again. She could hear moans from others caged like her and felt their fear all around her. She stood then, holding her arms close to her body. She was dressed in only white linen. It felt like some kind of hospital gown. She looked to the left and right of her. It was dark in the caves, like night she could barely see through. She closed her eyes and tried to shake off the drug she could feel in her system. It felt like evil coursing through her veins.

There was a woman in the cage next to her. Luna tipped her head in wonder and edged closer. The woman was lying on the floor, her back turned towards Luna up against the bars of her cell. Her back was bleeding from wounds under her gown.

Luna knelt next to the bars. The woman's hair was short and golden blonde, with stripes of bright gold shining, that had been cut jagged and short at the ends.

Luna looked further in her cell. The woman wasn't human, Luna could feel it. She remembered what Jeremy had told her about the prisoners held here.

"Hey there." She called out to the woman who slowly turned her head over her shoulder.

"Luna?" She whispered softly, making eye contact with her void less eyes.

Luna's heart fell. It was Talia.

"Talia!" She exclaimed, reaching through the bars to touch her shoulder.

Talia slowly rested her head back on the floor.

"Oh, Talia, what have they done to you?"

Talia sighed in the darkness. She was broken. Her wings had been cut off at her back bones. Her hair had been stripped out its angelic glory. "You have been asleep for a long time Luna."

Luna swallowed the venom back she felt pooling in her mouth. She tried to control herself, but anger raged through her for her friend. She looked around her cell again. There was nothing she could do for Talia. They were both caged, like animals, powerless. She breathed in an unsteady, shaking breath.

"They captured me and took me away from home."

Luna looked back at her questioningly. "Who Talia?"

Talia pulled herself up. It hurt, but she had to see her friend. She had to tell her everything.

Luna watched in disbelief as her friend sat up, aching and turned towards her. Talia had stained tears on her cheeks from an unknown length of time weeping in sorrow.

Talia showed Luna home. What it looked like now. What all the guys had done to save the pier, and the people there they loved.

"Like I said, you've been asleep for a long time." Talia continued, letting Luna see her mind so she could understand. "I was struck down, fighting beside Darryl in this war. God revealed to him everything, He allowed us to be together for a time, so I could heal at home." Talia lowered her head remembering the time she had spent at home in Luna Pier. She had been reunited with her family there.

"Asher had taken Darryl and some of the others to save Emie."

Luna watched as Talia showed her the strength and power in Asher and Darryl now. Luna was glad for it, but she feared what would come next from Talia.

Talia cowered at the sound of another cell door opening. "He's coming." She whispered quickly, afraid. She started shaking uncontrollably.

Luna followed Talia's gaze, and felt her fear. "Who?"

"The one who took me. Hide Luna." She whispered to Luna, not taking her eyes off what she feared most.

Luna crept back to a corner at the sound of the monster coming towards them. She had never feared anything before, but Talia's fear crept into her, so Luna backed away.

His steps felt like thunder. He walked like a beast with a purpose. His head was like that of a bull, with sharp horns and his body standing up right was like a wolf. Powerful with might in his bones.

His face though…. Luna reached with her eyes to see through the dark as he came near. When she saw his face, she was taken back.

Luna covered her mouth in fear so she wouldn't make a sound. She bit her lips shut and squeezed her eyes closed.

It was James.

No. No! She begged. It couldn't be the man she feared it was. It couldn't be him.

Could it?

Luna opened her eyes again praying, looking for the beast. She saw him standing there before her door. The sneer on his face told him everything she needed to know.

Luna licked the fear from her lips and felt like she needed to crawl in a hole. It was James.

Luna looked around her again. There were so many cells around her, like cages. So many others were locked inside of them. Humans, vamps, wolves.

The more she looked at them all, the more she trembled in fear.

"What have you done James?" She looked at him then, the beast-monster that he had become.

James lowered his eyes. He wanted to grab the bars and pull them off the cell just to get to her. But he was forbidden to touch her. His masters wouldn't allow it.

"For years, I wanted your powers. I wanted your strength."

James spoke with an edge in his voice like a deep, hungry growl. It was different than anything Luna had ever heard before.

Luna could see it there in his mind. The evil that had always been, that she had denied in hopes of saving him.

"But you wouldn't love me!" He shouted at her. Spit drooling off his lips flew at her like he wanted it to. "You wouldn't look at me like you did Jesse. And for that, you will pay."

Luna stood then. She didn't understand why her strength or powers were weak, but she stood. She faced the evil James had in him.

"I would have saved you. I would have loved you!" She screamed at him. Just looking him in the eyes, the face she had come to love over the years, shared by the man who meant the world to her. "There was something inside of you though. Something so… dark and cold. James, what have you done?"

There was no saving him now, was there? She wondered softly.

James scoffed at her. "I am not the monster Luna. You are."

And with that, he walked away from her, dragging his claws across all the cells that line the walkway where she was. She heard, when he was out of sight, another cell door slamming open and the screams of another he was after.

Luna fell to her knees. She bowed her head, listening to the roar of his growl. She tried to block it out shoving her fingers in her ears.

It wasn't until the sounds stopped and the darkness filled the void of the silence that Luna felt safe enough to relax.

"Luna."

Luna looked back at Talia. Talia was pointing to the cell next to Luna.

Luna looked to where Talia was pointing. Her mother, Linda was kneeling there near the bars of her cell.

"Edoa Toi Waya." Her mother called to her.

Luna wept like a child and ran to her mother next to the bars. She reached through and placed her hand in her mothers.

"My child." Linda whispered.

"Mother." Luna wept.

Linda was smiling, but Luna couldn't see why. She was broken also. She was weak and tired.

"Why are you smiling mother?" How could she have found peace in this hell?

"Look around little Waya. Everything you have been searching for is right here."

Luna looked, but all she seen was death, or the coming of it. She looked back to her mother, bowing her head. "I don't understand."

"Luna, look again." Linda told her as she cradled her face in her hand.

Luna opened her eyes, and this time in her heart she could feel it. Everyone down here was her family. Ancient, generations of her tribe. And the tribes of her people. Luna had searched for them for years and they had been here all this time.

"God was showing you the way, and because you never stopped, he's brought you here to save us."

Luna shook her head. "How? I- can't mother." She felt weak. Like she had been stripped of everything.

"He will provide a way." Linda promised her.

Luna had never not believed in that, but she feared for everyone now.

"Remember the stories I told you when you were little, Waya? The stories of the sparrows."

Luna nodded her head at her mother. She remembered. Whenever Luna doubted or worried, her mother would take her to the woods. She would show her the birds and the flowers. It was the sparrows, in their flight, scattered and unsure where to go, that her mother would point out to Luna.

Linda quoted the old parables for Luna like she had when she was a child. "Therefore I tell you, do not be anxious about your life, what you will eat or what you will drink, nor about your body, what you will put on. Is not life more than food, and the body more than clothing?

"Look at the birds of the air: they neither sow nor reap nor gather into the barns, and yet your Father feeds them. Are you not of more value than they?

"Consider the lilies of the field, how they grow: they neither toil nor spin, yet I tell you, even Solomon in all his glory was not arrayed like one of these."

"He tells us to fear not child, for He loves us so much more than the sparrows or Lily's of the valleys."

Luna bowed her head with her mother. They prayed there in the silence. She didn't know how, or when, but she knew. God would save them. In this life or the next.

Days later...

Asher knew the moment he got back to the department he needed a smoke. He had been out on the beach with everyone trying to console Darryl. Now that he was back at the department he headed up to the roof so he could be alone with his pack of smokes.

Emie came with him. And that suited him just fine, he thought kissing her hand as they walked out onto the roof. He watched Emie bathed in the sunlight God now aloud them to be in. She was spinning around and dancing in it.

Asher wondered if it was possible to love someone more than he did Emie.

Darryl had lost Talia a few days ago. Asher didn't understand it all. He didn't understand why she had left while they were gone rescuing Emie.

They had won the fight. He and Darryl had killed both Victor and Axel. New York was now ashes under the fire he had lit on the city. But had it been because of Talia? He wondered. Had she been there, fighting with them?

Asher reached for his smokes and lit one with his finger, smiling over at Emie who was leaning over the ledge looking at the sunrise sparkling on the lake from up here. Just as he was about to sit down on the ledge next to her and let his body relax, he heard moans.

Asher turned his body and looked by the door that led back into the fire hall. He didn't see anything so he turned back around shaking off the feeling. He noticed Emie didn't see anything either.

"Asher." Jesse weakly gasped.

Asher turned then and threw his smoke away. That time, he had heard Jesse. He went looking for the sound of Jesse's voice he had just heard. It was faint, but Asher could feel Jesse's distress.

He called to his brother, desperate to find him when he didn't see him right away. "Damn it Jesse, where are you?"

Jesse crawled from behind the door and reached for Asher.

Asher went to his knees on the floor and pulled his little brother to him. Emie was right there next to him helping him.

Jesse's skin was hot and a dark, black ashen color. There was a wound on his neck he was holding. Jesse had wings stretched out behind him that looked like demon, rubbery bat wings, unlike Asher's own angelic feathered wings.

Asher moved Jesse's hand, prying it away from his wound. It was a deep, jagged cut. The meat hanging open looked black and diseased.

Emie gasped at the sight of it. "He's been poisoned Asher."

"Jesse, what happened?" He demanded of him.

Jesse tried to gulp down the pain so he could speak, but the poison inside of him was destroying him.

Emie touched Asher's hand that was holding his brothers. "Let's take him to Joseph. Joseph can help him Asher."

Asher picked up his broken brother and flew through the department with him down into the meeting room. Once there he laid him on one of the tables.

Joseph was already there waiting for him. Everyone else came running into the room, all talking at once wanting to know what had happened.

Asher looked at Joseph. "What happened? How long has he been up there?" He demanded of Joseph. "You were supposed to be protecting them, damn it!"

Asher felt like in that moment he had been gone longer than just a week.

Joseph touched the side of Jesse's shoulder. He reached inside his mind and begged Jesse's to remember the details of what had happened to him. He watched as Jesse replayed it all for him.

Emie was clinging to Asher's side. She was afraid to let go of him. She had seen the demons like what Jesse was becoming while she had been in New York. She never would have guessed that they had once been innocent humans turned into evil demons.

Joseph looked at Darryl, knowing what he had to reveal to everyone was going to be so hard. The war wasn't over yet. It was here. It had taken Talia and now Jesse.

"Asher." Joseph looked at him and begged his attention. Asher had been looking at his brother, holding his arm, trying to console him.

"You need to listen to me-"

"Tell me what happened Joseph!" Asher demanded. "I don't have the patience for you to beat around the bushes right now. I want the absolute truth and I want it now!"

"Talia didn't return to the realm like I thought." Joseph breathed in a deep breath. He hadn't known any of this. "Jesse was trying to save Talia two days ago up on the roof. She was being kidnapped by demons. He was cut by one of them. Like one of the ones from the mansion."

Joseph looked down at Jesse then, trying to understand it all. "He's been poisoned by it. It's turning him into one of them."

Asher looked down at Jesse. He was angry with Joseph now. "Can we save him?" Asher asked slowly across the table over his brothers body, looking at Joseph, growling heavily, yet he was demanding his answer of Joseph.

"There's only one way."

Asher looked at Jesse who was now in the fetal position clinging to life. He was facing Asher. Shaking and struggling to breathe.

"Just kill me. It hurts- so bad Asher!"

Asher looked at Joseph almost pleadingly. "He didn't want to become one of us."

Joseph couldn't believe Asher was thinking of killing his brother. "It's your decision Asher. But he's becoming one of them. It won't be long now. You would have to do this right now."

Jesse grabbed Asher's shirt. "I don't want this. Kill me!"

Emie touched Asher softly. "He means he doesn't want to be a demon. Not that he doesn't want to be one of us." She had to make sure Asher knew this.

"Are you sure?" He couldn't read Jesse's mind like they could.

"Yes. Are you sure he didn't want to be one of us?" She questioned him honestly, not understanding why he was waiting.

Asher looked to Curtis then.

"He said he was in Asher. He wanted to help us, join us. Do it. Don't kill him."

Asher knew how James had felt. Somehow Asher had just assumed Jesse didn't.

Asher looked at Jesse then. He needed a minute to think.

Jesse couldn't wait anymore. He couldn't take the pain. He pulled his gun out and aimed it at Cristina who was behind Asher. He knew someone would kill him if he did it, the poison reached his heart and he could feel it bubbling inside of it, pumping through it. He couldn't stop the bullet once it left his gun.

Cristina felt inside of her the moment the evil reached Jesse's heart. The evil wanted a sacrifice. It was taking over Jesse's soul. He was going to kill her.

Her eyes became large when see saw what Jesse was doing now. She screamed as she slowed time down, stepped in front of the bullet aimed at her and grabbed it.

They couldn't wait any longer, she ran up and made the choice for Asher. She attacked Jesse, biting into his wound pushing her venom inside of him to stop the poison. Like Joseph had done for her when she had been attacked.

Asher couldn't believe his own eyes. What was happening. It wasn't like Jesse to pull his gun, unless he was threatened. The seconds that passed as he watched his brother sacrificing himself made him pause in awe. Then Cristina attacked him and there was nothing more he could do.

Joseph looked at Asher. He touched Asher's arm and showed him the plan God was showing him. It was time.

Joseph spoke to everyone. "It has to be a lot of venom to over power the poisons that are in him. He needs all our venom, all our abilities to fight this. We all need to help him, or he will die." He reassured them.

Joseph lifted Jesse's arm, knowing what they were about to do to him was going to make him scream louder than he was now. He pierced Jesse's artery on his wrist with his fangs and let his venom seep into Jesse. He pushed his ability as far into Jesse as he could.

Jesse screamed so loud the humans in the room had to leave. He felt the piercing of his skin as Joseph sank his jagged fangs into his wrist. He felt his artery bust open bleeding. He felt the way Joseph sucked, pulling the poison out of him, and pushed his molten venom inside of him that burned worse than the poison.

Cristina was doing the same thing at his neck. Followed by Jeremy, Jordy, Curtis and Shelley. They bit into him, causing Jesse to struggle for his freedom. It was the first time they had all done something so unnaturally untamed, using their venom and their abilities together like this.

Izzy stepped forward to Jesse. Asher wondered why, but knew it was her brother she was trying to save. She looked back at Asher then.

"I was given the abilities of shielding and knowing." She turned back to her brother and placed a kiss gently on Jesse's forehead, knowing how he felt. He was withering, tossing in pain she couldn't bare to watch. She bit into the other side of his neck. It was the first time she had ever done it to someone.

Asher looked up to the ceiling away from it all. Emie reached for his hand drawing back his attention.

Emie gave him the will to see the truth. "He wants this. I promise."

Asher trusted her with his life. He watched as she let him go and walked over to Jesse. Her abilities he had learned about her were ones Jesse would need now. Jesse would be able to control the minds of the demons and make them not see him. He would be able to walk undetected anywhere he wanted with them, and make them all do his bidding.

Asher watched as Emie found Jesse's biracial artery in his upper arm, it was closest to his heart. She bit down and Asher knew she had sealed Jesse's fate.

Darryl walked over to Jesse. It was his turn now. Darryl had strength and combat abilities. A heightened sense of a hunter.

Asher had an ability unlike anyone else's. When Darryl lifted off Jesse's body wiping his mouth like everyone else, Jesse had went still staring off. It was working. Asher prayed his abilities would make Jesse strong enough to become what they needed now.

Asher walked closer to the table that his brother was laying on. Jesse looked up at him in return.

"It hurts so bad brother!" He hollered out loud.

Asher spoke to Jesse and apologized to him for not being here to protect him from what had happened to him, but also for so much more, as Jesse screamed and cried out in pain. Asher should have helped Jesse a long time ago.

When he bit into his brothers arm, he pushed everything God had given him into his venom. He prayed it worked for Jesse and that it wasn't too late.

Jesse needed this. He needed to become strong enough to defeat whatever else came their way.

All Jesse wanted in this life was to love Luna and be with her. Asher felt it now that he was connected to Jesse. Now Jesse could go find her, save her, like Asher had Emie.

Asher stepped back, wiped his brothers blood from his mouth. He went to Emie and picked her up in an embrace he wasn't about to let go of.

He buried his face in her hair. "I never wanted to do this to any of them Emie."

Emie hushed Asher holding the back of his head to her shoulder.

"Stay with him Asher. He is going to need you now." She told him sweetly.

Joseph looked at Asher when he let go of his sister. "He is going to be ok Asher. We will all help you train him when the time comes."

"Yes!" Jeremy and Jordy exclaimed as they shared a fist bump. They both liked Jesse. Now he was one of them.

Cristina took her leave and left the room followed by Joseph. Curtis put his arm around Shelley and they both left the room also, followed by everyone else.

Asher was alone with Jesse now. He dragged a chair over to the table and sat next to him holding his hand.

"Asher!" Jesse whispered aloud grinding his teeth against the pain. He didn't know if he could take the pain anymore. It was worse than before.

"I know little brother." Asher understood Jesse even though he couldn't read his mind.

Asher bowed his head praying the poison in Jesse's heart would be taken over by all their venom.

Jesse looked for Asher again through the pain, shaking their hands Asher was holding.

Asher tried to smile at him. Tried to reassure him. "You can do this Jesse. I've been where you are right now. It's hard, but you gotta fight."

Jesse closed his eyes. "When does it stop?" He asked through his gritted teeth, his whole body was shaking now.

Asher hated this part. "It doesn't."

Jesse turned his head quickly at Asher. He almost bound off the table to strangle him because of what he'd said, but Jesse knew it was just the poison making him feel like that.

Asher remembered what had gotten him through it. The only thing that had gotten him through it. He adjusted in the chair and he had turned it backwards sitting back in it and looked at Jesse in all seriousness. "Is she worth it man?"

Jesse took a deep breath his lungs he no longer needed. It burned so bad he vowed to never do it again. He was so mentally frustrated! He didn't want to be alive. He didn't want to fight.

Thoughts of Luna crossed his mind. She had become his own personal wonderland in his mind lately. He knew if he fought this, he could finally be with her again.

"She's worth it." Jesse told him simply. Honestly. She had always been worth it.

Good, Asher thought. "Then fight for her Jesse. Fight this and come back from it."

Jesse was afraid to ask what was next, but he had to know. If only to distract himself from the pain. "What happens next Asher?"

Asher sighed deeply. "You have to die."

~ *Twelve* ~

Be still, accept your fate

Asher could still hear Jesse's heart beating. He hadn't died yet.

Jesse looked at Asher. Struggling not to breathe, trying to stop the shaking he couldn't control. He couldn't believe what Asher had just said.

"When you finally die, you will wish you were truly dead. I'm not gonna lie Jesse. It gets worse."

Much worse, Asher thought quietly.

"What happens?" Jesse tightened his grip on Asher's hand in his. He took ahold of Asher's wrist like a strength endurance hold. He needed something to hold onto when Asher couldn't answer his question.

"Don't leave me Asher! Keep talking to me." He begged his brother, looking him in the eyes intently.

Asher grabbed his brothers wrist like Jesse was doing to him. He held him like a big brother should do.

"I got your six man." Tears started form in his eyes, he had to brush away. He'd never had Jesse's six. Now he did.

Asher felt ashamed he couldn't hold it together in his brothers eyes. Having Jesse's back now while he went through this, holding his bothers wrist stronger then in reassurance, he felt like he was finally doing something right in his life. "I'm not going anywhere Jesse. I swear it."

He kept talking to him. "Our venom will seep into your heart like the poison did, your heart will pump it into your body. Everything it touches it will destroy. You will die, from the inside out, Jesse."

Asher almost lost it when Jesse fell silent. When he stopped trembling. Asher wiped a tear off his cheek and covered up his mouth that was dripping venom. Jesse had died right there in front of him. His hand even let go of Asher's. But Asher grabbed it and held their hands together in both of his.

Asher was determined not to let his brother go. "Then your heart will start back up. Pumping only venom through your veins that is multiplying inside of you now and it will become a source of life for you that will heal you.

"It will restore your body, strengthen it. God is recreating you now Jesse. Accept it."

Please, Asher prayed as he bowed his head while he waited for it to happen.

He wanted his little brother back. He couldn't lose Jesse.

"Not Jesse." he pleaded with God. "Please don't take Jesse."

Asher shook off the hopeless feelings and continued talking for Jesse like he had wanted him to do. "The venom, it will crave things, like blood. It's ok though. It will over power your mind that will be hard to control. But I'll help you learn how Jesse." Asher shook his brothers hand. "I swear it Jesse."

Asher listened as Jesse's heart started beating again. It was pumping out the venom that had killed it. His body was now healing and working again.

Asher lifted his head heaven ward. He thanked God and waited for Jesse to wake back up.

Luna heard the slamming of the main gate that lead to her cell corridor. James was coming again.

She was tired of being frightened by him. Sitting in the back of her cell, Luna looked up and waited for the moment he would pass by.

She was tired of not fighting. Determined, she started to stand up when he got nearer.

She was tired of watching James drag off others, being helpless and a little relieved that it wasn't her. She didn't turn away this time. She refused to fear him any longer.

Luna sighed when he marched past her cell. She walked over to her cell door quietly. She peered out and craned her neck so she could see what has happening down the row of cells.

James was opening another set of cell doors. He was in someone else's cell. She couldn't see what he was doing in that cell until he came back out into the hallway. He was dragging someone using a steel hook that he put into their feet to connect them together and trap them.

There was no escaping James when he used his steel hook. Luna wanted to shake her cell when he walked by to get his attention. She had to make him stop, if only for a moment to give the person he was dragging away a chance.

Luna had been trying this for weeks. Trying to get his attention so he would stop what he was doing, if only for a moment. Nothing she tried ever worked.

"Was she worth it, James?"

Luna got his attention. There was nothing else she could say to him that would stop him from his purpose so thoroughly. She had literally stopped him in his tracks.

"Was she worth all this James?" When he looked at her over his shoulder Luna continued. "You asked me once why I couldn't love you. I didn't stop trying until her."

James turned on her then. Luna didn't flinch or move from her purpose. She prayed the poor soul he had in chains could make amends with God before they met their fate. James never brought back his human recruits.

"She was nothing." He cocked his head at her, trying to remember through the fog of his human memories. "She meant nothing to me. Like you,". James walked closer back to her. "she was just a means to an end."

James laughed at Luna then. "Are you still trying to save me Luna?" He laughed louder then. A bellowing laugh that shook his whole body. "There is no saving me Luna." He stepped closer to her cell then. Closer to her.

Luna had to swallow the venom that was rising in her now. The steel bars of her cell held her powers at bay, but her venom was still ever present inside of her. She longed to sink her teeth inside of James and destroy him with it.

James reached through her cell door, faster than she expected. He reached through the bars and grabbed the back her hair pulling her up against the cell bars so she could face him and the steel of the bars could burn her face.

He said slowly to her, making her hear every word individually, knowing it would finally break her of her illusions. "I never loved you Luna." His hatred for her was there in his eyes. "I do miss that body of yours though."

James started drooling on her, looking down at her body. He licked her face and saw the distress it caused her. "One day, I'll have you again. You can count on that."

James dropped Luna and let her fall to her knees. He watched her cup her face and enjoyed the sight of her in pain that the bars had caused her. He lifted his next victim and put it over his shoulder walking out the main cell gates, slamming it firmly to scare Luna again.

"Why do you do that with him? Why do you try to save him?"

Talia hadn't gotten off the floor of her cell in days. Luna wasn't sure if that was a good or a bad thing.

Luna knew the burn on her cheek would last for hours. It burned like she was still pressed up against it. "I don't know, honestly."

"You should stop, Luna. You are only angering him and delaying the inevitable for his victims."

"I know." She whispered softly back. "I just can't sit in here like this anymore."

Talia rolled over and looked at Luna. "You can't escape."

Luna sat down on the floor then and faced Talia. "I know Talia."

And she did know. She couldn't think of anything else but that some days.

"Then why do you do it?"

Talia had laid her head back on the floor again. Luna knew Talia was weak, and didn't expect an answer to her question. It was more of a statement. It made Luna sigh and look heavenward. "Because it's the only thing keeping me alive."

Hours would turn into day, and day would turn into night. Before Luna knew it, weeks had went by that added up to another month.

Luna closed her eyes and rested it against the floor like Talia was doing. Sometimes it was the only comfort she had.

In restless, timeless dreams, Luna would turn away from dreaming about Jesse. She couldn't do it anymore. She couldn't look at the man she wanted to feel in her pleasant dreams. It would crush her into oblivion. She had to live in the reality that was here. In this place.

She couldn't go to him in his dreams. She couldn't give him hope that couldn't be. They couldn't dwell in what was, or what had been. Time couldn't erase the past. The silence, there in the truth of it, was breaking her immortal heart.

Luna laid in the stillness. She longed for the quiet. She understood now why Talia did it.

James would come and go with every passing day. He would slam the main gate knowing it was close to her cell. Then he would drag his claws across the doors as he went by. He would make a bigger spectacle with his victims then he needed too, just to scare her.

Some days it worked, crippling her, his ugly sneer would haunt her, worrying when her time would come. Other days she would turn away and think of Jesse, just wanting to die inside.

She learned James could read her mind now. It would drive him so mad when he would pass by her cell when she was thinking about Jesse, he would even forget to close a door or two.

When Luna learned how it worked on him, she started doing it more often. Even though it was killing her. She even carved Jesse's name in her cell door. On the outside of course, so James had to look at it every time he passed her door. When he would scratch across it with his claws as he passed by, she would find another spot to carve it in until James would leave it alone.

She would stay awake for days doing it. Giving back the punishment he sought for her. But she could only take so much. She wondered when it would finally break her apart.

And then it finally did. Like the end of a song as it drifts off into nothing.

Someone was holding her. Dancing off into the moonlight with her. Luna slipped into the oblivion she thought would destroy her. It was a heavenly state that took her towards a light she had only found in the presence of her dreams.

Opening her eyes wide in realization of what was happening again at the sound she heard, chanting, that didn't sound heavenly. Things her mind was trying to forget brought her back to life. She wanted to scream. She couldn't do this again.

She felt herself being laid down on a wooden table.

Luna tried to fight the hands that were holding her down. She could feel steel spikes being pierced through her feet and arms nailing her to the wood table she was on, then a steel chain being wrapped around her neck. Luna screamed in an unholy voice she didn't recognize at the pain she had to endure again from the steel going through her.

Someone placed the steel mesh inside of her mouth that had trapped her before. It cut inside of her mouth as she fought it opening up wounds that the poison soaked mesh could fill.

Luna whimpered out loud. It was burning her. Her eyes opened and took in everything around her. She was in the big room of the caverns now. The one she had been searching for a year ago.

Had it really been a year now? She almost wept thinking about it.

Luna looked into the waterfall she had known was in here. It made her see the failures in her life. If she had only made it down here then. She could have wiped them off the face of this earth. Forever banished in her wake.

She could see the royals there all around her. Chanting still. A sight she had feared but never saw before.

They were dressed in white bloody robes. They wore masks on their faces that made them look like hogs. James stood next to one of them. It was all odd to her, like she was still lost in a dream state from the poison.

She rolled her head away from looking at him. It must be her time she told herself. She prayed God would make it quick.

"You must take her mother." She heard them say to James like they were trying to convince him of something.

Luna swung her head back. Her mother was standing next to James, held by steel chains Luna knew were burning her. Luna fought against her own chains. She tried to raise off the table.

She struggled to fight with the mesh in her mouth so she could scream at him. She knew he could hear her, because he looked at her.

Luna put her head down, trying to think. She had to be still and listen to what they were saying.

"Linda is the first of her generation. The strongest. She will meet our purpose now. Breed with her. Kill her. Drink from her powers and become stronger than all of them."

Luna started breathing heavier, she tried to rein in her powers. Tears fell from her eyes down her cheeks into her hair when she couldn't shake the helplessness she felt. The steel wouldn't release her.

A chill swept over her, she was drenched in bloody tears and damp cold from the waterfall.

"The Whitby's have taken our strong hold in New York."

Luna stopped fighting at that. What had they just said?

"You must do this, now James, so we can destroy the Whitby's and take back what is ours."

Luna tried to bolt. She tried to scream at them all. It weakened her more. All she could do was look at James.

James, look at me. Please. When he did, Luna rejoiced. Not her, James. Take me. You want me!

It was all she could do to save her mother. Try to speak to him with her mind. Remind him that he wanted her.

She was so weak and powerless, she worried if he could even hear her.

"No." She heard him state simply. "I need Luna."

Luna closed her eyes, believing it had worked.

"Luna is stronger than all of her tribe. She's more powerful than any of the Whitby's. I've seen it."

Luna looked at James in disbelief. He was going to use their past to undo them completely.

"I've witnessed her power. She is a majestic werewolf and a monstrous vampire hybrid. A creation that will give me powers to bury all of them under our weight!"

Luna watched as James walked around the room, making himself known as a leader now.

"She will give me her destructive force. One that will give us a new ability to resurrect the evil we seek within the earth! We can take back this land, and from there take over the world." His voice was like a deep, empathic growl.

Everyone in the room was chanting now. The sound of it defeated Luna further.

Luna wanted to destroy herself in that moment. Heaven felt so far away. Tears unlike she had ever wept before stung her eyes and blinded her. She screamed through the mesh and begged with God to take her life.

"Look at her now. Nothing can stop her, but me."

The chanting got louder. The screeching from the demons surrounding them flowed around the room above them like circling bats. Like a demonic wave.

Luna felt more hands upon her, releasing her from the spikes and chains that bound her. She couldn't fight them even if she wanted to. She let go, because her strength was gone now. She was weak from the pain and the poison that was killing her. She felt the moment in the darkness when James picked her up. The chanting got louder. He turned her and presented her to the royals.

"I will take her out on the sacrificial rock, in her moonlight, for all the earth to witness her end, and my beginning."

Luna couldn't weep any longer. She couldn't feel anymore. All she could do was beg him not to do this as she fell inside of his arms.

James, please. Don't do this.

Luna opened her eyes while he was walking with her through the caves. She saw the writing on the walls, the legendary writings of her people seeking freedom from their enemies. New painting's now that spoke of death and hell.

Cells lined the endless hallways. She couldn't believe how many people were down here. It was like walking through an asylum, listening to the moaning and habitual pleas of the victims. The smell was so grotesque Luna wished she could cover her nose.

Luna breathed in the fresh midnight air as James walked out into the mountains with her. All of the royals and demons followed him. She couldn't hear the chanting anymore. Her ears filled with the silence inside of him as he walked her to the rock on top of the great smoky mountain.

She hadn't felt the coolness of the earth upon her skin in forever it seemed like. The darkness of the night, the stillness that was around them, like all the creatures of the earth had fled from the evil mountain that was here in this place. It called to her.

The wolf inside of her wanted to be released. Wanted to run away as fast as she could.

Luna started clawing at his chest. She couldn't believe this was going to happen to her. She looked for the rock he had spoken of. When it came into her view, Luna thought her lungs would bust with the scream she couldn't contain.

There in the light of the moon, stood a flat lying rock, long enough to be a table. It shined brightly in the silver light. Millions of stars shone through the treetops lining the horizons.

Luna reached up and touched James face. She tried to make him look at her. You don't want to do this James.

James wouldn't look at her. She looked at the rock again, the closer they got to it. She started flailing in his arms, trying to escape him.

No. This couldn't be happening. James hated her, that much she knew, there was no way he would do this to her. No way he would force her to do this.

He better have a lot more drugs for her if he thought she was going to let him do this without a fight. She had never been rendered useless in the face of danger.

Evil surrounded her now chanting her destruction.

Oh God! Luna begged looking at her future. She was doomed.

James laid her down upon the rock. Her body was weak, paralytic now. She couldn't even move her arms to reach out to him. She cursed the darkness and closed her eyes to it all.

"She's mine!" James growled into the night as he climbed unto the rock in the form off a human man upon her.

When he looked at her, picking her body up into his, Luna lost it. She was stunned into a reality not of this place. Time was being held still for her in this moment.

He winked at her. And in that moment, she knew. It wasn't James.

Jesse could feel the moment Luna realized it was him. He didn't know whether he was happier she had found that peace in his arms he had wrapped around her now pressed against his body, or if it was the fact that only she could see the difference between them. Whatever it was, he was thankful for it.

Edoa toi Waya. He whispered to her heart and mind, letting her know he knew this now. I got this Babe.

Jesse laid his body upon hers on the rock meant for this night. He looked down at her body he had craved all this time. He looked down at her lips and secretly took out the steel mesh in her mouth that was holding her powers captive until this moment.

Jesse leaned down and kissed her lips softly. He whispered to her soul again to be still.

In that moment all the royals and demons were captivated by him, still controlled by Jesse's abilities. Jesse let a force take over him. A power she didn't know he possessed. He thrusted into a shift that transformed his body into a werewolf. More powerful and stronger than even her.

Jesse reared his head back and howled. He took powers from the heavens and looked back to the earth at all the evil he could see within his abilities.

Luna had feared the day this would happen to Jesse. The day when he would give up being human for her. There had always been a secret side of her though, that had truly wanted to know what it would be like if he could be a wolf like her.

And here he was. Right above her. Standing guard over all he loved, protecting her. Saving her like he had promised. Becoming all she had ever wanted him to be.

Jesse howled into the night, in a low, deep growl, throwing his head back again, that echoed into the night. He used mind powers to control the royals and the demons. He evoked a fear in them that distracted them long enough for God to reign down fire and brimstone all around them.

He watched as every single one of them that were up here on the mountain, turned to ash, swept away by the wind.

Asher and Darryl walked past them when God was done. Followed by Darryl's men, the Whitby's and firemen that Asher had brought with them. They walked into the caves and released all the prisoners, killing anyone who stopped them.

Jesse got down off the rock. He paced around the rock Luna was on. Making sure there was no threat left to her.

Luna lifted up and watched the strength and power in Jesse. Her abilities returned to her, weak at first.

He looked more like a bear than he did a wolf, she wondered. The way he shook his head in defiance and took up a stance next to her, defying anything that might strike against him.

Luna leapt off the rock. She ducked under his neck and wrapped her arms around him. She cried out his name as she held him.

Jesse let the shift that he couldn't stop take over. He became the man she needed. Well, the vampire, he reminded himself.

Luna pulled him tighter into her embrace. Daylight blinded her. When she looked around, they were no longer on the mountain.

She looked at Jesse questioningly as the waves of an ocean crashed into the sandy shore they were standing on. She had no idea where they were, and suddenly she didn't care.

Jesse smiled down at Luna, moving a stray black hair the wind had landed on her face. "It's just a moment. A place in time I promised God I would bring you back too."

Again Luna looked at him questioningly.

Jesse took a moment of his own. He had to kiss her again revealing all to her that had happened to him. He lifted her off her feet as he kissed her passionately.

When God had watched enough he coughed silently next to them.

Luna turned, taken back by His presence so close to them. He was dressed in a plain woolen shirt, a plain pair of pants and his feet were bare in the sand like theirs.

She looked at him questioningly also like she had Jesse.

Her savior was there before her in her midst. What was He doing here? Where were they? Why were they here?

"Be Still my child." He told her impatience. "Walk with me, Luna."

Luna looked at Jesse then. She didn't want to let go of him.

"It's ok. Go. I'm not leaving you, Babe." He told her touching her cheek in reassurance.

Luna sighed and lead the way down the beach, with God walking next to her. Their footprints in the sand behind them.

"I have brought you here Luna so I can share with you what I need you to tell your people. My people. The past, the present, and now the future I want for them."

Luna thought about that. "Why me? Why not Joseph or Emie?"

God smiled at that. He was using them now to do His will back in Luna Pier and all around the world.

"Jeremy and Jordy are going throughout the world, recruiting their kind, fighting against the evil left in this world. Joseph and Emie are gathering those in Luna Pier until the time has past that I will take everyone home to be with me.

"Then I will have victory over this evil that has sought to take what's mine. But,"

Luna almost laughed when he paused. He had learned something from Jesse. Or had Jesse learned it from it God? She wondered quietly.

"Until then, I need you to prepare your people. Protect them. Live among them. And wait."

God stopped walking and reached out his scarred hand towards Luna. Luna knew what this meant. Joseph had done it to her in the past. She waited though. She needed to know something first.

"Jesse?" She questioned as she turned back to see him standing in the waves, looking into the crystal clear day, the sun that was rising in the east.

God sighed following her gaze. He had to shake his head at what his children did when it came to love.

"I will leave you two here. A honeymoon as you call it, for a time." He looked back at her when he had her attention.

"You would allow me to marry again?" She questioned Him.

"Again? I never married you the first time."

Luna stood in confusion at that.

God looked back at Jesse. "When you came before the altar to me with James; the deceit in his heart, you wanting Jesse and not him. You both hated what you were about to do. How was I supposed to bless that?"

Luna saw the way God looked at her. It was forgiveness. He had given her mercy that day.

Luna bowed her head then. "What happened to James, Lord?"

God looked away from her. "I tried to save him Luna. He didn't want to be saved. He tried to kill Jesse when he came to save you. So I let Jesse take his life. I'll deal with him later.

"For now." And this time God took her hand, not letting her have her way anymore.

Luna knelt there in the sand before her God. She saw the creation again in her mind. But this time she felt it in her heart. God's unending love. She watched the scenes he played out for her. All was revealed to her.

There was a time when the land she was standing on belonged to her people. The royals, the evil creation that had left their God, overtook them and drove them off the land.

This place, where her knees were resting in the sand, belonged to her people. God wanted to give it back to her people. It had remained untouched by man, government, evil. A secret place in the earth that man had coveted because of its beauty. But God never allowed it to become theirs. He kept it safe for her people.

He showed her how he wanted her to bring them here. For a time of course. He would be back soon.

Luna rose her head to ask how she would do this, but he was gone. Only one set of footprints were left there in the sand. Hers.

Jesse knelt down next to Luna. "No. Their His. He was carrying you, healing you. When you knelt down he made you whole again."

Luna looked at Jesse. She smiled at him in awe of God.

"You can read me now."

Jesse grinned at her like she always made him do. Sometimes he couldn't stop it. It was the way he loved her.

He placed their foreheads together. "I was born to love you Babe."

He pointed out into the water for her. There was ship out in the water waiting for them.

Luna looked in disbelief. It was big enough to carry everyone back here to this place.

Jesse took her hands in his. "But not yet." He picked up her hand and kissed it.

Luna noticed the sun got bigger. The light was shining all around them. Heavenly host were gathered around them. Witnessing what Jesse was about to do.

Jesse got down on one knee there in the sand and looked up at Luna. He slipped a gold ring on her finger that was engraved with the image of a cross, surrounded by diamonds. He felt the moment in his soul when her soul responded to his undying love for her.

It was there in her soul he would find rest. Forever.

"Luna Waya, will you promise your life to me, stand next to me forever.

"Be still!" He chuckled at her stubbornness winking at her. "And never leave me again?"

Luna had waited for this moment forever it felt like.

"Yes Jesse! Yes Baby!" She promised him.

Jesse couldn't stop the smile that took over his soul. He stood up, took Luna in his arms and kissed her. He danced there with her in the sand while the heavenly hosts above them sang their love song. He took her into the water and made love to her there on the ocean floor. In the waves, where they were always destined to be.

~Epilogue~

Juliet closed the book she finished writing. She looked up into the bright, misty ocean breeze around her. The sounds of Luna's people in the distance living together with the Whitby's and the Stones, filled her with joy.

They were being loving, being saved, and being still.

Jeremy told her she could do it; write the love stories of the Whitby's. She hadn't believed she could, but there it was in front her. Written with love for her new family.

All the Whitby's had ever wanted was to be loved.

The feel of the man she loved wrapped his arms around behind her and playfully whispered to her, "Did I ever tell you the story of Grim and Helana?"

Author's Note:

      Sometimes all we have left are the memories of yesterday and the time we spent together. Sometimes those memories are all that connects us to each other over the distance between us. We can wish upon a star, hope that great void within us won't destroy us with the pain we feel so deep in our soul that's tearing us apart. But if we learn to remember, if we hold tight onto faith, then one day it will all make sense and we will learn to understand that everything happens for a reason.

      I will always love you. Always love me.

Made in the USA
Monee, IL
27 November 2019